UNFORGIVABLE

A HIGH SCHOOL BULLY MAFIA ROMANCE

EMPIRE ACADEMY, A NEW ADULT MAFIA ROMANCE SERIES

MONIQUE MOREAU

MEET MONIQUE!

Join Monique's Newsletter (and receive goodies and
release information) https://bit.ly/SteamyReadNewsletter
Join Monique's FB reader's group
Possessive Alpha Reads
Like her Facebook Page
https://bit.ly/MoniqueMoreaufb
Follow her on TikTok
@moniquemoreauthor
Follow her on Instagram
https://bit.ly/MoniqueMoreauIG
Follow her on Book Bub
http://bit.ly/MoniqueBookBub
Learn all about Monique's books
MoniqueMoreau.com

PROLOGUE

LUCIAN

Silky blonde hair, in two perfect pigtails, coast down the back of the girl in front of me as she grasps the bar of the jungle gym. She shakes it hard, as if testing its strength.

Always so careful, this one.

Is she afraid the metal won't hold? Jeez, what a scaredy cat.

That thought makes me itch to yank one pigtail.

I *will* yank it.

Make her squeak.

Make her turn around and glare at me with her dark eyes, so different from the cheery, bright yellow of her hair.

I like the black sparks in her eyes when she looks at me like she hates me.

I like it less when I shove her to the ground, but that's the way it ends between us sometimes.

That's how it will end today.

I push her.

She falls on her hands and knees, crying out as she scrapes her palms and knees against the pebbled concrete of the schoolyard. There's black rubber underneath the jungle gym, but she fell just passed it on the hard, rough ground.

Oh well.

I tried to be nice once. Once. But she ignored me.

No one looks down on me, so I hit her and screamed at her, and called her *stupid* and *ugly girl*.

She cried, but I felt much better after.

"You took too much time climbing up that thing," I blame her, pointing at the jungle gym. "Slow and stupid, that's what you are."

I don't mean it, but I started this and I need to see it to the end. That's how things are between me and her. That's how they always are, and I'm okay with that.

She glares at me over her shoulder. Her eyes are red. Her cheeks are pink from shame, but she doesn't cry. She's cried before, but this time, she won't give me the satisfaction. I don't mind. I like her mad better anyway.

"Hey," says Crina, stepping into my space. She's the boldest of the girls, a tomboy. "Leave her alone."

I shove Crina hard. She stumbles back, her arms flailing like windmills. Her rump slams down hard on the black rubber.

Marku hovers nearby. He's torn because I'm his best friend, but Crina's like a sister. I give him a look, telling him I'm not here for Crina.

My gaze returns to Star. I want to see what she'll do next.

She scrambles to her feet, coming up to protect the girl who stood up for her. Her tights are torn at the knees. Her palms are scraped and bleeding. A crumpled, dry yellow leaf rolls past her feet like a tumbleweed.

I feel a twinge of something in my chest, but I slap the sore spot and shove the feeling down.

Kids have stopped playing and stand to watch the drama.

My muscles are loose 'cause I know I'll win this battle. Even if she stands up to me, I always win. There's no choice since Daddy got sick.

"Stop it," she speaks low, almost too low to hear.

But I hear her.

Her voice is soft and clear like chimes, even though she just gave a command. I hear it in my dreams; it chases the goblins away.

I place my hand in the center of her chest. A braid slips off a shoulder as she stumbles back a step and twists her ankle. She rights herself, putting weight on it, but holds herself upright with a grimace.

"Who's gonna stop me?" I demand.

Fury darkens her eyes to a pitch black, the flags of pink on her cheeks redden, but she remains silent. She's too weak to go toe to toe with me. It's something I count on.

I shove her shoulder again.

"Not you," I say.

Crina rushes to her feet and links arms with Star. This is their way of showing a united front.

I roll my eyes.

My gaze flicks to Crina. "Or you."

I side-eye Marku to come in and get Crina before I'm forced to do something he won't like.

He steps forward, but before he has a chance, an outraged "Hey!" rings out behind me.

It's an adult one this time. We freeze.

"What is going on here, Lucian Popescu?"

The teacher on recess duty strides up to me. She takes in the situation, pausing a beat as she sees Star's knees, the smudge across her cheekbone where she swiped her white-blonde braid away from her face, and the tear on the sleeve of her blue checkered dress.

"Who did this to you, Star?"

Her question is met with silence.

I glare at Star, shooting her warnings of revenge if she doesn't cover for me. *Not good enough, Star.*

"N-no one, Ms. Dimitriu. I f-fell," she replies, too little too late.

"Hmm, fat chance." She stares at me and sighs, then points to the entrance to the school building. "To the principal's office, Lucian."

I groan and throw out my hand toward Star. "I didn't do that. This isn't fair. Just 'cause I'm a boy, you think it's me."

She twirls around fast and bears down on me, but I hold my ground. "No, *not* because you're a boy," she emphasizes. "Because you're *you*. Ten years old and you already have a reputation for acting up and bullying other kids."

A gasp comes from some other kid behind me.

I swivel my head over my shoulder to see who it is. I clock the kid's face. It's Dan. He pales when he realizes he's gotten my attention.

"It wasn't him. N-not this time," tries Star again, stepping forward to block the teacher's glare on me.

Ms. Dimitriu turns her gaze down to Star. "I might believe you if we were talking about anyone else." She leans over, past Star's slim figure, and orders, "To the office, Lucian."

Normally, Ms. D is easygoing, but Star rakes up protectors like fallen leaves in autumn. She has that effect on people.

Her tone hardens. "Now."

I growl low as I pass Star before stomping off. A brisk wind blasts my face as I trudge through the crowd of kids that part like the Red Sea.

Marku gives me a smirk. I glare at the kid who'd reacted to Ms. D's comment. Marku gives me a nod. He'll join me at the principal's office soon enough.

* * *

"THANKS FOR SHUTTING DAN UP," I tell Marku as we turn out of the main office in the lobby and head back to our classes.

"We're brothers," he replies, but levels a hard stare at me and adds, "But Crina's mine. If someone's gonna hurt her, it's gonna be me."

"Yeah, I got it," I call out as he turns and takes the stairs back to his classroom.

Not in a rush to get back to boring class, I amble down the empty main hallway. I trail my hand over the ugly green tiles on the bottom half of the wall, while my eyes skim over the drawings and paintings tacked up on the walls.

I pause in front of her painting. I tilt my head to the side as I take a moment. Green hills are dotted with brown bears, lynx, and lots of wolves. Lots more wolves than anything else. Makes sense considering they're the namesake of her *Lupu* clan.

As I peer up at the blobs of brown and gray paint, my lips turn down in a frown. It doesn't feel so good to make her cry anymore. It did when my father went away to the hospital, but not since she lost her daddy.

5

I like her better mad. The spark of anger in her eyes chases her sadness away.

A teacher coming out of one of the rooms waves me away with a warning that I'd better get back to my class. I head up the main staircase and I've just hung a right toward my classroom when I freeze.

Is that crying?

Pausing at the doorway of the art room, I peer in and scan the empty room. Three rows of long tables each have identical red chairs tucked in. The papers, paints, crayons, and markers are carefully organized on counters at the back of the room. The walls are covered with artwork. A large carpet with squares in rows lies near the front of the white smartboard.

I hear another sniffle.

I step into the room. This new angle gives me a better look at the corners of the room. Star is tucked away in one corner. She's on the floor, getting her pretty, blue-checkered dress dirty, with her knees tucked against her small chest. Her face is buried in her hands.

I quietly close the door behind me. She doesn't hear me. She lets out another big cry. It shakes me up a little inside and I rub my chest to ease the feeling as I walk up to her.

She still doesn't realize she's not alone.

I tap the toe of her black patent leather Mary Janes. The glittering rhinestone in the center of the little embroidered black flower on the top of her shoe quivers.

Star gasps and plasters herself against the whitewashed brick wall, staring at me, terrified.

"Shhh," I say.

I put my hands out in the calming way my Mama does. "It's okay. It's alright."

Her gaze darts around the room. Before she can scurry away, I drop down beside her.

Dust spreads out beneath me and I sneeze a little. Humph, they don't keep things clean like my mama does. Lazy.

Palms on the dusty floor, mouth agape, she watches me, ready to jump up and sprint away any second.

I wrap a hand around her knee, the tip of my finger grazes over her skin where there's a rip in her stockings that I caused. I squeeze her knee, commanding her to stay still.

"I know what happened to your dad," I said, the fight forgotten in the face of real problems. Dead or sick dads are real problems, playground pushes are not.

"You do?" she whispers.

Her eyes instantly drop to her shoes; tears fall to the ground. Is that shame? She shouldn't feel shame. He didn't dishonor her like my daddy did me. I heard how the Bratva slaughtered him, the bastards.

"He died in battle. He died with honor," I tell her to make her happy.

She lets out a whimper, as if I've hurt her more.

Not the reaction I'm expecting.

I frown down at her, wiggling my index finger in the hole at the knee of her stocking.

Her dark eyes turn to me, so much sadness and despair in the dark pools of brown. Her eyes are like the ones on the teddy bear my little sister sleeps with. I don't like to see her teddy bear eyes so sad.

The sides of her mouth turn down; her bottom lip trembles. "I hope you're right."

I take her hand. Her skin feels soft and I squeeze it. "I know I am. I know everything that goes on with the big people. It's my job to know because one day, I'll be *consilier* of my clan like my tata was."

She starts crying again, tears tracking down her

cheeks. "I don't know what's going on. No one tells me anything," she wails. "Mama cries all the time, and my brother's scary he's so mad. He stays out all night. I wait up for him to come home. Last night, he didn't return until three o'clock in the morning. I saw it on the clock on my nightstand."

"He's avenging your father's death," I say confidently, puffing out my chest a little.

That's what good *mafie* men do. They avenge wrongs. That's what I will do one day.

She shakes her head. "It's war, and if something bad happens to him, I'll have no one."

"You have your mama."

She shakes her head, staring at my finger playing with the frayed strands of the hole in her stocking. "My mama is weak."

I know what she means. It's the men that keep families safe.

Her voice drops down to a whisper. "I'm scared he won't come back…like my dad. I creep around and try to listen in to their conversations, but—"

Fear spears my heart.

Fear and a jab of pain. I do the same thing, eavesdropping on the grown-ups. But I'm a boy, and I'm the head of my family.

She's a girl, and she shouldn't do that.

It's her brother's job to protect her. He's probably too busy to notice she's slinking around. But I get why she does it. The fear gets so strong, you want to know what's going on, what's going to happen. It feels like…control.

I want to protect her, but I'm not in her house so I threaten her instead, "Don't ever do that. You shouldn't be sneaking around the house trying to be a grown-up. It's your brother's job."

Her mouth firms in mutiny. "But what if he dies, then what?"

"He won't," I insist.

He could die at any time, but I don't like her scared, and I'll do anything to take the fear out of her eyes.

She looks at me skeptically.

"I don't lie."

She lets out a little sigh of relief, but her lips press rebelliously. Stubborn girl. I didn't know that about her.

I pause and argue what I think might work to make her stop. "You don't want your brother to catch you listening in on the grown-ups. He won't like it."

Her eyes widen, another layer of fear. "I'm quiet. He won't know."

"He's smart. He'll catch you."

She considers my argument for a moment, then hangs her head in defeat.

"He could," she agrees.

"Leave him alone," I tell her. "He needs to fight and go to war, not worry about you. You're a good girl, Star. You're a good sister, so stay a good girl. Stay a good sister."

She looks at me quizzically. "You do it. You sneak around and find out what the grown-ups are up to."

"I'm a boy and my daddy's gone. I'm not like you." I push my chest out. "I'm like your brother."

She looks at me under her lashes. I feel a pang in my gut. "Why did you come here, Lucian? You always make me cry, so..."

She leaves it hanging, and so do I. She's a smart one, but I'm not going to touch that question.

"It's not good to cry alone," I reply, wrapping an arm around her slight shoulders.

The cherry vanilla scent from her hair drifts over me, making me feel warm all over. Cherry vanilla is the fragrance of ice creams and lotions that girls lather over their skin when they get out of a bubble bath. A bath with too many bubbles.

"We're Romanians. We should never cry alone." I release her hand and stand up, giving her a stern look. "But that doesn't mean when we leave this room, we're friends or nothin'."

There are rules for a reason. Might not know what those reasons are, but rules are rules. This is just a moment suspended in space and time, but when we get back to the real world, we return to what we were.

Later, back in the classroom, the glossy blond braids call to me again. I snake out my hand and tweak one.

She angles her head slightly in my direction, eyeing me from the side, giving me the attention I want.

From now on, I will tease and bug her and she will get mad at me, but I will make sure to do just enough to make her mad. Only mad, not sad. I can control this and make it work, like I make everything else work.

I'll do it for her, not just for me. And that makes me feel better.

CHAPTER 1

LUCIAN

"*A* tutor?" I spit out.

Irritation thrums through me and I flick my wrist, repositioning the cuff links of my shirt to align with the button of my jacket.

Anton, sitting on the red couch, snorts. Marku lounges back in his chair, the brown leather creaking under his hefty weight. He gives me that classic smirk of his.

Cristo, my cousin and the second-in-command of my clan, asked us to stay once the weekly meeting was over and all the other soldiers and officers cleared out. We sat back down and he dropped this bombshell.

I must've heard wrong because… *Hell no.*

Anton chuckles and I have the urge to cuff him upside the head. Of course, he'd never abide such disrespect and we'd end up in a scuffle. Eyeing the fancy Persian rug dubiously, I wonder how Nelu would handle us breaking shit up in his office. Not well, I imagine.

Suddenly, my fantasies of revenge are overtaken by another thought.

"There's a fucking war about to explode with the Russians and you're worried about my high school grades?"

"Yeah, no thanks to you," Cristo grumbled half-heartedly.

I wave off his complaint. "It was inevitable and you know it."

"That's beside the point. You're failing, you dumbass runt, so you can't talk yourself out of this. Graduating is nonnegotiable, Lucian, and at this point, you're not going to," Cristo warns. "How are you gonna marry Roxie, knowing the kind of family she comes, without a high school degree? She's sure as hell gonna have one. That's not a good look for anyone, but especially not you."

Leveling me a hard stare, he threatens, "You either comply or I break every bone in your body, get me?"

He gives a shrug as he lights a cigarette. "If it's any consolation she's pretty to look at."

I don't give a shit about what she looks like. Me and my boys have single-handedly taken over the Jersey shore's drug routes from the Bratva, and now I'm gonna get tutored by some loser girl?

Nah, that's straight-up embarrassing.

Marku's one-sided smirk spreads into a full-on grin.

Bastard.

"A girl? And a Lupu one at that. Are you trying to humiliate me?" I sputter out, shifting the seat I'm sitting on so that the outside leg lines up with the side of Cristo's desk.

I glance at the intricate red handwoven rugs covering every inch of the floor, following the design in the matching hangings on the walls. If nothing else, I can appreciate the symmetry of the office Cristo shares with his father, Nelu. As anyone can tell from the decorations, it's a different world out here, across from the sparkling skyscrapers of Midtown Manhattan.

We'd be a better fit for a Habsburg castle in the old country rather than twenty-first-century New York City. Every piece of furniture is ornate carved mahogany, from the two desks facing each other to the vintage ruby-colored velvet couch.

"You've succeeded in doing that on your own…by flunking," Cristo reminds me.

Anton makes a choking sound of holding back laughter and I throw him a killer glare.

Placing my elbows on my knees, I glower over my steepled fingers, as warm, dusky light filters through the three stumpy windows hovering at street level. One can even hear the clip-clop of heels from a woman passing by on the sidewalk outside.

It's bad enough that I have to get a tutor, but to have it be a girl is infinitely worse. A smart girl at that. And he said she's pretty. I'm torn on that last bit. I've had plenty of pretty women. I don't need help finding myself a fucktoy.

"Who the hell is she?" I bark out.

"Watch your fucking mouth with me, whelp," he snarls in my face. I snarl back.

We Popescus are savages and proud of it. With the kind of brutes we breed, it's easy to pick fights, although touching a prince like Cristo is unusual.

But not unheard of.

"Up till now, you've gone above and beyond to prove yourself as a top dog in this clan. You keep harping on about how you want to be my *consilier*. How's that gonna work if you don't graduate high school? 'Cause no way in hell is my *consilier* a high-school dropout. Talk about a fucking embarrassment to the clan."

My heart plummets. When it comes to my goals, intense is my resting bitch face. I may only be nineteen years old, but in a world where boys are inducted at the ripe age of thirteen, a man my age is ready to carry the world on his shoulders.

I wasn't inducted this year, when a kill would be easy, what with violence bloodying the streets.

No, I came up six years ago, when this city was squeaky clean. When Bushwick was a fucking artist's' colony and Times Square had been chewed up and spit out by a Disney princess, farting out fairy dust instead of pollution. The epitome of gentrification.

Fuck, he's got me and he's got me good. The Popescu clan is my life. I've finally schemed and definitively fought off Dimu, my main competitor for the position. I'm on the brink of bringing my family name back to the top after my father shunted it into a ditch. I'm not going to become the *consilier* my father once was, I'm going to be *better* than the *consilier* he once was.

"And before you argue with me, no, I'm not going to let you squeak by. I want you to fucking prove to me that you can do this. I'm not asking for Honor Roll here, but for fuck's sake, no straight D's either."

That was exactly where I was about to go, damn him. I stare at him incredulously. "Since when do we care about *grades?*"

"Since we've partnered with the Lupu clan."

I know this, but I'm going to fight him just to win the point. Any point.

"Why? Because they're into graduate degrees doesn't mean we have to follow. I'm your toughest solider. I have a cadre of men under my command. I've wrestled territory from the Bratva that we've panted after for decades. I've already proven my worth."

"Goddammit, Lucian, I'm not asking you to go to Harvard and become a nuclear physicist."

Cristo expels an impatient sigh. "We have a reputation to uphold. You graduate from Empire Academy with decent grades and marry Roxie, and I'll fuck off without you saying a word. But until I get what I want, you'd better bet that on your mama's life, I'll be up your ass."

He bares his teeth at me. "Oh, and Lucian, in case there's any doubt in the matter, I always get what I want."

He's not wrong.

It's one of the many reasons I admire him.

Ignoring the growing smirks on my friends' faces, I push off the chair and pace up and down the small, cramped office. Five steps, turn, five steps, turn. "Fuck, okay, I'll accept your tutor. Get a Popescu girl and keep it in the family."

"I wish I could, but you're so fucked they're not good enough. You know how obsessed those Lupu are with education. The best tutors are from that clan, but don't worry, I've got just the girl for you."

The silence seething between us is punctuated by Anton's howl of amusement.

I give him the evil eye before turning my suspicious gaze on Cristo. I know every student at Empire Academy, home of the children of killers and sinners, aka the Romanian *mafie*. We've all been stuffed in one fancy, shiny new brick building off Park Avenue in Manhattan. *Thank you, Alex Lupu, for pioneering that move.*

"Who is the bitch?"

Cristo pauses, as if for emphasis.

My shoulders hunch forward.

Then, I motion with my hand to hurry him along. "Stop with the suspense already. Who is it?"

He places four small red-and-gold drinking glasses on the tabletop and unstops a matching glass decanter of *țuică*. He pours healthy doses of the strong plum brandy.

Holding up a glass in a toast, he gives me a shit-eating grin and replies, "Starlene."

I blink.

My belly flip flops with tumultuous anticipation at the mention of her name.

Star? The geeky girl? But Star's the kind of nerd-girl you jack off to in the shower, imagining her puffy red lips wrapped around your cock, her long blond hair wrapped around your fist, and her somber dark eyes staring up at you with that unforgettable mixture of fear and sadness.

There's attraction, but I wish it were only that. Since high school, I've made a point to stay away from her precisely because everything in my core gravitates toward her. I've slipped here and there, but I eventually right myself and withdraw back to safety.

Star won't like this plan, I know that much. Not after the way I've treated her over the years.

Then again, she won't be given a choice.

At a loss for words, I declare, "She's a nerd."

Cristo's eyes harden. "You'd be so lucky to snag a nerd, asshole."

Touched a nerve, did I? For an old man over thirty, I see how he flitters around that strawberry blonde Lupu geek.

Excitement lights up inside me and I shove it down. Pulling the cuff at my wrist until the cuff links are lined up just right, I reply, "Alright, whatever. Star it is."

Cristo narrows his eyes at me, scrutinizing me.

He stands up, rounds his desk until he's facing me, and takes hold of my shoulder. I sigh internally as his grip pulls the sleeve of my jacket, messing with the alignment of the button and cuff links.

"Don't you dare fuck her," he threatens, locking eyes with me. "I'm serious. I have plans for her. With the recent Bratva threats, another Lupu-Popescu alliance would be helpful right about now. She's Tatum's sister, which makes her close to royalty. I'm thinking of matching her up with Simon."

Simon? That pussy?

My stomach churns, but I hide it with a grunt. "Christ, I've got enough women to fuck, I don't need to stoop that low."

"Shouldn't be a problem," Marku helpfully pipes in. "If he'd wanted to fuck her, he would've already done it."

"You're an asshole, you know that," Cristo says to me, with a shake of his head and a fond chuckle.

He releases me and I tug on my sleeve.

"Yeah, that's what makes me your favorite cousin." I give him a wide grin. "What's the point of being a Popescu if you're not an asshole?"

CHAPTER 2

STAR

"*I* got in," squeals Gabby as she waves the acceptance letter high above her head.

We celebrated days ago, when she saw she'd been accepted online to the American Musical and Dramatic Academy, but there's something special about holding an honest-to-God snail mail letter in one's hand.

"Three more months and we graduate. Free to live our best lives. After everything we've been through these past four years, we'll be done. Done! No more being lorded over by our parents and teachers. Next year is our year to shine."

Dropping to my bed, I peer out the window at the bright sun hanging in the azure sky, and harrumph. Worry for Gabby dampened my initial excitement at her acceptance.

Music drifts in from a car passing below, the notes from an oldies station blaring through the open windows. *MC Hammer?* The song reminds me of the stories my brother used to tell me about my father smuggling DVDs of American music back in the old country.

Wearing a pair of ripped, cut-off jean shorts and a crop top, I'm not looking forward to going back to a uniform for the final months of school after spring break.

"The sun may be shining, but that's about all that's good about spring," I grumble, half to myself. "You talk about teachers, but have you forgotten the kings? Talk about lording it over everyone."

Speaking of the kings, a shiver works its way down my spine at the thought of one particular king.

Lucian.

To think that once upon a time, he checked off every bullet point on the 'Imagine My Husband' game we used to play as little girls.

Olive skin. Check.

Dark hair. Check.

Light eyes (gray, to be exact). Check.

Square jaw. Check.

And that's just his face.

As if his looks aren't irritating enough, he's bad-boy catnip to a fixer like me. From the moment I loved him from the moment I set eyes on him in kindergarten.

My heart is a twisted puzzle when it comes to Lucian Popescu. With the way he's treated me over the years, you'd think I'd be ashamed by how much I crave his attention.

Crina looks up from her place at my desk, and says confidently, "It's the end of the road for the Big Bully."

I roll my eyes. "And you know this how exactly?"

She gives a little dismissive shrug. "He's got Roxana draped all over him with her octopus arms, staking her claim. They'll be engaged any day now, and once he's engaged, he can't continue doing the weird shit he does to you."

My stomach clenches at the reminder of his imminent engagement.

Falling on the bed beside me, Gabby gives an exaggerated fake shudder.

"As if any of us would want a man like that," Crina continues, scribbling away in the diary she carries with her everywhere. Candy wrappers litter the desk. "Let the spoiled brat have him. I might hate her guts, but she has her uses. And distracting him in her bid to become his queen comes in handy. Did you see her dripping in Gucci from head to toe at Easter mass?"

"So trashy," chimes in Gabby.

I hate to love him and yet, something happened to my insides when I caught Roxana slobbering into his mouth behind the church. Like Crina said, I should be happy that he'll soon be engaged. Instead, I fantasize about the dark murderous prince who bullies me. There are no boy-meets-girl love stories in my world, and to harbor any fantasies of Lucian is practically an act of self-harm.

Always the optimistic one, Gabby insists, "What do we care about Roxie or the kings? Remember the poem we read by Robert Frost about the road not taken, Crina?"

"*Two roads diverged in a wood, and I— / I took the one less traveled by, / And that has made all the difference,*" she recites with a sigh at the end.

"We're going to do that," she promises, tapping the acceptance letter laying on the bed. "Our lives aren't going to stop at the big Romanian wedding. We're going to grow up to be something more than boring little wifies."

Yes, yes, we made a pact to apply to colleges together. Crina and I are still waiting for our letters. Me, for a program in art curation. Crina for a writing program.

"But I want to do something now," I grumble as I grab the small coffee cup on my night table and take a sip of Turkish coffee.

The small cup, a little larger than an espresso cup, has the words "Best Brother Ever" wrapped around it in cursive. Tatum left it behind in his hurry to leave, and I'm glad for it. It reminds me of him.

Gabby perks up. "What are you saying, Star?"

From my position, seated with my back to the head-board, I pull open the drawer of my nightstand and grab a sheet of paper.

Waving it in the air, I say, "My bucket list."

Crina lunges across my room onto the bed.

Laughing, I jump to my feet and lift it high out of her reach. "No looking!"

I scramble off the bed, stuff it back into the drawer, holding it closed with one hand while warding her off with my other hand.

"Behave," I warn Crina.

"Oh, come on. You're no fun."

"Ha, as if you ever let us read your diary," I throw back at her.

She sniffs. "It's a journal."

"Whatever. The point is, it's private. You wouldn't want me reading your *journal*."

"My life is an open book," she exclaims. "Ask me anything and I'll answer."

"Same here," Gabby pipes in.

I stand firm, giving them my best I-mean-business glare. Crina retreats with a grumble and plops back down on the chair by my desk. "So what's the biggest thing on that list? The thing we absolutely need to know."

I purse my lips. I can tell them anything, it's just that I haven't said it out loud yet. I've thought about it more times than I can count, but it's scary to say something forbidden out loud.

"You can tell us anything, Star. You know my darkest secret," says Gabby, with her uncanny ability to read my mind.

She has a good point. In comparison to what she's hatching up, my plan looks like child's play. College may be on her radar—or she could be on the run for her life.

"I don't want to get married right away." Turning to Crina, I said, "I know our plan was to get into college, get married, and then convince our future husbands to let us attend, but I don't want to get married just yet. I want to go to college first. I want to work. I want to learn hands-on what it's like to *live*."

With a surprising lack of well…surprise, Crina nods but then asks, "Work? What kind of work? Like in a museum?"

"Or a gallery," I add.

"Gallery? Have you ever been to a gallery?" Gabby asks, appalled at the idea that I've done anything so unusual without her.

"Well, no. Not yet," I reply. "But I will. I want to go to real galleries. The legendary ones in Chelsea or the cool ones on the Lower East Side. Or in Brooklyn. Sadly, there aren't many left in Soho anymore."

"I'll come with you," Gabby suggests.

I crinkle my nose at her. "You're not interested in art."

"Not really, but it's not safe to go alone."

"Okay, that's not true," Crina asserts. "I go to poetry and spoken word readings in cafés. Our parents have brainwashed us with scary threats about the Bratva when really, it's an excuse to keep us away from outsiders. I've snuck out and gone as far as Williamsburg for a reading. Let me tell you, there's no Bratva in Williamsburg. Pretentious hipsters, yes. I had an Uber meet me a few streets away, went to the reading, and took an Uber back. Practically door-to-door service. No subways. Not much walking. Zero risk."

Gabby's mouth drops open. Mine's not far behind.

"Umm, and why are we only hearing about this now?" I ask.

Crina turns her back to us and scribbles in her journal. "I don't know…Gabby can't risk doing anything with what she has planned with her sister, and you're a good girl."

My shoulders slump forward.

She glances over at me. "Sorry, it never occurred to me you'd be interested."

A crash on the landing outside my bedroom has us freezing in place.

Gabby's gaze dashes to mine.

Holding our breaths, we listen to the muttering on the other side of the wall.

"Shouldn't you go and help her?" Gabby whispers softly.

My eyes dart to the door. I shake my head and mouth *no*.

My mother would be horrified if I went out there, with my friends visiting. It's better to pretend I don't hear anything, but God, the humiliation makes me itch to run away. Ever since Tatum left, she drinks herself into a stupor. Mama knows I have friends over, but that doesn't stop her. I don't know how much longer I can live under the same roof as her, but who will take care of her, if not me?

We wait her out as she struggles to her feet, stumbles, crashes into the wall, and then slowly drags herself across the long runner covering the parquet floor.

"Is she—" asks Crina, a deep frown marring her forehead as she's trying to figure out what my mother is doing.

I cringe, knowing exactly what's happening.

"Yes," I reply grimly.

Yes, she's crawling to her bedroom.

"Does your brother know?" Gabby asks in a loud whisper.

"My brother's *gone*," I answer, barely refraining from snapping.

Ugh, why does everyone automatically ask about him? I'm the only one here, holding down the fort.

We remain silent, listening to her slowly drag herself to the bedroom.

After what feels like an excruciating amount of time, her bedroom door finally closes.

Mortification burning my cheeks, I lift my chin high and say, "Things have changed since he left."

Crina's eyes turn soft. "I know it's been hard on you."

You have no idea.

Their pity triggers a surge of frustration. Quivering with rage, I declare, "Now that Tatum's gone, I have no one to be good for but myself, and I promise you, from now on, I'm taking the road less traveled."

The last interaction I had with Lucian flashes before my eyes. At Cat and Luca's wedding, he caught me in an empty hallway near the women's bathroom. I don't know if he was drunk—he definitely tasted of alcohol when he pushed me against the wall and smothered me with a searing kiss. He cut it off as abruptly as he'd started it, ambling down the hall as if nothing had happened.

And that wasn't even our first kiss.

But it was the aftermath that got me.

Standing off to the side of the dance floor, I overheard him being teased by some guys for the smears of lipstick on his mouth. At that moment, Anton happened to scan the room, stopping on me. His gaze dipped to the smudged lipstick on my own lips.

Lucian, facing Anton, followed his friend's stare. Twisting around to find the focus on me, he said, "You're dreaming. I haven't kissed any bitch."

The shame of that memory burns deep in my gut and I spit out, "As for the kings, I'm not going to let them step all over me ever again. This time, I'm fighting back."

Gabby's mouth pinches tight; she's struggling to keep it shut.

To break the tension, she rolls onto her tummy, props her chin on her hands, and asks in a light teasing tone, "Oh, and how are you going to do that?"

"Not sure, but I'm not going to lie down and just take it anymore. I'm going to give back as good as I get."

Tilting her head, she warns, "You'll only make yourself more of a target, and you don't have Tatum here to protect you."

"I don't need Tatum," I bark back.

"Wouldn't it be better to lay low and hope Lucian doesn't notice you? Get through the year and escape?" Her eyes glaze over. "I don't want a repeat of what happened in the fall."

Of course, she doesn't. Not after the meltdown she had with Anton, the blackhearted bastard.

Gritting my teeth, I glare at the map of the world on the wall facing my bed, dotted with pushpins. I have a bucket list this year, and by God, I'm going to do everything on that list if it kills me.

I cross my arms over my chest. "Not me. No more. I'm fighting back."

Gabby lets out a resigned sigh next to me. "Oh boy, then I guess there's gonna be no peace."

That's my girl. Always has my back.

Crina twirls around in my spinny chair, making a soft noise of derision at the back of her throat. "I'm not afraid of those bastards. Never was. Marku especially. He can go fuck himself, and you know I'll tell him that to his face."

And she has. Unlike me, that girl is fearless. I may never be a Crina, but I'm determined to shed the old Star.

Since Tatum left, I'm coming to understand that life means taking risks, and it's past time I started taking some.

CHAPTER 3

LUCIAN

"*Y*ou want me to do *what*?" Star asks, eyes wide as she stares up at the head of the Popescu clan.

I stand beside her, facing Cristo like a good soldier, while he lounges back like some modern-day Roman Emperor. Even the ornate crimson leather couch he's sitting on looks fitting for his regal pose. The large windows of his Tribeca loft rise behind him like mountains. The setting sun strikes the panes and spills into the expansive room, setting the bright ruby-red of the massive modern paintings of jagged mountains on fire.

I hear her swallow.

Out of the corner of my eye, I catch her tugging at her crop top in an attempt to cover the sliver of flat belly showing.

I get it, glancing down at my own attire with irritation. I didn't get a chance to change into a suit, because when a boss calls, you come running.

The fact that she's not only wearing a crop top, but oversized sweats and a pair of coral-colored Air Jordans tells me that she flew out of her house when she got his summons. But fuck, even dressed like a typical teenager, Star is nothing but fucking stunning.

Star. Only one syllable, it's such a simple sounding name.

Simple as it might sound, it's a perfect expression of who she is. Stars may look small in the sky, just pinpricks in a huge expanse of black, but they're immense. Fiery and explosive. Yeah, I bet she'd explode under my touch. Better yet, under my tongue.

Whenever she steps into a room, I just want to go to her, to bring her attentive dark eyes on me, and I want to keep them there. It's gotten worse over the years. Every one of those instincts is wrong, wrong, *wrong.* So instead of satisfying my burning desire for her, I expend every ounce of energy I have to crush it. At times, I have to crush her in the process. Collateral damage.

Cristo scowls.

I second his irritation.

Star's not stupid enough to outright dismiss the Popescu *şef's* request, but what the fuck? Did she actually question him? Is she pushing back because we're Popescus?

I shift slightly so that I have each foot planted fully on an entire paisley in the design of the rug. Fucking Lupu snobs.

Cristo has more patience than I do, because he schools his features into a marginally less vicious expression and says, "Tutor him, Star. You're the smartest girl in your grade. You can do it."

"B-But, I'm a Lupu," she has the audacity to argue, even if her voice doesn't rise above a rasp.

"Lupu. Popescu," Cristo replies with a dismissive wave of his hand. "It's not like before. We're at peace. Our families are friends. My sister married a Lupu, for Christ's sake."

Yes, his sister Cat. How could I forget her wedding?

That kiss.

But he's also making a point, one with an underlying threat: *Do you dare insult me? There's peace, but it only takes one match to light a fire.*

Her gaze darts to me.

I return it and get lost in her inscrutable dark eyes. I love her eyes. They're like whirling black seas of onyx, mysterious and impenetrable.

They bore into me with unmasked determination. Seeing the stubbornness in them burns the back of my neck. She's acting like I'm a monster or something. The longer she holds off agreeing, the worse she makes me look, and that's really starting to piss me off.

I harden my face and lift one of my eyebrows in a challenge.

Her gaze snaps back to Cristo.

She stammers, "I-I'm sure...you can get one of his... friends to help him."

She's wringing her hands together, clasped in front of her in a sign of desperation. I let out an irritated sigh. Is this playacting payback for what I said after the kiss?

Cristo snorts. "He'll spend his time fucking these so-called friends, not studying. That's why it's gotta be you."

He flicks his index finger up. "For one, you're jailbait."

Not true, but he doesn't know her real age and neither of us bother correcting him.

Another finger ticks up. "Secondly, Tatum is the only Lupu who doesn't loathe me. I won't risk pissing him off by letting Lucian fuck with his little sister."

He angles his head slightly and eyes Lucian. "Isn't that right?"

"Yeah," I grind out.

For the love of God, why the fuck are they acting like I'm going to jump her or something? Okay, maybe she has a point, but Cristo?

Star's shoulders abruptly slump down as if Cristo just popped her bubble of bravery.

Hmm, must have been the mention of her brother. It's no secret how close the two of them were. He was more like a father to her.

"Whatever," she mutters into her chest, stomping her foot lightly.

"I'll take that as a yes," Cristo grumbles. Then he looks her in the eye and warns, "Just do it, Star. I need him to graduate, okay? Don't cross me on this." His tone drops an octave. "You'll regret it if you do."

She gulps audibly and she's right to be nervous. By agreeing, she's making a tricky commitment. This is the *mafie*. For whatever reason, my *şef* chose her and now that he has, the burden is on her to help me pass. Failure is not an option.

Having gotten what he wants, Cristo slaps his hands on his knees and raises himself to standing.

Dismissing her, he claps me on the shoulder, leans in, and mutters a harsh warning in Romanian, using gutter slang to tell me what's what.

I nod dutifully, but I'm still irritated by it. As if I'm some beast who'd physically harm her. And he's fucking insane if he thinks a warning would stop me. *Şef* or not, I do what the fuck I want.

Cristo gives me a curt nod and says, "I'll let you both get on with it then."

He disappears, leaving us to stare at each other like two cowboys readying for a duel.

Throwing her shoulders back, she glares at me, putting every ounce of strength she has in it.

Cute.

Cute on top of gorgeous, because at that moment, as the sun descends below the horizon, a ray of gleaming light strikes her head. Her ice-blonde hair, normally the color of pearl dust, lights up like a halo. Other than her platinum-colored hair, most people don't notice her because she's always hiding in the wings, trying to meld into the wall. Yet, I've noticed her from the beginning.

Only…

I tilt my head to the side and study her carefully. Her shoulders are pushed back instead of slumped forward like usual. Her eyes drill into me as opposed to darting away. She stood up to Cristo instead of promptly agreeing to his request.

Something has changed… Intriguing.

Star swallows and the old show of nerves makes me smile inwardly.

"We don't have to be enemies, you know. We can be friends," she says, although I distinctly hear the begrudging tone in her voice.

I laugh, a bitter one. "There's no such thing as friends. This world is made up of three kinds of people: family, competitors, and enemies. Friends are an American concept, a sheep's clothing for one of the latter. Competitor or enemy, take your pick."

"If that's how you feel, why pick me? Any other girl in your clan would do," she asks crossly.

I languidly move closer. She tenses.

I take a step closer.

And a wave of cherry vanilla hits me.

My stomach clenches. It's the fragrance of innocence, of childhood, of the shampoo little girls with flaxen hair use in their baths.

A childhood I know nothing about. I have no need of false memories, memories that exist in other kids' lives. My own memories are filled with white walls and the stink of antiseptic. With grasping hands. And with blood. It always ends with the scent of blood.

I press my eyes closed and breathe it in deeply, this unrelenting cherry vanilla fragrance.

I snap them open. She hasn't moved a muscle, standing stock-still, like prey on the alert.

I'm the Big Bad Wolf to your Little Red Riding Hood, little girl. I'm your biggest nightmare.

"He has his reasons for choosing you," I reply.

Fuck if I know what they are, but my *şef* never does anything without a purpose.

Circling her tightly, I exhale, and my breath flutters a few loose strands of her hair. I watch a shiver course through her delicate frame.

Be afraid, little girl. Be very afraid.

I breathe her in.

My heart skips a beat.

I breathe her out.

My heart pounds.

"He's using you for his purposes, and I'm going to use you for mine."

Her head turns slightly in my direction. "To become *consilier*, you mean."

I still midstep in the tight, hovering circle I've made around her. I've never made any bones about my intentions within my clan, but she isn't a Popescu. The only way she can know something like that is if she's sought out intel on me or watched me closely.

And is that bitterness I hear?

"That's right. And you know what that means, don't you, Star?"

I pause a moment.

She shakes her head, frustration marring the smooth perfection of her forehead.

"That means I have a future to fight for, so we can never be friends. Get that idea out of your head. I can fuck you." She swallows. "I can rut you." Her gaze skates away. "Hell, I can even breed you, but I can never marry you, and I sure as hell can never be your *friend*."

I spit out the last word like it's a curse.

Her hand swings out, swift and firm, but I catch her wrist before her palm connects with my cheek.

My gaze burns into her, although inside...inside I'm fucking *laughing*.

Little girl got herself a spine over the break.

"Let go of my hand."

Using that very hand, I drag her closer until our lips are a hair's breadth away.

Her dark eyes widen, pupils blown out, in fear or lust I don't know. "Don't touch me without my permission."

I huff. "Ironic, that. You were about to touch me without mine."

"You deserve it. You may be a king at Empire Academy," she grinds out, "but you don't own me."

In a silky tone, I contradict her, "Oh, but how wrong you are on both counts. I am the king and I do own you. Test me, girlie, and I'll have you over my lap in a heartbeat."

God, would I love that.

Scandalized, she tosses her head and yanks her hand hard.

I tighten my hold.

"Let go of me," she grits out between clenched teeth.

I get back into her face. Another whiff of sweet dark cherries glides over me, but I fight the urge to taste her, and reply, "No."

Her chest flutters up and down, almost heaving. Our gazes clash.

She shakes her fragile wrist, manacled between my long fingers.

I stand firm.

She shifts from foot to foot and rolls her eyes. "Are you done already?"

"Not yet," I snap back.

"I could break you, you know," I say softly. Soft, but menacing.

Her lashes flutter, her only reaction. But it's enough. I've stood close to her long enough. Star may normally be demure and quiet, but she's a lethal combination of strength and innocence, all wrapped up in the body of a siren. A man like me would devour her tempting innocence raw. I'd tear at it and crush it between my jaws till it's been ground up and spit out.

I savor one last beat of heaven before I release her and step away. The move is so fast, she wobbles in my absence. I wait for her to regain her footing and then ask for her phone.

She blows out a sigh from her full, suckable lips and grabs it from the side pocket of her over-sized joggers, encasing a tight ass the shape of peaches. I should know, I've stared at it enough times.

She opens her phone and shoves it into my open hand.

I call myself and put my number in her contacts.

Handing it back to her, I angle my head toward the front door and say, "Now get out of here."

She doesn't need to be told twice.

She hitches her backpack over her shoulder and rushes

out the front door without a second glance, like the prey she is. Light glints off the many buttons pinned to her backpack just before she disappears.

Star always was the smartest girl in the class.

I see some things haven't changed.

CHAPTER 4

STAR

Gabby, Crina and I meet up in the morning to take the train into Manhattan. After getting off at the 86th Street subway stop, on the Upper East Side, I pick up a donut twist at the shop on the corner.

Biting into it, I'm about to step onto the crosswalk when a bus roars passed me like it's on a high-speed car chase. Crina yanks me by the back of my uniform shirt, and I barely escape getting mowed down. A gust of dirty exhaust blows in my face.

Hacking, I shout into the wind with my fist in the air. Pedestrians rushing past me barely glance my way. Gabby grabs my elbow and tows me across Lexington Avenue. Afterward, I trudge behind them moodily the few blocks it takes to arrive at the gate that leads to our high school.

Kids stream into the small cobblestoned courtyard, the scattering of black wrought iron benches, tables, and chairs already swarmed by hordes of students. Each of the kings is leaning against the brick wall near the entrance, coolly surveying their subjects like the royalty they assume themselves to be. Roxie is among them, hanging all over Lucian.

I grimace as I loop arms with Gabby and walk past them. Crina comes in right behind us, and when Marku makes a comment to her, she growls and snaps her teeth at him. His deep chuckle reverberates in the packed courtyard.

I've just passed the double doors of the entrance when Lucian leans toward me a fraction and murmurs, "Music room. During study hall."

Ignoring him, I wipe the white donut powder from my mouth with the back of my hand. Roxie glares at me over the expanse of his chest. She may not have heard him, but she doesn't like his focus being sidetracked to another female. Knowing how Roxie is, Gabby protectively tightens her grip around my arm and tugs me away.

I was hoping against hope that Cristo and Lucian would've forgotten about me, but I'm not surprised Lucian's initiated contact; two days into the first week back from spring vacation and assignments have already been handed out.

Later that afternoon, I knock on the door of one of the soundproofed music rooms in the basement. I try the handle. I softly push the door open and glimpse inside.

Lucian is sitting at a small table he's pushed to the center of the tiny room, and his head is cradled in his hand as he studies the laptop in front of him. A paperback is lying facedown beside him. There are a few music stands and plastic folding chairs carefully arranged in a corner. The white walls are interspersed with beige acoustic panels and one sorry-looking vintage poster of a crying geisha for *Madame Butterfly*, at The Metropolitan Opera.

Jeez, this must be one of the most depressing rooms in the school.

Without looking up to check who he's talking to, Lucian grumbles, "It's only been a couple of days and Ms. Sava hasn't wasted a second of it."

"It's Ms. Sava. What do you expect?" I reply, dropping my worn backpack on the carpeted floor.

The multitude of pinback buttons covering my backpack make its reassuring clattering noise. I carry a metal chair from the corner and drag it to the rickety table. Facing him, I pull out my notebook and the paperback we're reading for English.

Lucian finally lifts his head and looks at me. "I need you to write the essay for me."

I blink at him.

"You want what?" I cup my hand to my ear. "I must have misunderstood because I swear I heard you say you want *me* to write *your* essay."

A faint smile lifts the corner of his beautiful mouth. "Stop acting smart."

Just as quickly, it vanishes. His voice hardens. "Just do what I say."

I make a little dismissive noise in the back of my throat. He's insane if he thinks I'm going to jeopardize my graduation by helping him cheat. Not only do I not have the time for this, but Ms. Sava is no fool. She'll easily catch us.

"That wasn't our agreement and that's not what Cristo wants either. You can't bribe these teachers. They're immune to getting paid off. Not only do they make good money, but they'll get fired and worse if they take a bribe."

Disappointment burns in my chest. "So this was your plan all along. That's why you didn't fight Cristo on this."

"What Cristo doesn't know won't hurt him," he replies shamelessly.

"Just do the work." Exasperated, I pick up the soft paperback with the yellowed edges and slap it softly against the hard white plastic table. "You're smart enough to graduate on your own. Put in the work, get the grades, and move on. Sounds simpler than trying to get away with cheating."

"I'm failing," he snarls at me. "And I have more important things to do than read fucking Shakespeare." He flicks a disgusted finger at his paperback. "After I leave school, I have to pull in a full shift for my clan."

He lightly slaps the book down on the table. "I hate English. Even if I put the work in, there's no way I'll get more than a D, and that's not acceptable."

Ignoring the last comment, I reply, "How can you say that?"

I tap the cracked cover of the book. "I bet you haven't even read Shakespeare. I bet if you gave him a try, you'd be surprised by how good he is. There's political intrigue, violence, family betrayal. Guilt. Remorse. All of them are lessons. *Life* lessons."

Seriously, some of Shakespeare reads like *mafie* clan sagas.

He lifts one brow. Tone dripping with sarcasm, he asks, "I'm going to find that in *A Midsummer Night's Dream?*"

I huff out an irritable sigh. "Maybe not in *this* play, but it might make you laugh. You might be amused. Did you think of that? This Shakespeare guy is a master. If you only put in the effort, you can do well on this essay and pull up your overall grade high enough to get a B."

"Listen, nerd, I can barely read his old-style English and it's *April*. Not only is it too late but I keep telling you, I don't have the time. I have *real* problems to deal with."

I resolutely overlook his nerd insult. I am a nerd, and proud of it. What's so bad about school? Shakespeare isn't everyone's cup of tea, but he's not that bad. Lucian can at least try, but instead he wants to whine like he's the only one with problems.

He clearly forgot that my father was Rudari, derogatorily called *gypsies* in the old country. The man had no easy life. Not only that but Tatum was ruthlessly bullied in school for it. Suffering is all around us.

We're *mafie,* for God's sake. No one is immune, and women usually have it worse. Just look at Gabby's sister. He'd never end up like Lana, would he? He'll never be forced to marry a monster. He's been saved that fate by the simple virtue of being born a man. For that alone, he has it pretty good.

Spoiled brat.

Unmoved, I reply, "You act like you're the only one who's ever suffered. Everyone struggles and yet we manage to do what's expected of us. We manage to get an education and most importantly, we manage to graduate high school."

In the flash of an eye, Lucian is around the desk. Looming over me, his closeness unnerves me. The alluring musk of man, with hints of spicy cologne, winds around me, luring me in to lean closer and take a deep whiff. Fighting the urge, I force myself to stay still. Very still.

"The fuck you know about my life?" he starts. "You lost your dad, but he had an honorable death. You can be proud of him and the legacy he left you. Your family name hasn't been dragged through the mud."

I bite my bottom lip and say nothing. I can't give him an inkling of the truth. A truth only a select few in my clan know about, and they're eager to keep it a secret.

"Your father didn't go insane and lose *everything,*" he barrels forward. "Leaving you to pick up the pieces and rebuild everything from scratch. With a target on your back, no less. Everyone expects me to go crazy like he did, the ignorant fucks."

His fierce, pained face hovers far too close, his eyes stark and stormy. He twists his upper lip in derision. That rare glimpse of vulnerability in Lucian makes me inhale sharply, drawing in a deep breath of his delicious scent.

I have this irrational urge to grab him and plant a kiss on his lips. Kiss him to distract him. Kiss him to comfort him. Kiss him to drive away the pain because I know that pain. I saw the same agony etched across my brother's face when he confessed our family sins to me. Those sins are now mine to carry, and they're terrifying. Worse than going insane and losing everything.

I finally break the silence and acknowledge, "He did lose everything. He did abandon you. I know it hurts and nothing I say can take away your humiliation, but your single-minded obsession with becoming *consilier* at any cost won't save you, you know."

A flicker of doubt glints in his eyes, but he waves away my words. "Of course, it will. It will make everything right."

"It won't make you whole."

His hand snakes to my nape, grips my hair, and pulls my head back. A thrill zaps down my spine. Like the captain of a ship flailing in a tempest, he takes control because he needs it. Another reason he should read Shakespeare; he is the Tempest.

"What will, if not that?"

I shake my head. His grip tightens on me. My insides shiver at his dominance.

His charcoal-gray eyes, locked on mine, are twin vortexes of agony.

I let out a soft breath; it coasts over his cheek. A few black curls shift in the disturbed air.

"Listen to me," I say gently. "You don't have to sell your soul to get what you want. There's no doubt you'll be the top dog of your clan, with the perfect Popescu princess at your side. But it will be an empty victory if you don't come by it honestly."

"That's where you're mistaken, my little Lupu doll. You're so damn naïve to think there's virtue in this world," he hums softly, his nose edging my jaw and drifting down the length of my throat to bury itself in my hair.

He lets out a moan. The stubble of his five o'clock shadow scrapes my skin deliciously, teasing me. My heart is in my throat, pounding erratically.

"There is," I insist forcefully. A world dominated by sin and badness… I can't live with that.

"You can have it all and know, without a shred of doubt, that you've earned it. It starts with school, but if you follow through, you'll win every challenge. And there will be challenges. It's the way of the *mafie*, but no one will be able to take away your honor. No one, but you."

A surge of power and determination sweeps through me, and I stammer out, "I-I believe in you."

He pulls away abruptly. His gaze drifts off for a moment, then homes in on me. "I actually believe you do."

The revelation in his admission makes my heart ache. I hear the yearning, the desperation, the palpable need to believe me. "Yes, I do."

"You know, you'll make some man the perfect *mafie* wife," he croons.

Annnd…that one phrase breaks the magical intimacy of the moment. A cold chill sweeps over my skin like a hail of icicles. It's meant as the highest compliment, of course.

I cough, covering my snort of derision.

His brows gather in confusion. "I've insulted you. I've told you what every woman wants to hear."

He's observant, I'll give him that.

"No, you haven't," I lie. "But being the perfect wife isn't everything."

I don't know why I speak my truth to him. More often than not, he's the enemy, but his comment embodies everything that's wrong with our values. And part of me is sick of holding back, sick of hiding.

One side of his mouth ticks up.

"What is *everything?*" he asks teasingly.

The man is conniving. Of course, he'd pick up on that. I should answer him truthfully. After all, I'm not a Popescu; he's not invested in policing my conduct. Nevertheless, I hesitate.

"It doesn't matter."

His mouth tightens. So does his grip on me.

"Speak," he demands.

"I'm only your tutor. I'm not your responsibility. Once you graduate, we'll never speak to each other again, so let's not pretend it matters to you what my thoughts and dreams are. They don't."

He frowns. "They matter."

I shake my head again, pulling against the fingers digging in my hair. It's a delicious pull, but I stamp down the flames of lust licking at me.

"It doesn't. I don't want it to."

"You lie. You want it to matter."

I glare up at him. That's touching too close to the truth and that's not who we are. There can never be an *us*. Not with his ambitions. Not with my newly formed plans. I can't afford to indulge in silly feelings or unrealistic fantasies of Lucian Popescu.

"No, I don't," I reiterate.

Ignoring my lie, he suggests, "It could matter."

My cheeks flush. It sounds like he's giving nothing

away, but that's quite a statement. Light shines on this neglected corner of my heart, the one reserved only for him. Is he serious or is he toying with me? Either way, he's propped open the door to this derelict room, and I can't allow that.

"It can't," I pronounce resolutely.

"A part of me has always wanted you, Star. You know that."

I suck my stomach in. Meanwhile, my core floods, needy and aching.

"I don't know anything of the kind," I reply tightly. "You've messed with me for years. You kiss me, then you insult me. It's a constant push and pull, carrot and stick. How can I possibly guess *what* you feel for me?"

He has the decency to look abashed. It's brief, but I catch his expression before he covers up with a retort. "You don't know much about men. Or boys. I messed with you because a girl like you—"

He cuts off with a shake of his head.

My eyes bulge. "A girl like me *what?*"

Shrugging, he pulls away and settles on top of the desk. His pose is relaxed, hands draped languidly over his knees, but he shakes his head once more, silently telling me to let it go and move on.

My teeth grind together. I stare at him, an eyebrow lifted in challenge. *Come on, you can't drop that and expect me to simply dismiss it.*

"Go on, speak. You were never afraid before. Don't start now," I taunt him.

He chuckles. "There's been a change in you recently."

If he only knew... "Just say what you mean, instead of talking in code."

"Feisty. I like it."

Another blast of lust sears through me. I'm almost preening from one simple compliment.

His gaze moves away from me to the wall above my head. His shoulders stiffen. He rubs the stubble on his jaw, deep in thought. Impatient, I shift in my seat waiting for him.

In the end, his eyes return to me. In a monotone, he says, "My goal is to restore my family's name and power. It's the only thing that matters, and to do that, I must be the strongest, the quickest, and the smartest made man there is. I must marry a clan princess from an influential family, and I must graduate from this fucking pretentious school by June."

My shoulders slump. I had expected something honest and real to come out of his mouth. Instead, he's backed off and reverted to the party line. The one he's bought lock, stock, and barrel.

Listening to him makes me want to pull my hair out in frustration. Rather than taking a risk or challenging himself to be better—*like I'm trying to do*—he retreats behind a brick wall. Like a coward.

I want to throw that in his face, but he'll only get defensive and attack me. Instead, I yield, "Okay, do what you need to do."

I may not be able to change his mind, but that doesn't mean I'm going to help him take shortcuts either.

"But I will only help you do it right. I will do everything in my power to help you graduate, but I won't help you cheat. You either do it my way, or you find some other lackey—I mean person—to help you."

He gives me a baleful look. "Lackey, huh? Nice try, but Cristo chose you for the job."

I throw up my hands. "There are others—"

"He's a busy man with many responsibilities. He chose

you, and in his mind, that's enough. There's no one else. Get it out of your head, already," he replies with an irritated huff.

There's more to this story, but either Lucian doesn't know or he won't share with me because it's clan politics.

He leans forward again, back in my space. It's even more unnerving when he captures my chin and concedes, "I'll do it your way—for now. But don't push it."

With that, he releases my chin, hops off the table, and grabs his book.

A little dizzy from his fast retreat, I still feel the ghostly burn of his touch. Apparently, I had gotten a little too cozy with him sitting so close to me, touching me, and wrapping me in his woodsy, masculine scent.

Taking his seat, he pulls up the assignment on Google Classroom. "Haven't done any reading yet, so let's start from the beginning."

I sit there, blinking at him as I catch up to the fact that he's agreed to my terms. I didn't expect it, but I'm not about to look a gift horse in the mouth.

He's following my advice. He said I could matter to him. He even admitted to wanting me. That doesn't mean we could ever be together, but I don't even want that, do I? I stuff down the answer bubbling to the surface.

Mutual respect is enough.

Friendship is possible.

It should be possible, shouldn't it?

It should be enough, no?

CHAPTER 5

STAR

I wait in line at the cafeteria lunch counter, going over our bizarre conversation in the music room last week.

I thought Lucian and I had moved to a place of mutual respect.

Until he ghosted me.

In the past week, he missed our tutoring session and he's ignored every text I've sent him. I even called him, which is just plain pushy in this day and age, but he didn't have the decency to pick up. I was busy with my own work, and quite honestly, I was also procrastinating. It's hard to run after a guy who you have twisted, complicated feelings for. And with each passing day he ignored me, my budding hope took a nosedive.

But the week is almost over and the deadline for the Shakespeare paper is tomorrow. If he doesn't hand it in, there really will be no saving him.

Looking over the array of lunch options, my stomach

churns with worry. I doubt I can swallow anything, but I point to some random item of food anyway. The cafeteria worker plops spaghetti and meatballs onto a plate and slides it over the counter.

I should've gone to Cristo, but the thought of approaching him was just *yikes*. Not only does tattling rub me the wrong way; it just goes against our *mafie* code. I'm also willing to do just about anything to avoid standing in front of him again, especially if it's to admit failure.

And this late in the game, that failure would be on me. I'm the smart girl here, so it goes without saying that I should've been smart enough to get Lucian to comply. Cristo won't be impressed by my arguments of honesty and integrity. He wants Lucian to graduate, end of story.

His earlier words ring in my ear.

Just do it.

I know what those words mean.

It means that I need to get it done, period. If I can't get Lucian to do it, then I should write the paper myself, slap his name on it, and submit it for him. That's what Cristo expects. I know it, and he knows I know it.

And you know who else knows it?

My blood simmers with anger.

Lucian.

Not only does he know it, but he's taking advantage of it. My face flushes hot with anger. My eyes flickers toward the entrance to the lunchroom and narrow on Lucian.

In every high school under the sun, the lunchroom is a war zone. Empire Academy is no exception. Lines are firmly drawn; certain tables are reserved for certain cliques.

The table nearest to the lunch counter, front and center of the entire cafeteria, is a prime location. And it's for Popescu royalty only. I couldn't tell you how it happened, but the Popescus have long established this table as theirs. A kid can't get a seat at this table without being inducted, which means that every one of these boy-men are certified killers.

Lucian sits on the tabletop like it's a throne, feet firmly planted on the bench seat, flanked by Anton and Marku. The rest of the table is populated by Popescu boys, or what I like to call *the minions*. Even Dinu, Lucian's primary competitor is there, with his crew. They may hate each other, but as high-ranking clan members, they divide the table, every inch viciously contested.

Lucian throws his head back and laughs without a care in the world. Yeah, of course, the lazy bastard is laughing; he's saddled me with his work.

White-hot rage boils over inside me.

Fuck him.

He did this on purpose. He was just appeasing me with his *I'll do it your way* business when he obviously intended to stick me with the work all along.

Taking advantage of me, yet again.

But this time, it's worse.

It's about more than just me and him. It involves Cristo, and that man can make my life difficult in ways I can't begin to fight off. With my brother gone, I have no protection. I've heard whispers of Cristo wanting to marry me off to Simon. If he pushed it, I'd have no recourse. And that's the least of what he can do. Bottom line, I'm at his mercy.

Lucian knows this, but he's screwed me over anyway.

My fingers curl around my tray, laden with my lunch. Adrenaline floods my bloodstream, making me skin feel prickly hot.

How could he?

Selfish bastard.

He won't get away with this. Not today.

It's a split-second decision, but instead of walking on, I find myself halting in front of the Popescu table.

Not only is the table like a throne, but he looks like a king. At well over six feet, he's bigger than any other man here. Even Dinu, who works out at the school gym like it's a religion. The cotton of Lucian's white button-down uniform shirt stretches over his wide chest, clinging to every defined muscle.

Standing stock-still as students flow past me, I hear my own heartbeat in my ears. *Ba-boom. Ba-boom. Ba-boom.* I burn to shove him in the chest, to feel the hard muscles under my fingertips. I'd curl my nails in, claw his hot flesh till I drew blood. That would teach him a lesson.

His shoulders bunch and biceps flex as he casually picks at the food on the tray beside him, brows drawn in concentration. I glance down at his plate. He's pushing his food into three distinct groups based on color. I frown, but briskly shake my head.

Focus.

I quickly check my surroundings for Roxie and her crew. Unlike any of these killers, the presence of one of those girls would make me pause.

Nope, she's nowhere to be found.

I turn my attention back to Lucian, staring daggers at his face until he feels my presence.

His gray eyes lift to me. They glisten like polished steel.

His gaze rakes over me like a physical caress. His scent drifts over me, balsamy and warm. Lush, like a forest of cedar and pine.

Muttering, he returns to his food. He might have mumbled a greeting, but it's hard to hear above the din of the cafeteria.

My rage seeps out of me. Doubt trickles in. He *did* acknowledge me…in a backpedaling way.

Shit, why is everything so complicated with him?

This is the moment of reckoning; I can either back away slowly and leave well enough alone, or I can take a stand.

I jut out my chin.

Remember the new me?

This is the new me and the new me will not back down.

A stand it is, then.

Clearing my throat, I glance around the table.

Every male has stopped talking and eating; their attention riveted on me.

Damn.

"Why are you here, Star? What do you want?" Lucian taunts.

Then one side of his lips tick up in a mocking smile.

It's that smile—provoking and spiteful—which brings my fury roaring back and has me blurting out, "The deadline is tomorrow. *Tomorrow.*"

His eyes widen.

Ha! I smile smugly to myself. He didn't expect me to confront him.

"You left me hanging for days," I accuse. "No text. No picking up my calls. No nothing. And now you expect me to do it for you."

I inhale deeply. "I won't cheat, I won't do it."

I breathe it out slowly. "You better make time to work with me or else you'll fail. And if you fail, you fail."

My words came out no louder than a rasp, but he heard them.

Oh, did he hear them.

His face morphs into rage. His unyielding eyes flash silver. A snarl rumbles low in his chest, the printed crest of

Empire Academy on his shirt swells and distends over his heart.

My survival instinct kicks in. I want to spin on my heel and sprint away, finally putting to good use the running tips from PE class, but his vicious glare glues me to the spot. And even worse—the worst thing, really—is that his anger shoots heat down to my toes. My skin crackles with electricity. The licks of steely fire in his eyes match the red-hot flames stoking inside me.

"What does she want, Luci?" Dinu asks, a deep smirk on his face. His turquoise eyes sparkle with malignant mischief.

Lucian stiffens at the question. The nickname.

"Shut the fuck up, Dinu, and mind your own business," he growls.

In stark contrast to the flashing meanness in his glare, Lucian employs a deceptively soothing tone of voice when he says nonchalantly, "Now I know there was a request in there somewhere. I suggest you rephrase and ask me…*nicely*."

That last word barely cloaks his icy rage, beneath the guise of calm. The hairs on my nape prick up, my lizard brain finally dousing my temper. My mind scrambles to catch up to the danger of the situation. He's in the wrong, but he can't appear weak in front of this pack of jackals.

Lowering my head in deference, I ask, "I was wondering when we can work on the essay?"

There I did it. I lowered myself to satisfy his ego in front of his men and to get his cooperation.

"On the *what*?" he sneers. "You must have me confused with someone else."

A few snickers bubble up behind him.

My face flushes with a blast of fury. One debasement is

enough. Two is pushing it. I open my mouth to answer when an angry feminine voice comes up behind me.

"What the fuck is going on here?"

My head whips around.

Standing right behind me is Roxie, flanked by Aurora and Luminita, two of the meanest bitches I know.

My stomach drops. I just stepped in a heaping pile. There's no getting out of this without stinking.

"I-I was asking about when we'll meet," I stutter, impressed that I strung a full sentence together. "To work on the essay."

Roxie bumps my shoulder, shoving me out of the way, and saunters over to Lucian. She scoots up on the tabletop and drapes an arm around his waist. His abdomen clenches in response, but otherwise he remains stock-still. He doesn't move an inch. Not toward her. Not away from her. By doing nothing, he declares a united front.

My stomach does somersaults. Disillusionment flutters through my chest. Stupid me, for having imagined there was anything between us. *Mutual respect, my ass.*

Roxie nuzzles against the underside of his stiff jaw. His teeth clench, but he still doesn't move a muscle.

Roxie flicks a hand my way. "Write it yourself, Lupu girl." Her eyes narrow on me. Tone hard, she warns, "Do it and go away. No one wants you here."

My head buzzes like a swarm of hornets. I feel and see everything at once: the clatter of silverware on the white porcelain plates, the grease swimming in the sauce on my plate, the blazing heat from the fluorescent lights above. The gray plastic tray I'm holding suddenly feels like a fifty-pound weight. My arm muscles tremble with the effort to keep it aloft.

Roxie must think we have a project to do *together* so I

blurt out, "I was just asking when we were going to meet for tutoring."

The snickering around me breaks off. A blast of tension plasters me like a gummy, wet blanket.

Uh-oh.

Roxie stops nuzzling Lucian's throat and turns sharply toward me. "Stop embarrassing yourself with your pretend tutoring. Lucian's way above your fucking pay grade. Crawl back into the gutter you slithered out of, Lupu bitch."

She plants a sloppy kiss on Lucian's perfect full lips.

My stomach cramps with disgust. Too much. It's too much. Before I tear Roxie off him, I turn on my heel. Taking a wobbly step forward, I use my elbows to push through the wall of mean girls.

Abruptly, a hard shove to my back propels me forward. My feet slip under me. The crowd parts. I crash headlong to the floor. The tray smashes against my chest, plastering me with sticky spaghetti, sauce, and meatballs. Hot food scalds my skin through my white blouse and splashes onto my face.

My gaping mouth pulsates with pain. Blood drips onto the sticky linoleum floor. My gaze skitters to the side and I see a glimmer of white.

A pearly curved chip of a tooth rocks gently next to a floating dust bunny.

Oh God.

I drag my hand from underneath me and pat the linoleum, feeling for the sharp piece of my tooth. A crystal encrusted Alexander McQueen sneaker smashes across my splayed fingers.

I arch my back and yowl in pain.

Wrapping my hand around my wrist, I tug to dislodge my fingers, but Roxie only tamps down harder. I curl around her foot, slapping at her calf to release me. She grinds her foot down, the sharp-edged lugs of her sole crushing the delicate bones of my hand.

Laughter and hooting boom in my ears. The sounds ricochets off the ceiling like in an echo chamber. I hear the pounding of forks and knives on tabletops.

"Disgusting," I hear Anton mumble.

"That it is. Serves her right."

That was Lucian.

My lower lip trembles.

Roxie cackles above me.

Distracted, she eases up a little and I manage to shove her off me. She teeters for a moment before she falls on her butt, eyes wide with shock. She lifts her hands, stained red with sauce, off the dirty floor into the air.

Hissing, she comes at me with claws out.

I scramble back, the linoleum squeaking beneath me. She lunges forward. I cover my face just in time to protect my face. Sharp nails score down my hands, my collarbone, and rip open my shirt. It flaps open, baring my blistered skin and stained bra.

Whistles and catcalls join the hooting and shouts.

"Cat fight! Cat fight! Cat fight!"

The chant rises and falls around me in waves.

Between the gaps in my fingers, I stare up at Lucian, begging for help.

Alarm crosses his face. He moves forward as if to help, but Anton grabs his shoulder and roughly drags him back to his seat.

Amid deafening cheers, Roxie lets out a shrill shriek and launches at me again. I squeeze my eyes closed and clap my ears, hunching into a ball. I jerk with each kick to my ribs. Rolling onto my tummy, I tuck my knees beneath me to protect myself. Roxie yanks my head back by the hair, tearing at my scalp.

My throat exposed, I gasp, my mouth wide open.

"Look at her teeth! She's toothless!" Roxie screeches at the top of her lungs.

Tears pour down my cheeks.

Howls and cackles explode and swell around the cafeteria, followed by a harmony of more shouts.

I struggle on my knees, moving where Roxie leads me as she flaunts her trophy in front of the whole school, gap-tooth and all. Spaghetti and bits of meat peel off my blouse, the gaping side displaying my soiled bra. Blood dribbles down like paint splashes of a Pollack paining on my shirt. Tears join the rest of the liquid tableau of my chest. I'm covered in food and blood and filth. The foul smell of acrid tomato, blood, and pain invades my nostrils.

Through the ruckus, I hear, "Enough!"

It's Lucian.

Maybe.

The chant dies down. It feels like eternity for the pounding to follow suit and peter out.

Sapped of strength, I sway, hanging from the fistful of hair in Roxie's grip.

"Let it go," comes a commanding voice.

Roxie squeezes hard once, tearing strands of hair from the roots, before thrusting me away. My hands slap on the floor, breaking my fall and saving my face from smashing against the floor once more.

Tears drop from my eyes to water the ground. The shakes take over, one full-body shiver followed by trembling. My gap tooth clatters against my bottom teeth and I clamp my jaws, but to no avail. My nostrils are blocked; globs of snot smack the floor.

I gag. *Gross.*

Shock sets in. My mind drops in a trance as I try to scoop up the food with my scraped fingers and place it on the tray, but it's hard to do through my blurry vision.

From the corner of my eye, I see Monica stand up with a sigh. She stalks toward the crime scene and turns on Lucian. "I don't know why she came up to you, but she must have had a good reason. You're a real asshole, you know that?"

Monica is a Lupu girl, but she has clout. Lucian glowers at her.

"This is between bitches. Since when do I step in on a fight between *girls*?"

"Yeah, well next time, control your bitch," she retorts with a toss of her head.

Roxie opens her mouth, but Monica raises her hand, stopping her in her tracks. "Don't even. I don't give a shit what happened, but whatever it was, it ends now. She's a Lupu, for God's sake. She doesn't want your man, Roxie. Stop acting like she's challenging you. You know damn well that one Lupu-Popescu marriage doesn't make a pattern. Get over yourself."

Glaring down at me, Monica says in disgust, "Leave it, already."

She grasps my elbow and hauls me up to my feet. I try to hold on, but the tray slips from my shaky grasp and clatters to the floor. With a quivering hand, I'm barely steady enough to sweep up the piece of tooth from the floor and tuck it into my pocket.

Bits and pieces of food fall off me as I crouch, plunking down on the linoleum floor with a wet plopping sound. Dazed, I numbly move to retrieve the tray, but she snaps, "For God's sake, you've done enough for one day."

I stifle a huge sob, letting it shudder through my frame.

As if it's not bad enough that I've completely disgraced myself, I've also disgraced my clan.

Despite my humiliation, I glance up at Lucian.

The muscle in his jaw is ticking a mile a minute. His gaze is lasering through the crowd of students, daring them to make a sound.

Boys leer at my chest and my shoulders curl inward.

Slashing a ferocious look my way, he barks at me, "Cover yourself."

As I grasp the sides of my shirt and clutch them together, he stares the boys down until they divert their eyes.

Monica yanks my arm impatiently and pulls me to standing, but I slip and crash back to the floor. Gleeful cackles ripple out behind me. Monica sighs with exasperation.

Shame burns through me. My face is hot, my cheeks are scalding like they're on fire. I swallow down a mixture of blood and saliva, grimacing at the taste. This is the taste of humiliation. *Why can't I just die?* Right this moment. I squeeze my eyes closed and pray to disappear, but when I snap them open, no, I'm still here.

I take a deep whiff of metallic blood and spoiled food and tears, and swallow down the bile that's gurgled up my throat. I lick my lips and get another nasty mouthful.

Breathe it. Taste it. Swallow it.

Never forget it.

And never forgive.

"Hey," says Lucian, directed either to me or Monica. I wouldn't know since I have my head down, fixed on one gray square of linoleum.

"Don't ever fucking talk to me that way," he warns.

His gaze rakes over me, a curl on his lips as if to say: *How could you think to approach me? Look at yourself, covered in blood and spaghetti. Embarrassing yourself. Embarrassing your clan.*

Oh, don't worry, I drill back into him with every ounce of loathing in my body. *I'll never talk to you again. Never approach you. Never look at you again. I hate you.*

I've kept to myself and tried to stay under the radar. I never asked to tutor him. I never asked to be around him. He pretends to treat me like a human only to screw me over. And then when I have no choice to approach him, he allows *this* to happen.

I glare at every arrogant line of his face, memorizing it. A sick, twisted part of me still wants him and I hate him even more for it. Rage and revulsion surges through me. Rage at him. Revulsion at myself.

Slowly, I plant my hand on the only dry patch of linoleum around me. Struggling to stand, I finally make it up and step out of the mess I've made.

I don't bother to grab my shirt again and close it. Let them stare. Let them see my peaked nipples outlined in my wet bra. It's a scarlet A—a bright, daring sign of shame—and I wrap it around me like a cloak. My humiliation *is* my strength. I will come back stronger and I will burn this school down to ashes.

As soon as she sees that I'm stable on my feet, Monica steps away—she doesn't want to be infected by my disgust-ingness.

Chin to chest, I stiffly toddle down the aisle between tables in my walk of shame. Popescu faces float in my vision, gloating faces. Then there's the Lupu faces, eyes darting away from me in shame. Like a death-row inmate being marched to the electric chair, it feels like the longest and most surreal walk of my life.

Swallowing the lump in my throat, I limp around the last table with the exit in sight when I trip over my own feet, my squeaking Vans the only sound in the eerie silence reigning over the cafeteria. I grab the rounded edge of a table and lurch toward freedom. One last glance behind me and I lock eyes with Lucian.

There's something there. Regret maybe?

Not caring, I turn away.

Fuck him. I hope he burns in hell.

CHAPTER 6

STAR

The next morning, Lucian and I stand in front of Cristo like two chastened kids, which I guess is what we are to him. We're back at his parents' cramped townhouse. Cristo is sprawled out on the couch, one arm looped across the top like a king at rest.

After getting out of the cafeteria, the first thing I did was call Crina and Gabby, but their phones were on silent. They were likely in the library. I crept to my locker like the pariah I was, grabbed a sweatshirt, and booked it down to the basement where I patched myself up and changed in a bathroom. Hugging the walls while praying no one noticed me, I slunk out of school.

Crina and Gabby rushed over once school was done, but a day later my eyes are still red from crying.

There's no rest for me on this gray, foggy morning. I'd received my summons from Cristo and had no choice but to drag myself out of bed and trudge the few blocks to his house. Even the blossoming cherry trees on his block couldn't cheer me up.

And now, shifting from foot to foot, I feel like my insides were scraped out and force-fed back to me.

My tongue slides over my chipped tooth.

Disgusting.

Just like Anton and Lucian had said.

I made an appointment with the dentist, but I won't be seen until midweek. Apparently, a chipped tooth is not considered an emergency.

I refuse to look at Lucian standing a couple of feet away from me. Still close enough for me to claw his eyes out, only this morning I'm much too raw to kill him. I need more time to lick my wounds—and get my tooth fixed—before I willingly suffer his presence again.

And then, it will only be to tear him apart with my bare hands.

After making us stand there long enough to feel sufficiently chastened, Cristo starts. "I don't know what the fuck happened yesterday but let me make myself clear. I don't give a shit."

He waves his phone around, the screen shaking too much for me to be able to see anything beyond the fact that it's our school's online grading platform. Guess he didn't get the viral video of me getting my butt whupped. I suppose I should be grateful for small mercies.

"The only thing that matters is the 'E' in English. That should be an "F," by the way." He gives Lucian the stink eyes. "I had a talk with your teacher and she did me the favor of giving you an extension. You're welcome."

His gaze swinging back and forth between Lucian and me, he asks incredulously, "You were supposed to take care of this. Christ, what the fuck happened?"

I'm not sure who he's addressed this question to, but I

want to sarcastically answer, *don't look at me. That's what happens when you miss an assignment in Ms. Sava's class, something I was trying to avoid by running after your little protégé.*

He waves his hand. "Never mind. I don't want to know. I have a business and a clan to run." He locks onto Lucian with a fierce glare. "I don't have time for this high school drama, understand?"

His eyes shift to me and the glare softens a fraction. Whether it's because I'm a girl, because I'm not a Popescu, or because he knows of the devastating incident in the cafeteria, I don't know.

Hoping it's the latter, and to appeal to his better nature, I say, "You heard how he treated me."

I instantly cover my mouth with my hand, the gesture bringing forth an upsurge of searing shame over my broken tooth, my humiliation. Shame morphs into fury and I fling my hand toward Lucian and declare, "I cannot work with him. You have to find someone else to do it."

Now his glare is back. And fixated on me. I tremble but clench my tummy to hold strong under his scowl.

Lucian moves in front of me, breaking Cristo's glower on me, and I hate that I'm grateful for the reprieve.

Cristo makes an impatient gesture with his hand. "Get the fuck out of my way. Don't act like you need to protect her from *me*. I'm not the one who embarrassed her in front of the whole school."

A wave of vindication swells inside me. *So he has heard about it.*

Lucian's shoulders bunch and he growls at his *şef.*

I slap him in the back, because, I mean *come on*, how dare he get mad at the truth. This whole mess is his fault. His tight back muscles twitch from my slap. He slides over a bit but still blocks me from Cristo's view.

I smack him in the flank, but he doesn't move.

"He's an asshole," resumes Cristo to me.

His voice softens. "In case you didn't already know, now you do. You don't have to like him, Star. Hate him for all I care—"

"Oh, I do," I whisper harshly, leaning around Lucian's bulk to speak to Cristo.

"Don't interrupt me," he warns, but his voice only firms up a touch.

His focus returns to Lucian. "I can't believe I have to bring you back in front of me like a wet-behind-the-ears boy. How can you be my *consilier* if you can't handle high school drama properly?"

Lucian stiffens beside me, and I cackle in glee inside. *Yeah, how is that, you prick?*

"Fucking apologize already," Cristo demands impatiently. "Apologize and deal with this, Lucian."

I cross my arms over my chest and tap my foot. I can't wait to see this apology. Hell yeah. I'm aching for it because I'm going to shoot it down so fast he'll get whiplash.

Lucian licks his lips, and says, "I will fucking deal with her, Cristo. I'll apologize as I see fit. When I see fit. You won't hear from either of us again. She's under my protection and I'll handle this the way I think best."

My eyes bug out of my head.

Oh, wow.

In my clan, no one would dare talk to my *şef* like that, other than his brothers. And from what Tatum has told me, only behind closed doors. Not in front of any outsiders like me. Of course, these Popescus are barbaric, so I shouldn't be surprised by this total lack of etiquette.

Unfazed by the challenge, Cristo looks at him dubiously, his lips pinched to one side. "Yeah, you think you can do that? From where I'm sitting, all I see are a bunch of Fs and a nice girl you've reduced to tears."

Preach, brother, preach.

Lucian glowers at him.

"Am I lying? Tell me if I'm fucking wrong, Lucian? Oh, and while you're at it, tell me how you're gonna make this right."

"I'll fucking handle it," he snaps. "She'll help me and you won't see another bad grade again."

I suppress a snort of derision and step to the side to watch Cristo's reprimand. While Lucian isn't squirming nearly as much as I'd like, I can still vindictively enjoy the show.

"You better *fucking handle it* because this is your last chance. Don't let me hear another word of nonsense and don't let me see another bad grade."

He leans forward, looking like a bad-dude predator ready to tear into the flesh of his own kin. "Believe me, you do not want me involved. You need to take care of this so you can get your head back in the game with business. Clan business. And as I've said before, your graduation is clan business, so for fuck's sake, just fix it."

He turns his attention on me and reprimands me. "You should've come to me earlier, Star."

I wince at his chastisement, but he waves my discomfort away magnanimously. "Never mind, you have a second chance to make it right. But next time you have a problem, you make sure to come to me."

Lucian grabs my upper arm. I gasp and swat at his hand, but his grip is too strong. Dragging my struggling form behind him, he contradicts his boss. "Nah-ah, she's under my protection. She doesn't come to you for anything. I will handle her and any issues that come up. Me. Only me."

I make a sound of protest from behind Lucian. Wiggling out of his grip, I finally break his hold on me and step away from him.

Cristo snorts. "If I didn't know better, I'd say you were claiming her."

I inhale sharply.

A laugh, the hysterical kind, bubbles up inside me and spills out.

I'd stake my life on the fact that Lucian Popescu would never claim me. *Never.* He can barely acknowledge me in public. He called me disgusting. He sure as hell didn't save me. None of those behaviors speak of a man who cares one ounce for a woman.

I'm no better than the dirt under his shoes.

He grabs me again, cutting off my giggle as he drags me back to his side.

Fury billows off him in waves, which isn't surprising since he doesn't have much of a sense of humor. He can't appreciate Cristo's joke.

But instead of rejecting me like I expect, he only repeats, "She's under my protection. There will be no more problems."

Humph, that's what he thinks.

I'd shake him off again, but I want to get out of here, and to do that, Lucian needs to show he has control of the situation. For that to happen, I'm willing to go along and let him think he's in control.

But there will be a price—a heavy price.

I may not be fighting him and throwing his hands off me, but I give him a glare of pure loathing.

Payback is gonna be a bitch, Lucian, and I won't stop until I've made you cry.

CHAPTER 7

LUCIAN

Satisfied with his scolding, Cristo leaves me alone with Star. I can feel her glare burning a hole into my face.

Fuck, it's easier confronting Cristo than dealing with an angry female.

Strife with women is not part of my daily life. As the man of the house for years now, my mother and kid sister defer to me. Sure, Zoe can be annoying, but when push comes to shove, she worships the ground I walk on.

The same could never be said of the woman standing at my side.

Ignoring the tension wafting over from her direction, I pick up her ratty backpack from the floor.

Inclining my head toward Cristo's front door, I command, "Let's go to my house and talk in private."

Her eyes narrow. Her lip curls into a snarl, unwittingly flashing me her broken tooth. I clamp my jaws together and bare my teeth to force out the breath painfully caught in my throat. I hate seeing her perfection marred like that. I hate knowing I had a hand in it. It may not have been intentional, but there's no denying I unwittingly played into Star getting hurt.

Star crosses her arms over her chest and snorts in disgust before she snatches at her backpack like she can't stand the fact that I'm touching it. I may be pleased by her little show of spirit, but I lift it out of her reach and give her a no-nonsense glare.

Yes, I know I fucked up in the cafeteria, but what did she expect?

Sure, it got personal between us in private, but *private* is the pertinent word here. I may have shown her my human side, what little remains, but that doesn't mean I'd tolerate having my personal business flaunted in public. What was up with mentioning the tutoring in front of Dinu and every other Popescu male in the vicinity? Was she delusional?

And she seemed to be under the impression that I was avoiding her.

I was working.

What would a precious princess like her know about having a nonstop, around the clock job on top of school? All I ever see her do is read her books or work on her laptop without a care in the world.

I sigh.

And what rare little bit of peace I felt with her is now gone. Around her, I didn't feel so exposed. I didn't feel the pressure to posture or fight. Hell, even when I made it difficult for her, she had a way of calming me with the weird bond we had.

She's acting like I'm a monster, like this was entirely my fault, but once Roxie showed up, everything spiraled out of control. It ramped up to a whole new level, one between women. Even if Roxie wasn't my soon-to-be fiancée, she's a high-ranking female in my clan. On clan loyalty alone, there was no way I could intercede.

No, Star was on her own.

And speaking of being on her own, what was she thinking standing up to Roxie? She didn't even have her two little friends to back her up. I mean, did she have a death wish or something? Was she into degradation? She should've just run out of there.

"Come on," I prod her as I move toward the front door, leaving her little choice but to follow.

I open the door, hold it for her, and shoot her another hard stare.

She tries to match my expression with a stubborn one of her own, but I hold it until she breaks. I suppress a sigh of irritation. I'll always win out in the end, but now there's this heavy tension between us.

She huffs as she breezes past me with her nose in the air like she can't stand me. I get it; there are days I feel the same way.

I follow her as she skips down the brownstone steps to the sidewalk.

Pointing to my house, I direct her. "The next one over."

Traditionally, a *consilier* lives close to the *şef*. There's currently no *consilier*, but since my father went crazy and killed himself, no one had the audacity to kick us out of our home, so we're still here.

She swiftly marches toward my house, leaving me trailing far behind. It's definitely a form of disrespect, but I let her go ahead. No need to antagonize her further when I need her help. If I wasn't holding her backpack, I'm not even sure I could get her to my house. But it's imperative we talk; I must get control of the situation and make sure we don't end up back in front of Cristo again. I didn't appreciate the tightness in my chest when Star was called up in front of him and I liked it even less when he butted into my business with her.

Star jogs lightly up the stoop and waits for me by my front door.

I look up at her, framed by the front door of my familial home, and jolt in place.

She looks so fucking pretty up there, glaring at me with sparks in her eyes. Her hair is glistening its pearl-white, blonde color. Star's soul calls to me—more than ever, since I've failed her—but so does my goal.

It's about my family name, yes, but it's also about my mother's and sister's futures.

Especially my sister's. Zoe just started high school. She's growing up and before I know it, she'll be getting engaged. I need to have solidified my family's status in the clan by then. I can never risk having her marry a man with problems, like my father. She's going to have the pick of the crop.

I take the steps two at a time. Turning the key in the lock, I pause to warn her, "My mother and sister might be home. Behave yourself. They know nothing outside of you tutoring me."

Star gives me a look of pure loathing. "Your sister goes to our school. I'm sure she knows all about what happened."

I cringe inwardly. Jesus, I'm going to have to have a talk with Zoe about it.

"Even so, behave yourself."

"Ugh, let's set the record straight, Lucian," she says in a haughty tone. "I'm not the one with behavior problems. I know how to treat people right."

I growl low. Little Miss Goody Two-Shoes. Fuck, she can be annoying.

Ignoring her, I put on a cheery face for the sake of my mother. The woman's suffered enough for one lifetime. I'm not about to add to it.

I step into the doorway and a wave of longing hits me. The house is preserved exactly as it was when my father was alive, a nod to the happiest time of her life.

From her perch on the burnt-orange loveseat, my mother's head swivels to the sound of the opening door. Zoe is beside her. They're framed in silhouette by the light coming from the window behind them. The strong sunlight is diffused by a set of long sheer white curtains, bordered with heavier curtains and valances. In contrast, the dark parquet floor, covered with a traditional rug, matches the exposed beams on the ceiling.

Light and dark, the story of our family.

My mother holds a small cup of Turkish coffee but immediately abandons it on the smooth cherry wood table at her side without taking a sip. Brows raised, she stands up to greet our guest, her hands clasped in front of her expectantly. Zoe rises belatedly behind Mama, her mouth open at seeing a Lupu coming through the front door.

"I didn't expect you back so soon— Ah, you've brought a guest," she says.

"Mama, this is Starlene," I explain as I reach her and drop a kiss on her cheek. "Star, this is my mother."

I ruffle Zoe's hair. She smacks my hand away with a fake snarl of irritation as I introduce her, "And this is my kid sister, Zoe."

I smirk. "She's a freshman this year."

Star reaches my mother and gives her a kiss on each cheek, before stepping back and patiently awaiting the inspection. She knows the drill. Mama grabs her forearm, keeping her in place as she gives Star the once-over.

She squeezes Star's arm, a gesture of welcome. "Are you hungry? Do you want anything to drink?"

Zoe gives a little snort. "It's eleven o'clock in the morning, Mama. She can't possibly be hungry yet."

Mama frowns down at my little sister. "You never know. It's always good to ask. Remember this, Zoe. You'll want to be a good host when you're in your own home."

Zoe rolls her eyes and Star covers her mouth to muffle a little giggle. The sweet sound makes my heart skip a beat.

"No, no," I quickly reply, cutting off the potential for any long, protracted interaction. "We're only here to get schoolwork done. We're going downstairs where it's quiet."

Star's smile slides off her face. I feel a pang of remorse. Damn her for making me aware of her every expression and gesture.

"Oh, okay," my mother replies, confusion written on her face.

I rarely bring people home through the front door, and now that I have, I shouldn't cut their first introduction short. My mother just finished rebuking Zoe about how to be a good host. Truthfully, I don't know why I brought Star in this way when there's a perfectly good back entrance that goes straight into the basement. Maybe it's because I only allow the women I fuck to come in through the back. Maybe it's to relieve the guilt gnawing at me about yesterday. Maybe it's my way of making restitution. Have her meet my family. Treat her with respect.

Feeling helpless after my abrupt interruption, I gesture downstairs to my domain and follow Star to the basement.

In the basement, I drop her backpack beside a worn, tufted sapphire-colored couch in the center of the room. My domain also doubles as a storage room for my mother's castoffs, which explains the excess of chairs and other furniture. There are random decorative ornaments like a series of colorful peasant dishes on the walls, carved wood sculptures, and even a chipped gold-painted icon of Saint George that found refuge in an abandoned corner of the room. We like to snort cocaine off it in our most sacrilegious moments.

I kinda hate this room because it's full of random objects that make no sense together, but not gonna lie, that part works well for hosting parties.

I leave her to get settled as I go to the back room to bring my laptop, notebook, and the paperback book for the essay.

On my way back in, I halt at the threshold. Star is standing rigidly near the base of the staircase, looking like she's about to flee.

"Sit down," I order dismissively, waving my hand across the numerous sitting options available.

She shakes her head. "Before I do, we need to get something straight."

CHAPTER 8

STAR

*L*ucian looks up at me sharply, his brows creased in confusion. Or is it irritation? Truly, I don't care. I'm not budging one inch, not lifting one finger to help him, until we get a few things settled.

He's not used to being spoken to the way I just spoke to him, but he sealed his own fate when he promised Cristo he would take care of *everything*—meaning me and the situation he's done nothing to fix.

And if he thinks bringing me in through the front door instead of the back door like everyone else—his basement parties are notorious—and introducing me to his mom is some kind of apology, he's sorely mistaken.

I'd like to think he sealed his fate when he left me out to dry, but that would be a lie. If it wasn't for Cristo's intervention, Lucian wouldn't care about what he had done to me.

My nerves are on edge, but my anger is righteous. It burns deep, rooted in the humiliation I've suffered at his hands. And in case he thinks to share the blame with Roxie, I put it solely on his shoulders.

I breathe in the anger, draw from the bottomless well of it in my soul, and find the courage to say my piece. "I'm willing to help you, but I have one condition."

He makes a noise full of scorn. "If you want an apology, you're not getting it. I didn't do anything wrong."

A white-hot brand of pain and fury spears through me.

"You did me wrong, you prick," I snarl as I charge into the room. "You should apologize to me. If you were a good man, if you were a decent man, you would."

I wave my hand as if batting away a mosquito. "But I don't expect that level of maturity from you. I don't want your stupid apology, so don't waste my time with one. There's only one way you can make this worthwhile for me."

"Oh, and what is that?" he sneers, a brow lifted in challenge.

"Mock me all you want, Lucian. I don't care. I've thought long and hard about this. There's only one thing that will get me to stick around, keep Cristo off your back, and get you your precious diploma."

In my bed, under the covers, I'd thought about what would make this right and what I could get from him that I couldn't get from anyone else. I require safety and secrecy —and he's capable of giving me both.

In the blink of an eye, he's in front of me. Taking my chin in his fingers, he snarls, "The fucking Popescu prince asks you to do something, you fucking do it. End of story."

I shake my head but can't loosen his grip.

Grasping his hand, I try to pry his fingers off. No use.

I stop fighting him but it doesn't prevent me from glaring at him with the full blast of my hatred. "I'll do it, if you give me what I want. Otherwise, I'll go to Cristo and tell him to find someone else. You swore to him that he wouldn't hear from either of us again, that there wouldn't be any problems. It will make you look weak if you can't control a woman."

The anger coming off him is palpable, but I lift my chin and promise, "But if you give me what I want, I'll be dutiful and quiet."

"Since when are you so stubborn?" he asks, his features twisted in exasperation.

He might be exasperated, but he's got nothing on me.

"Since I'm sick of being good. Good equals stupid equals getting treated like you're nothing, and I'm done with that. The good girl is dead, so get used to it."

He shakes his head a little but doesn't relent on his grip of my chin. "You're talking in riddles. Spit it out already and tell me what you want."

I wrap my fingers around his hand and he finally allows me to pry his fingers off. "If you'd let me talk, I'll explain."

"Go ahead then," he snaps.

God, I hate him.

Considering just how much I hate him, it's a wonder I'm about to propose this to him. But my choices are limited, I remind myself. As horrible as he is, he's still my best option. Okay, let's face it—he's my only option.

"After graduation, I want you to help me escape," I blurt. "I'm doing everything I can to get into a good college far, far away and, when I get accepted, I'm going to leave this hellhole. You help me get out without anyone finding me and in exchange, I'll help you with your reading assignments, essays, and preparing for tests. I won't help you cheat, but I'll be at your beck and call."

I gulp. "Anytime you need me. Day or night."

Shock spreads over his face.

I pause and take in a deep breath before emphasizing, "But only if I get what I want."

He stumbles back a step.

"Oh, come on," I huff. "Don't act so surprised. And before you ask me any stupid questions, the answer is yes, I know what I'm doing. Yes, I'm aware that I'm ruining my chances of a good marriage."

His face morphs into shock.

"God, stop looking at me like that. I won't get married. So what?"

"*So what?*" he asks, outrage reverberating through his tone. "Why in the fuck would you do that?"

Men are so dense, it's a wonder they're the ones who rule the world. They must think we're incredibly dumb. How could we possibly be interested in anything but the stupid rules they've set out for us? His shock is almost laughable.

I cross my arms over my chest and reply, "After the way you've treated me, I'm not sharing anything with you. Just to be clear, Lucian, I don't want *any*thing else from you. I don't want an apology. I don't want friendship. I don't need you to respect me or my choices. I'd have to care enough about what you think for that to happen. In case I didn't make it clear, if you help me, I'll disappear forever. You'll never see me again, God willing."

If possible, his expression only turns darker. I thought he'd be pleased with that last bit, but whatever. I'm beyond caring what he thinks.

His face is stiff, but I ignore it and keep going, "This is an arrangement to get me where I want to be, and that's all it is. The only thing I ask is that you maintain the utmost discretion. No one finds out about our arrangement. Not Anton. Not Marku. Not your sister. Not your mother."

He jeers, "My family knows nothing about my life."

I roll my eyes. "Your sister knows plenty. She's not an idiot. I'm sure she knows you're a manwhore."

"Hey," he snaps.

I wince. Ugh, why did I say that? I sound like I care. Which I don't.

Fluttering my hand dismissively, I continue, "Whatever, it's none of my business. Do we have a deal?"

"Just tell me why you want this," he demands. "You answer, and I'll consider your proposal."

I sigh.

He doesn't deserve to know. He's done nothing to earn it, and I don't want him using any additional information against me. I've already put everything on the line by divulging my plan to him. The less he knows, the better.

"I'm serious," he warns.

I scrutinize him carefully. His clenching jaw tells me he's not going to let this go. *Fuck.*

I huff out a sigh. "Fine, you want to know? I'll tell you. You get to do exactly what you want to do. I want the same thing."

He pulls back in confusion.

"Does this have to do with your brother's move to Cali? Before that, you were just another good girl. Now you suddenly want to leave your clan and abandon your mother." His brows lower. "Is this a cry for help?"

Jesus, he thinks this is silly rebelling because my brother's gone. Sure, Tatum's confession about our father's treachery, and then him leaving me to deal with it alone, triggered a seismic change in my life. But why couldn't this just be about fairness, ya know? About the fact that he can do what he damn well wants whenever he wants and I can't?

I stiffen. "I'm not talking about my brother with you. You wanted an answer and I gave you one."

I flick my index finger between us. "There won't be any heart-to-hearts between us, Lucian. There's nothing between us except the time we study together and the times we plot my escape."

He drops to the couch, which sags deeply beneath his bulk. The springs on that thing must be gone.

Dropping his head in his hands, he mutters, "Christ. You're just a girl. You can't make it out there alone. You'll get hurt."

Irritation rattles through my chest. I'm not his family or clan. He doesn't care about me. In fact, he thinks I'm disgusting. What's his problem?

My hands twitch from wanting to wrap my fingers around his thick throat and throttle him.

"Oh, puh-lease," I reply. "Stop acting like a fussy prude. And stop pretending you care. Just 'cause you're a man doesn't give you any proprietary rights over me. If it did, you would've acted on it in the cafeteria. You would've done *anything* to protect me." I pause and remind him, "Which you didn't."

I take a deep breath and get into the groove of scolding him. "Don't be a hypocrite. I'm not family. I'm not clan. I'm not dating an outsider, which might give you a reason to tattle on me. Stay in your lane, Lucian. God knows, that's how I plan to treat you."

His gray eyes turn dark. He looks thwarted. Frustrated. Almost...*hurt?*...by my speech.

I chuckle quietly to myself.

This selfish guy? Impossible.

Lucian only cares about three things. Being *consilier*, marrying Roxie, and besting Dinu. That's it.

"You owe me," I say softly, going for the jugular. "You owe me for what happened in the cafeteria and you'll owe me for doing everything possible to help you graduate. It's a debt, Lucian. Are you the type of guy who leaves a debt hanging between you and a girl? Hmm? 'Cause that's not the made men I know."

He's doing that thing he does when he's thinking hard, looking far off into the distance even though we're in a cramped basement with a low-hanging ceiling above our heads.

His gaze swings back to me, his eyes burning, almost angry. Is he upset because I'm finally getting something out of this arrangement that up till now held no value for me whatsoever?

God, what a jerk.

I tap my foot impatiently. "Come on, Lucian, enough with the suspense already."

"You have a mouth on you, you know that?"

"Oh, *I* know. This is new to you because *you* don't know me."

Ignoring my little jib, he argues, "You can't leave your mother. You're the only person she has left."

My spine stiffens and I draw myself up tall. "You know nothing about me and my mother so kindly keep your mouth shut."

A rumble comes from his chest.

He stands up, steps close, and looms over me. He circles around me, face a bit slack as if he's seeing me for the first time. My stupid body reacts to his nearness.

Stupid, stupid hormones. Damn them.

He makes one circle, then another, and stops in front of me. He tucks one hand under his arm, holds his chin with his other hand, finger tapping on his bottom lip as he thinks, likely considering every angle of our agreement and how he can exploit it to his benefit or get out of it altogether.

"If we enter into this oral contract, then we do things

my way. I'm in control. I make the plans. Think you can handle that, with your sassy mouth and witchy attitude?"

The elusive scent of freedom passes beneath my nose. Exhilaration strums through me to my nerve endings. I can almost taste the freedom. I can, but I lock it down tight and reply, "I can handle anything you dish out. Think I've proven that, no?"

He gives a ghost of a wince at my little dig but sticks out his hand to seal our deal.

I place my hand in his.

Electricity shoots through me.

I try to pull away, but he holds tight. "Don't fuck with me, Star. You'll regret it."

A spark of anger fires through me, but I laugh it off. I've gotten what I want. He's just being a sore loser. He thinks I'm a silly girl, but I've given this plan a lot of thought. In less than three months, he'll go his way and I'll go mine, and we'll never set eyes on each other again.

Giving him a smug smile, I tease, "I promise to be good, this one last time."

I yank my hand away, and he lets me take it back.

With that out of the way, I'm finally ready to focus on the essay he's missed, along with the next assignment Ms. Sava already posted on Google Classroom.

Satisfied, I plop down on the couch and sniff. *Eww.* The smell.

Turning my nose up at him, I look away as I swallow down the nausea.

Beside me, he grabs his book and pauses. "What's wrong?"

Still facing away, I stifle a gag and ask, "Isn't this where you party?"

My gaze flicks to the glass top of the side table to my left. I'd heard how it's covered in white with cocaine for his wild parties. There's a jar on the table that gets filled to the brim with the highest-grade Molly on the market. Of course, it's easy for him to supply his debauched parties since his clan sells anywhere there's a beach in the tri-state area. Rumor has it that's the exact wording in the treaty between the Lupu and Popescu clans.

Of course, beneath the question is another, more pertinent one. *Isn't this where you have sex with the many women you fuck?*

"Yes," he answers. There's no point in lying when it's common knowledge.

"Georgina, Marina, Joanna. Sofia and Cici. And let's not forget Roxie," I say bitterly. "Unless, of course, you haven't had sex with her yet because you need to wave the blood-stained sheets around the morning after."

"She's a virgin," he confirms.

Relief sweeps over me before I shake my head ruefully.

Gag, I'm acting as if it matters whether he's fucked her or not. One day soon, he will. By the end of the school year, if the gossips have it right, and they do because it comes straight from the horse's mouth. Roxie. According to her, they'll be engaged the day after prom.

Not my problem, I remind myself firmly. I'm here for the escape plan and nothing else.

Along with the tension between us, it's dank and stifling down here, which is not helped by the fact that I've always had a sensitive nose. It smells so bad, of urine and rancid sex no doubt, that I want to puke. I blow out a breath to hold off a wave of nausea.

He grabs my hand and stands up, tugging me up with him. "Come on, there's another room. One that's clean."

Holding my breath, I follow him because, really, what choice do I have?

He leads me down a hallway and opens the door to a

smaller room. There's soundproofing on the ceiling like the music rooms in school, just bigger and cozier, which isn't saying much since this room is spare.

There's a large wide window overlooking the back garden, a row of rose bushes filtering the strong sunlight from the south. One entire wall is covered with shelves filled with vinyl records. There's an old record player on a low bookshelf sitting beside a new turntable with a canary-yellow base. I spot a black box with two circular things on top, which I don't recognize.

Knowing me and my curiosity, he offers, "It used to be my father's music room, where he practiced his trumpet. Now it's mine."

The way he says it, low and almost melancholic, touches on a poignant undercurrent beneath his simple words.

He waves to the double bed and explains, "After my father died, I stayed down here till late in the night. Listening to music till I fell asleep on the sofa. Finally, my mom put a bed down here."

Other than that, there's an old desk, with a chair and a couple of single file cabinets, like one would find in an office.

"I'd sit for hours while he practiced or played music. More than half of this collection is his," he says fondly as he tenderly reaches out and touches a few records.

"Did you cry alone when your father died?" I let slip, thinking back to the time he'd held me when my dad died.

I wave my hands in apology. "Sorry, not my business."

He grabs my hand and hauls me closer to him. "Yeah, I did," he replied. "I cried alone."

His proximity, with his enticing scent of a pine resin, sweet, yet sharp and tangy, addles my brain.

He wraps his arms around me, linking them at the base

of my spine. I remember the day in the art room, when he found me crying over my dad. That day haunts me still. It's hard to forget one of the worst times of my life when Lucian was somehow able to make everything better.

"You said never to cry alone," I whisper.

"I lied. For you, I lied. I didn't want *you* crying alone," he replies, his voice a husky rasp. He shrugs one shoulder. "Me, it's not so important."

"You make no sense, you know that. You sit with me when I cry over my father, but then you humiliate me in front of the entire school."

"I had my reasons for doing what I did."

"What was your reason back then?"

He looks down at me quizzically. "To comfort you, of course."

I expel the breath I was holding. "And in front of the entire school?"

He pauses for a long moment, his gray eyes turning stormy again. "To protect you."

"From whom?" I prompt. "Roxie?"

"Among others."

I tilt my head, examining him, really trying to look deep, because I don't know whether to believe him. He says he did it to protect me. Could be true, could be a lie. Ultimately, it doesn't matter. I would do well to remember that these moments of intimacy are meaningless. He won't protect me when it matters and I'm here for business, nothing else.

Anyway, no one ever comes back from coercion and extortion. No relationship can grow from a poisoned well, that much I know.

After all, isn't that how I want it?

CHAPTER 9

STAR

"He's going to help me," I explain to Crina as I slide my student MetroCard through the turnstile and push the metal bar forward. Passing through the turnstile, I turn around to catch Crina's reaction as she follows me onto the subway platform.

Her eyes are wide, eyebrows high. "You went to him? Gabby and I could've helped you, ya know. You didn't have to go to anyone else."

The local subway rattles into the station with its green luminescent number 6 in the front. A gust of hot air swishes my hair off my shoulder. We don't get on since we're waiting for the express train to Grand Central Station, where we'll transfer to the subway heading toward Queens.

As the silver-colored train rolls out of the station, giving us a moment of blissful quiet, I continue, "No you couldn't. You and Gabby will be the first suspects and they'll break you down. Believe me, the less you know, the better."

"I know you want to leave," she points out. "But getting help from him isn't smart."

"Yes, it is. That's what I'm trying to tell you. There's nothing to trace back to him. After the cafeteria incident, no one will link us together. You read mysteries. No one would believe my bully helped me. And Lucian won't come forward and sabotage his chances to become *consilier*."

"In Agatha Christie mysteries you look for the guy who no one suspects," Crina points out, leaning against a cobalt-blue-colored column. "That would be him."

Getting frustrated, I ask, "Why are you being so negative? I expected you to be more supportive."

"I am supportive, but I don't see how this is going to work. You're a softie. How are you going to do this alone?"

The number four express train pulls in. We take a couple of seats at the end of the car, which is relatively empty at this hour in the afternoon.

"I'm tougher than you think," I reply stoutly.

"I thought I was rebellious just thinking of convincing my future husband to let me go to college like Cat, but you're giving me a run for my money."

I let out a sigh. "I have nothing keeping me here except my mother. Gabby's going to leave. You know her sister's only hanging on until she graduates."

Her voice sounds forlorn. "What about me?"

The conductor's garbled voice comes on the speakers in the car as the train pulls into the next station.

I wait for the racket to stop and declare, "You'll be married, and to a good man. Your father will make sure of that. What am I supposed to do here? I won't be shackled to a husband. While you live a happy life and have children, am I supposed to watch until I die an old maid with my drunken mother?"

An older woman sitting across from us looks up from her hardcover book and frowns at me. I boldly return her look. She quickly schools her face, drops her gaze to her book, and scrunches her forehead together as if concentrating on what she's reading.

Reading my ass.

She was eavesdropping, not that I can blame her. In a city as big as New York, people eavesdrop all the time. Calling my mom a drunk wasn't a nice thing to say, but I'll never see her again. I don't care what she overhears or what she thinks about it.

"I hear you…" Crina replies hesitantly.

The difference between Crina and me is that she has a father who has her best interests at heart. She may have ambitions beyond marriage, but regardless of whatever happened between her and Marku, her father will make sure she marries a solid, decent man. Well, as much as that's possible in our world. He'd have to be a made man, of course, to be able to protect her. And her father is all about protecting her.

Do I feel jealous? Not exactly, but I have to put myself first. Crina will be fine. *Me?* Not so much.

"There's no hope for me here. I've got to go," I repeat. "And he's going to help me."

A surge of determination—a pure victorious wave of power—sweeps over me. I'm going to use Lucian to get my way and get the hell out of here. I'm going to treat him the way he's treated me—like I'm disposable.

Crina's not convinced, though.

Canting her head to the side, she gives me a speculative look. "I don't know…this could turn into a nightmare.

What if Roxie finds out? What if she thinks you two are fucking?"

"What if she does? It's not like she doesn't know he has sex with other girls."

"Yeah, but you're different."

I shake my head vehemently. "I'm not."

"You are," she argues. "He's had a thing for you for years."

I burst out in laughter.

Pulling away from her, I look at her like she's crazy. "You do realize he's bullied me for years, not pined over me. The man has no heart, and he sure as hell doesn't care about me. The cafeteria incident more than proved it."

"He's not set in stone, Star," Crina chides me. "People can change. People *do* change."

I look at her incredulously. "We've known Lucian our entire lives. He's worked hard to get the rep he has. He doesn't want to change."

"People shouldn't get labeled for life for things they've done in high school," she contends.

"First you say that he cares for me. When I blow holes in that argument, you say that I should forgive him because he's somehow going to change. Following that line of thinking, then Marku should change, right? You should forgive him for what he's done to you."

"That's different," she snaps.

Crossing my arms over my chest, I look at her smugly. "Hmm, touched a nerve, I see."

"I know that guy inside out," she claims. "There's no changing the direction he's gone in. He's bad to the core. He has no sense of remorse. No soul."

"He, Lucian, and Anton are the same."

"I see redemption in Lucian," she says emphatically.

I freeze, shock reverberating through me. Dammit,

she's dropped a prophesy. It's hard to explain, but Gabby and I know when it happens. Sometimes things pop out of her mouth and they turn out to be true. She does a special tonal thing with her voice. The air shifts and...her words ring true.

Neither Gabby nor I have spoken of this to anyone. They would think we're downright crazy or worst-case scenario, they'd believe us. Our *şef* would figure out a way to exploit her talent. *Mafie* clan bosses are ruthless and if anyone could figure it out, it's Alex. That man is brilliant. Scary, but brilliant.

But I reject her prediction. Even if it turns out to be true, it's no concern of mine. Redemption or no, Lucian hurt me. He's proven that he cares nothing for me. That will never change, even if he does.

The subway pulls into Grand Central and we jump off. People stream out, rushing toward various exits. We make our way through a maze of underground stairs and halls that we know like the backs of our hands. It's like the board game Chutes and Ladders, only dingy, dirty, and crowded. While some students get driven to school by chauffeurs, we like to keep it real. And nothing screams real like rats running along train tracks.

We make it to the 7 train that will take us to Queens, but just before stepping onto the subway car, I get an urge to go downtown. I want to wander around in Washington Park, near the main campus of New York University. Sit on a bench and watch students and hipsters walk by or check in on the old guys playing chess.

I tug the back of Crina's shirt, preventing her from boarding the train. Once it leaves, I tell her my idea. She's quick to agree to our new adventure and shoots a text to her mom with an excuse for returning home late.

Giddy with excitement, we retrace our steps back to

the local train and we get out at Astor Place in the East Village. The station has an old-timey look about it, with faience plaques and art deco enamel work on the walls.

From underground, we take the stairs two at a time up to the street level, which is encased by a fancy, decorative cast-iron and glass subway kiosk. With its domed green metal roof and cast-iron shingles, it reminds me of my summers in the old country.

We find ourselves on a small island in the middle of a plaza. Cars zip past us on Lafayette Avenue and Fourth Avenue. We clasp each other's hands, giggling with glee. Not only have we escaped our parents, but this is the first time Crina and I have ventured off together, taken the road less traveled, just like in that poem.

"I've been to Bowery Poetry Club for open mic night," Crina reveals to me.

A slow grin spreads over my face. "Oh really? Let's go there now," I suggest, bouncing on my toes.

"Okay! It's too early for any readings, but we can grab a cappuccino and hang out. Pretend we're artists and poets."

"Hell yeah," I agree as we turn away from NYU and head east.

"They have the best knishes there. We can get different ones and share," she suggests as we cross the street and pass Cooper Union, a prestigious art college in the center of the Village.

As we walk past the huge ornate brownstone building, Crina stops and looks up longingly at the façade.

"You'll get into their writing program," I encourage her gently.

Crina glances at me as we turn toward the Bowery, or what was once known as skid row, and shakes her head sadly. Her shoulders slope down. She looks so dejected it makes my heart ache. "I should've heard by now."

"You don't know yet," I press on. "There are a few days left, and you could get wait-listed. Nothing's certain yet."

"Even if I get in, then what? My mom won't hear of me going to college. She wants me to get married, have children, blah, blah, blah. If she even saw a letter from a college, she'd toss it in the trash."

I grab her hand and stop her.

Tilting my head back to look up at the huge façade of the building, I reply, "Stop it, Crina. You don't know what life has in store for you. Everything's online nowadays. Your mother doesn't have to know you applied or got in, and you will get in. I believe it, whether you do or not."

She squeezes my hand back and says, "I don't know…"

"Keep the faith, Crina. Promise me."

Silence. She purses her lips. Her gaze drops to her feet, where she digs her toe into the sidewalk.

"Come on…" I prod.

I grab her other hand. We stand in the middle of the sidewalk in front of the glass doors of the entrance, facing each other. A stream of students part around us, flowing by to go wherever college students go after classes are done for the day.

Crina's eyes drop to the pavement. "And what happens if I get in and I can't go? That will literally kill me."

"You'll convince your husband to let you go. And if he dares give you trouble, talk to Cat. She'll support you in front of your husband. Along with Luca. He might not be *şef*, but as the second oldest, he has clout. Gabby and I will help you, I swear it."

"You and Gabby won't be here to help," she notes. "That's why I need it more than ever. I'll have nothing but school."

I'm about to answer her when I feel a weird prickling on the back of my neck. I glance past Crina's shoulder and freeze. A familiar pair of gray eyes are glaring at me from across the street.

"Goddammit," I curse softly.

Crina's head whips around. "What the hell are they doing here?"

She releases my hands and turns around fully, her shoulders hunched forward as if preparing for battle. Flicking her thick hair over her shoulder, her voice is hard when she shouts out, "Are you following us?"

Marku's face turns deadly.

"What the fuck are you two doing here?" he shouts over the traffic.

"None of your business, you imbecile," Crina sneers.

Marku steps into the street. A taxi blazes past him with a long blare of its horn. He steps back cursing and waits for a break in the stream of fast-moving vehicles. At the first lull in traffic, he sprints across to our side.

"Like hell it isn't," he growls as he stalks up to us, Lucian following close behind. "Does your mother know you're here? 'Cause I bet you lied to her. No way she'd be down with this."

"Fuck. You," she shouts, shoving her face in his. "Don't you dare bring up my mother."

"Oh boy," I whisper as Lucian strides right up to me.

Grabbing my upper arm, worry creases his forehead as he asks, "You okay?"

I jerk my arm, but he doesn't let it go. Of course not, he never does. He treats me like a rag doll, like an object he can toss this way and that.

"Of course," I snap. "We're just going for a cappuccino."

Befuddled, he responds, "You can get one at Adrian's Bakery."

Marku's and Crina's voices rise high beside us. They're really going it at it now. Crina is in a pique and there's no shutting her up once you've triggered her fight mode.

I let out a sigh of vexation and, dripping with sarcasm, reply, "Yes, I'm aware, but that's in Queens. We wanted to go somewhere new. You understand the concept, no?"

"And why did you stop in front of here?" he asks, glancing up at the building.

Shit, they'd spotted us long enough to watch our heated discussion in front of Cooper Union.

"No reason," I say stiffly.

His eyes narrow on me, not believing me. "Were you meeting someone—"

"Of course not, don't make up crazy stories." To divert his attention, I drop to my knee and lie, "I had to tie my shoelace." I quickly tie my laces and return to standing. "What are you doing here anyway?"

He tilts his chin toward a small falafel hole-in-the-wall. The Middle Eastern guy manning the stand is watching the scene between Marku and Crina. His gaze touches on Lucian and just as quickly flickers away in fear.

"Taking care of business. I told you I work once school ends."

I jut a thumb at Marku. "Why's he so upset? It's not like we're Popescus. You have no claim on us."

His nostrils flare.

His expression shutters, but just before it does, I catch a flicker of something. If I didn't know better, I'd say it might be fear, but that can't be right. The man cares for nothing but himself and his clan.

Tilting his head toward Marku, he says, "That's not how he sees it. Anyway, Popescu or not, you're a female and you're alone."

"Oh, come off it, already. I'm not alone. I'm with Crina. It's broad daylight and being a woman's got nothing to do with anything." I wave my hand around. "Look around. Women everywhere. No one's getting attacked. Not one's getting harassed. No one even notices us."

His voice drops low, controlled. "There's Bratva everywhere."

"Oh, yeah, the big bad Bratva crawling out of the woodwork." I point to the gutter. "Oh, there goes one, rising out like a Mutant Ninja Turtle. Ooo, scary." I point to the sky. "Oh, here comes another, parachuting down from space. Watch out, it's an alien. Coming to get me! Ahh!"

"Hardy-har-har," he mutters.

I push him in the chest. His hard muscle flexes under my touch and I immediately regret touching him.

Disgusted with myself for having any kind of reaction to him, I gripe, "Go back to your business, Lucian. We'll go home when we're ready."

He stiffens. "That won't work."

I get up in his face, stare into his granite-colored irises, and declare, "Too bad. You're not the boss of me."

"Fuck, you're just begging to be put over my knee. I'm itching to swat your sweet ass like the brat you are."

I pull back, gasping.

A tingly sensation spreads over my body, but I steel myself against it. God, I'm so weak when it comes to this man, and it makes me boil with anger again. He's *still* kryptonite, and my embarrassment at my reaction only fuels my hatred.

He swipes a hand over his face. Scrubs the hair on his head like he's irritated. "That shouldn't have come out of my mouth."

"Damn straight," I mutter begrudgingly, his admission soothing my pricked pride. I still cringe at my bodily response to his comment, but thank heaven for small mercies, he didn't notice. I shouldn't be surprised. When has he noticed me?

"Boss or no boss," he continues, "now that I've seen you, I can't let you go. I need to see you and Crina home. It's the decent thing to do."

My lip curls. The gall of this guy. "Oh, come on. Since when is the word *decent* in your vocabulary? You didn't feel a sudden pang of this so-called decency in the cafeteria but suddenly *now* you're worried about my safety? Just stop it."

From the corner of my eye, I see Crina stalk away and Marku yank her back before she steps out into the street. Meanwhile, Lucian's spine snaps straight like I've insulted him or something.

"It's not the same," he counters.

I jut out a hip and plant my hand on it. "Like hell it isn't, you hypocrite."

He grabs my arm and says, "That's it. You're going home."

"Hey, get off me!"

I struggle to get him to unhand me, but his grip only tightens as he calls out to Marku, "You take the car, you're gonna need it. I'm taking the subway with her."

I open my mouth, about to scream bloody murder when he turns to me and warns, "I'm not letting you go. Make a scene if you want, but I swear to God, you'll regret it if someone calls the police."

I snap my mouth closed and shoot him a furious look, because Popescu or Lupu, he's *mafie* and getting the police involved is downright taboo. "That's low, even for you."

"You want to be the reason I find myself sitting in jail, keep going," he adds carelessly, amplifying the indignation burning in my chest.

I might not be able to scream but that doesn't mean I'm all out of fight. I pull back on his tugging so that he has to drag me across the avenue toward the subway station. I glance over my shoulder at Crina and see her gaze snapping between me and Marku, who's got a hand on her as well. I shake my head. She lets out a little scream of frustration but thankfully stops fighting him.

They've got us and they've got us good because they know we won't violate the *mafie* golden rule. He's just added to the reasons I want to leave this community: protecting our men from outsiders. When you've grown up in a society like ours, it's bred in you to trust no one outside of your clan.

Outside of our *mafie* world? Well, that's out of the question.

When we reach the subway kiosk, I trip over my feet. Lucian interprets it as me increasing my struggle and chides me, "As if I need to remind you, I told Cristo you're under my protection. What do you think that means, Star? It means you're as good as a Popescu."

I inhale sharply and he glances back at me with a frown. "Oh, what? We're not good enough for you, huh?"

"That's not what I think and you know it, Lucian. It's just like a Popescu man to take insult when none was given."

"Please, now you're the one being coy. The Lupu are snobs. We moved the school from a perfectly good building in Sunnyside, Queens just because the Empire Academy Board, filled to the gills with members of *your* clan, complained about fake problems so that they could move to a fancy building in Manhattan."

"Everyone has a reputation," I retort. "Lupu are snobs. Popescu are violent. Ionescu are good with money. Albu are expert snipers. But we're individuals too, you know. To hear you claim me as one of your own was a shock, that's all."

Of course, I don't believe him. He'd only said that as an excuse to drag me off like a naughty child. He didn't really mean it.

He stops halfway down the stairs leading to the station.

Staring up at me, he says something but I can't hear him over the rumbling of the subway train in the station below.

"What?" I ask, cupping my ear.

"I said, Popescu or not, you're mine."

I stumble back, almost busting the back of my head on a metal stair behind me, but Lucian's other hand whips out, grasping me around the waist and steading me.

Standing a couple of steps above him, we're eye to eye when he breaks the spell by saying, "I told Cristo you were mine. If something happens to you, it looks like I can't take care of what's mine. And anyway, if you're gone, who's going to help me graduate?"

I roll my eyes at him. "Of course, it's always about you. How will *you* look to your *şef*? How will *you* graduate? You, you, you. Always you."

"It's about you now," he grumbles. "I have more places I need to check on, but I'm cutting it short to take you home."

"No one asked you to take me home, and you just said you're only doing it because of how it will make you look, so don't put this on me."

"It's not just that, but…fuck it, you're impossible to talk to," he mutters as he tugs on my hand to resume going down the steps.

That's rich coming from him.

"*Me???*"

Great. Now I have a long train ride home shackled to the guy I hate, who's doubling as my prison guard.

Knowing him, he'll walk me right to my door. I'm not so worried about my mom. She should be napping off her liquid lunch right around now, but if Ms. Ana is looking outside her living room window like she does every day, I'll have to answer her question of why "that Popescu boy" was walking me home.

When we get back to Queens, I'll shoo him home with the excuse that he doesn't want anyone linking us together, what with me tutoring him and him helping me escape.

If that doesn't work, then I'll stomp on his foot and make a run for it. Hopefully, he'll be in too much pain to run after me. Bottom line, there's no way I'm walking down my street with him by my side.

To think that once upon a time, that was my fantasy.

Now, I shudder just thinking about it.

CHAPTER 10

LUCIAN

Star and I are back in my sacred music room, the one I've never allowed another person to enter. Not even Anton and Marku. Since we can't meet at school and the sofa smells something awful from the debauchery it's endured, I have no choice. I mean, I don't even like to see Star on that sofa, much less sit on it with her.

I liked it even less when I caught her in the Village the other day. Fuck me, but I thought I was seeing things when we left Mamoun's and spotted the girls across the street.

In the 'hood, *mafie* women and girls roam the streets in relative safety, but when I saw them, alone and vulnerable, my stomach dropped to the floor. I glanced over at Marku. The horror on his face matched my insides.

Okay, I'm not insane.

Even if that's what the girls seemed to think. Instead of being mortified at getting caught roaming so far out of our jurisdiction, they were indignant. I still don't get it. Sunnyside is Romanian. Brighton Beach is Bratva. Bay Ridge is

Italian. Washington Heights is Dominican. And Chinatown is well…Chinese. Anywhere else is up for grabs. And they could have been literally grabbed right off the street.

What's more worrisome was their total lack of concern, as if this wasn't their first time out. Which begs the question, where else have they been? Jealousy simmers in my gut. And are they still going out, despite the harsh warnings Marku and I gave them?

I glance over at Star, her head bent over her laptop. Silky strands of hair hang down, half hiding her face. Streaks of white blonde shimmer in the dappled light streaming in through the window.

Unaware of me, her smooth forehead wrinkles in concentration. Her lips pucker to one side. She clasps her plump bottom lip between her teeth and I stifle a groan.

Fuck. What the hell is she doing to me?

I glance down and get my answer. My sweats are tented in the crotch. No way am I going to stand up anytime soon. Should've worn heavy denim jeans 'cause this girl drives me fucking crazy.

Of course, the irony is that she hates me more than ever now.

I moodily stare across the table at her. She's got more spunk than I gave her credit for. And stubbornness. A stubborn streak a mile wide has cropped up. Ever since her brother left. The reminder that she lives alone, with only her mother as protection, unsettles me. Recently, I've had these odd surges of protectiveness toward Star and it's got nothing to do with my promise to Cristo.

She purses her glossy pink lips as she flips the page of the book and peers down, squinting her eyes slightly as she re-reads a phrase. God knows what she finds fascinating about a book with characters named Puck and Bottom. Christ. It doesn't matter, though, 'cause my cock pulses from watching her move her lips around. It sees them and knows what they could do, imagines what they would feel like wrapped around its length.

Cheeks hollowed out.

Long pulls.

Eyes on me.

Begging for guidance. For praise.

Hell yeah.

Combined with that sassy innocence and… Oh, fuck, do I want that. My balls feel heavy with the urge to spill inside her and coat her womb. There's a hard, undeniable tug of need, a need almost as strong as the need to get my family name back on top.

I brutally stamp it down, but it still leaves me with an uneasy feeling swimming in my chest. I'm irritated by how enthralled I am with her, especially now that she doesn't seem to know I exist.

Star grabs a pencil, flicks the tip with her pink tongue and scratches something in the margin of the book.

Oh, for Chrissake…

I growl low.

On top of being generally sexually frustrated, I'm equally frustrated by the sheet of study questions she slapped on the desk when she first strolled into the room. These questions are meant to prepare me for the English test, but they're ridiculous. Questions like what does Puck do to Bottom and what does that say about Puck's attitude toward humans? Who gives a fuck about a fairy and a man named *Bottom*? And why doesn't Star notice that I've abandoned the stupid study guide and spent the past five minutes staring at her?

A few more long minutes pass. I shift in my chair. It makes a loud creaking sound.

Finally sensing my rapt attention, Star stiffens slightly.

The pulse at her throat quickens, making the tiny beauty mark above it flicker.

A reaction.

Fucking finally.

She looks up at me warily and demands, "What?"

She glances down at the half-eaten muffin on a crumpled paper bag she came with and swipes at her beautiful, perfect lips. "Is there something on my face? Crumbs?"

Her hot cocoa eyes widen, bright and naïve. She's so damn clueless how fucking gorgeous she is. If I wasn't so fucking thankful that it kept other men away, I'd be downright pissed off about it.

"No," I rumble.

Irritability flares bright in my chest. Is that why she thinks I'm looking at her?

She squints her eyes at me for a moment. Her head dips down to the ever-present grape-colored backpack covered with pin buttons. For the first time, I peer closer to see what they're about. There are a few humorous buttons, but most of them are about...*art?* I recognize one by the iconic "M" of the Metropolitan Museum of Art.

She bends down and pulls out a small mirror, making a little satisfied sound as she determines she doesn't have traces of muffin on her face.

"You don't believe me?"

"No," she grunts.

Growing more insulted by the moment, I ask, "Why would I lie about something as stupid as that?"

"Why do you lie about anything?" she throws back at me with a hard glare. "I don't know why you do anything you do. Scratch that." She gives a little shrug. "I don't think about you. You're not worth my time."

Annoyance snaps inside me like a live wire. I sit up

straight. Fury and indignation beat at my chest. *Oh, is that right?*

I scooch my chair over until I'm right beside her.

Her eyes flare in alarm.

"You don't think about me, huh?" I start, placing my hand on her lithe thigh. My hand covers the entire width, it's so slim.

Her thigh muscle jumps on contact.

"W-what are you doing?" she demands, jerking back.

I wrap my hand tighter around her thigh, holding her in place. "Seeing how you don't think about me, how I don't affect you in any way, you wouldn't mind me touching you, then."

"Y-Yeah, that's right," she stutters.

Uh-huh, sure.

But I'm nowhere satisfied with a timid little touch.

I'm not a timid guy.

Far from it.

I slide my hand to the crease where her thigh meets her pussy, and before she can react, I grab her by the nape, bring her close, and crush my lips against hers. I flick the seam of her lips and bubblegum flavor explodes on my tongue. I nip at her bottom lip to open.

She gasps and I plunder her mouth hard and fast like the punishment she deserves. Teach her who she's dealing with. Reprimand her for not noticing me. My nostrils flare as her cherry vanilla scent penetrates my nose and I can't help but greedily drag in more. Fuck, I'm in heaven.

Groaning, I cup her pussy, and goddamn if it's not hot to the touch.

My heart pounds in my chest. Lust pumps through my bloodstream.

She makes angry little sounds, which goads me to hold on tighter, delve in deeper. Those indignant gasps make me harder, and I swallow them down like they're the finest nectar. This will teach her not to dismiss me again.

I push my tongue farther in, drawing in more of her cherry-vanilla-bubblegum taste, amping up my desire. I mean for the kiss to teach her a lesson, but one taste and I'm spiraling down a rabbit hole of need.

And then she bites me.

I taste the metallic tang of blood and suppress a laugh of glee. This little bitch has some bite to her and I fucking *love* it. I don't pull back as she expects and her teeth stop their compression, releasing my lip just a little bit, as if testing me.

Test me, little girl. See what you get.

Confusion clouds over the sharp black flames in her pupils. I didn't react like she expected and she doesn't know what to do about it.

She slowly unclamps her teeth and breaks our contact. Drops of blood coat her bottom lip, urging me to lick them or bite them in return.

I smirk at her, tasting my own blood.

I imagine my smile must look garish because she pulls back with a wince. "It was a warning. I didn't mean to hurt you."

I huff out a laugh. "You didn't hurt me. You made me hard."

Her eyes pop out in alarm, darting down to my cock. Still cupping her, I squeeze her tightly. She lets out a yelp.

I withdraw my hand, but warn her, "Be careful next time, baby girl. Your bite only provokes me to dominate you."

Her mouth drops open. She snaps it shut and swallows, but her eyes dilate, letting me know more than she probably knows herself.

She's fucking perfect for my tastes.

"Ahh, you like that."

She straightens her spine and denies it. "I do *not*."

"You haven't had sex yet," I say matter-of-factly, since that explains everything.

"So?" Said with indignation as if it wasn't obvious that she was a virgin.

"You don't know how it can be between a man and a woman. How good it can be, the mix between pleasure and pain. There are different…how should I put it…tastes…in the bedroom. Some men like to dominate. I'm one of them. If you're ever tempted to—"

"I'm not," she interrupts.

"If you're ever tempted to experiment," I go on, "then you should know that I like to be in control. You think you can handle that with your sassy mouth and attitude?"

Two bright splotches decorate her cheeks. She shakes her head vigorously. "Nothing's going to happen between us."

I smile a knowing smile. "Never say never."

"Believe me, it's a never," she says with utter conviction. "I'm not giving up my virginity to a *mafie* guy. I'd rather give it up to the man at the corner store."

I'm confused and…insulted. What she said is like a slap to the face, "What do you have against *mafie* men?"

"I can't afford to lose my virginity to a *mafie* guy who might find his conscious and force me to marry him. I'm leaving, remember."

There she goes again with this so-called *leaving* business. I promised to help her because I needed her cooperation, but I didn't think she was serious. A whisper of fear brushes over my nape, making it prickle with alarm, but I stoutly ignore it. She's not my responsibility, I remind myself.

The prickling only intensifies.

I clap the back of my neck to dislodge the disturbing sensation. She's *not* my responsibility, I repeat fiercely.

Granted, I made sure to never fuck a virgin for that very reason. I didn't want to get roped into marriage with a fuck buddy when marrying a princess was part of my grand plan. But looking at Star, with her hair rumpled from where I grasped her nape and her lips stained red with my blood, the thought of fucking anyone but her makes my skin crawl.

I return to her comment that nothing would happen between us. I think back to her dismissive attitude. She was never like this before. It's ridiculous to blame me when she's the one that approached me at lunch and started rambling on about tutoring in front of my men and Dinu, of all people.

"What did you expect from me in the cafeteria?" I demand.

I can tell my question has thrown her off, but she rallies quickly. Her face turns to stone and she replies snidely, "Oh, I don't know. A bit of decency, maybe."

"You blame me, but you refuse to see your part. You came up to *me* in public and babbled on about our tutoring. I could've handled my men, but Dinu and his men? Don't act naïve. You know the rules, Star."

"I do know the rules, but I also have a life and Mr. High and Mighty was too busy to show up to our meeting, too busy to read any of my texts, too busy to pick up the phone. You thought you could dodge me and I'd do the assignment for you, even though I'd told you I wouldn't cheat. But no, you had to strong-arm me into it. You're not my only responsibility, you know. I have my own future to think of. Entrance into a good college won't fall in my lap. I need to work hard to keep up my grades."

"Your brother's as rich as sin. He can donate a wing and pay your way in."

"Who says my brother knows about my plans."

My entire body tightens like I got jabbed with a cattle prod. I drop my voice low. "If you're not going to your brother in Cali, who the fuck are you going to? Who's going to take care of you?"

She shoves her face closer and hisses, "*Me*, you Neanderthal. I don't need any man."

I swallow. My heart skips a few beats and then speeds up like it's trying to hammer a hole in my chest. My skin is strangely clammy. "That's not safe. I thought I was helping you escape to reunite with your brother."

She wipes the remnants of blood-saliva mixture off her lips with the back of her hand. "Well, you're not."

"I don't understand you," I explode. "Your father was slaughtered by the Bratva and I find you carelessly wandering the streets of the Village. Now you want to roam the globe on your own. How can you be so irresponsible?"

She looks at me strangely, canting her head to the side.

She smiles and her smile broadens with glee until she belts out a deep laugh.

I frown. "What's so damn funny?"

"Oh my God, Lucian. No one wants me." She swipes a couple tears of laughter away. "Why would the Bratva go after me? I'm a woman, and barely an adult at that. As far as they know, I've got no father or brother. No husband. You have to be valuable to make it worth their effort. You have to be a shoe-in. Even if they snatch me, who's going to pay my ransom? Alex?" She shrugs casually. "Maybe, maybe not." She lifts her brows to her hairline. "Oh, maybe, you're thinking it'll be my dead father, my absent brother or my drunk mom?"

She snaps her fingers in front of my face. "Snap out of it, Lucian. I'm not a valuable pawn to the Russian mafia. Not everyone is worth the same in this world. I'm not being irresponsible when I walk around the city. I walk around like that because I'm not worth anything. You count so you think everyone does, but news flash, dude, I don't."

Her words jar me.

For reasons I can't explain, her reasoning makes me angry. If she got hurt or kidnapped, I'd fucking lose it.

She should matter, dammit, the way she matters to me.

That realization jars me, but I stuff it down because I'm overwhelmed by a wave of powerlessness. It's the same helpless despair I felt around my father. After he got sick and lost his position as *consilier,* he stopped mattering, and I hated it because I was helpless to make him matter again. And he mattered to me and my family so damned much. He might have been sick, but he was the glue that kept us whole. I've tried to be that glue ever since, but many days I know I've failed. No one can replace him. Sure as hell not me.

There's an unrelenting jangling in my chest.

I'm panting fiery breathes of anger.

Her face hovers closer to mine, worry lines creasing her forehead.

I grasp her neck again, only this time, I take her by the front. I collar her throat, and it looks pretty in my hand, covered with my clan tat of the crowned eagle with an Orthodox cross. It's like the eagle is tatted over her skin. That image does something to me.

I drag her until our lips are practically touching.

Her eyes bulge, bewilderment marring her smooth skin.

Breathing harshly, I say, "Don't ever fucking say that again. *You matter.*"

Star tries to shake her head within my grasp, denying what I've said.

"You matter. You matter. You matter."

And then my lips are on hers again. She tries to wiggle away, but I tighten my fingers ever so slightly and she stops instantly. I'm forcing a kiss on her, but I can't help it. And this time, bite or no bite, I'm not pulling away until I get my pound of flesh. Her bubblegum taste is back in my mouth, her cherry vanilla scent filling my nostrils. I breathe and drink them in like the starving man I am. Hunger pounds through me, leaving me dizzy with need. My cock is hard as fuck, harder than it's ever been for any woman.

With a moan, she begins to return my kiss and soon our tongues are sparring, trying to outdo the other.

Unhinged, I tear at her shirt, buttons popping and pinging against the tabletop and the floor. I unclip her simple white bra, a solitary silk rose in the center. I duck my head and find one perfect pink bud, suck it into my mouth and it's delicious. *She's delicious.*

Her breasts are high and bouncy. Goose bumps break out over her arms and she arches her back to feed me more. Her fingers grip my hair, pulling me closer. I thrum the other nipple for a bit before pinching it.

She groans low, but suddenly her seeking fingers change to pushing my head away. I don't want to let her nipple go, and I give her a warning bite. She doesn't heed it.

"No, Lucian," she rasps out hoarsely.

I inhale more of her beautiful breast, moaning around her areola, desperate and greedy for more.

Her fingers slip away and her tone hardens. "No."

I squeeze my eyes together and release my suction on her breast. Fuck, her nipple looks glorious, blotchy and pink from my ministrations. I can even see the faint arc of my front teeth from where I bit her. My teeth. My mark. *Mine.*

I lift my gaze to her. Her eyes flash with anger. She turns away from me, hiding that beauty from me, and tosses a withering glare over her shoulder. "Thanks a lot. That's the second school shirt you've ruined."

With jerky movements, she throws her hoodie over her torn shirt, stuffs her books and laptop into her purple backpack, and hauls out of my sanctuary like a bat out of hell.

I slump into my chair.

That went about as well as could be expected.

CHAPTER 11

LUCIAN

Star plasters herself against the wall of the art gallery, doing her best to blend in.

She eyes the crowd, her gaze passing over the entire gallery, including me, but she doesn't notice me. Thank fuck, she was in the gallery by the time I got inside, otherwise there would be hell to pay. Who am I kidding, there's going to be hell to pay anyway. She was wandering the city again, in direct defiance of my order.

I'm still livid from when I caught her slipping out of her house. She's been ignoring the texts I sent asking when we should meet up for tutoring, but that's not why I was standing guard outside her house.

Don't ask me why. I refuse to ask myself that question, knowing I won't like the answer.

I did a double take when I noticed the fancy dress she had on. Where the hell was her mother? Star mentioned that she drank, but everyone drinks in our world. That's no excuse for not watching over your only daughter.

I barely refrained from lunging forward to reprimand her, stepping back into the shadows just in the nick of time.

My head almost exploded when I followed her to the corner and saw her wave to an Uber, which was obviously on standby, and slip into the back seat as if it were nothing. I had surreptitiously installed a tracking app on her phone after I found her in the Village. It didn't take long for me to get into my car and follow the dot to the far western end of Chelsea.

The neighborhood looked deserted, except for a bodega at the corner and an art gallery with people spilling out into the dark, empty street. Slipping into the gallery, I easily found her and kept my distance, simmering with anger.

The gallery's an enormous, converted warehouse with three huge rolling garage doors. It might've once been a humble old building, but inside, it's a cathedral-like space that breathes luxury. Aided by the skylight crossing the upper part of an entire wall, the light and airy space accentuates the photographs on display.

I don't recognize the exhibition of self-portraits that look like old Hollywood film stills, but then again, why would I? I don't do art. I may not know what's going on, but this retrospective must be a big deal because the place is packed. I catch Star stamping her feet in delight and her eyes glisten with excitement as she takes everything in.

A waiter passes her carrying a tray of champagne flutes. She snags one and takes a big gulp of liquid courage. Smart girl that she is, she swipes a puffed pastry thing from another passing tray.

I'm torn between being spellbound by her, impressed by her pluck, and downright pissed that she snuck out alone in the middle of the night.

Star pops the puffy thingamajig into her mouth. Her eyes close as she savors whatever she's eating. They pop back open and she does a double take.

Fucking finally.

I've been spotted through the wall-to-wall throngs of people. I was wondering how long it would take her.

"*Lucian*," she mouths my name.

Choking down the rest of her food, she takes another large swig of champagne. I see her mind working. I'm here, at a gallery opening, on the western extremity of Chelsea. Not someplace a guy like me would be.

Which means, I'm here for her.

Damn right, I am.

Irritation flashes over her face.

Star pushes off the wall and slips through the crowd. Stopping by my side, she takes me in for a moment. Her lashes flutter unconsciously, letting me know she likes what she sees. The jacket I'm wearing is snug. It's one I happened to have in the back of my car and I threw it on over my black jeans, in an attempt to blend in a little. Not that my clan tat can hide who I am. It's a calling card to anyone in the mafia, but of course, no one in this trendy place would know that.

Star notices a gaggle of women beside me blatantly checking me out, and that douses the desire on her face.

"What are you doing here," she demands.

My gaze flashes over her, my only sign of acknowledgment. My jaw tightens, the muscle at the base pulsing in irritation. Fuck, how can she ask me that when she's the one in trouble?

"I'm serious, why are you here," she continues haughtily.

Her tone of voice triggers my temper.

"Be quiet," I snap. "I'm furious."

My gaze cuts to her again.

"*Furious*," I hiss.

She jerks back in surprise. "With me? You're kidding me, right?"

Indignation blasts through me. My hand shoots out and wraps tightly around her upper arm.

"Never fucking go out alone," I snarl as I drag her closer to me. "For the love of God, I thought we covered this last time I caught you roaming around in the Village."

"Okay, first, I was not *roaming around*. I was there with Crina and we were going to a poetry café. But that's not relevant. What is relevant is that you had the audacity to follow me."

"You're one to talk about audacity," I reply, my eyes narrowing into slits.

"We've discussed this. I'm perfectly fine going out alone, and anyway, it's none of your business. I don't know where this misguided sense of obligation is coming from. I'm not even from your clan, but you act like you own me or something." If possible, my jaw clenches tighter. "I *tooold* you, it doesn't matt—"

I press an index finger firmly on her lips, cutting her off.

"Don't say it," I warn, shaking my head in slo-mo. She's seriously working my last nerve, and I'm seconds from snapping completely.

Enraged, I glance away, unable to look at her without wanting to throttle her. I won't let her finish the ridiculous statement that she doesn't matter. I can almost hear her finish it in her mind and it rings in mine as if she's said it out loud. Goddammit, it drives me to the edge when she says things like that.

"We're leaving," I say abruptly, tugging at her arm.

She digs her heels in, trying to get out of my grip. She's surprisingly strong, but no match for me.

"We are not," she declares, gesturing toward a wall with three large photographs mounted on it. "You can leave, but I just got here and I haven't even checked out the exhibition."

"I'll haul you out over my shoulder if I have to."

The pulse at her throat goes a mile a minute. Her nostrils flare.

Seeing the mutiny on her face, I put my finger an inch away from my thumb, and warn, "I've been patient, but I'm this close. Don't test me, Star."

"Since when are you patient?"

Eyes to the ceiling, I retort, "Oh, you have no idea." I snap them back to her. "But you will. By the time I'm done with you tonight, I swear to it, you will."

She draws back from me, or as much as she can with my fingers cuffed around her arm.

"Don't you dare pull away from me," I seethe. I feel myself unraveling, and clench down on it to regain control. Control. Need control. "You drive me crazy, you know that? And that's not a good thing. Crazy was my father, not me."

She yanks her arm harder. "You can leave. I'm not your responsibility, remember? Let me go."

"Never. You're mine, whether I have the right to you or not. You disobeyed me and there are consequences for that."

"Like hell there are. Get off me," she shouts.

My hand rises and falls across her ass hard. God, that felt good. She's asking for it and I'm more than ready to give it to her.

She gasps in outrage. "Did you just—"

Cutting her off, I warn, "Naughty girls get spanked."

That's when she really starts to struggle. I tighten my hold on her, but people pause their conversations, glancing our way. Fuck. The last thing I need is a public scene, but I'll be damned if I let her go.

"You're being a bully," she cries out as she whacks at my grip.

She opens her mouth to scream, and I slap a hand over her mouth.

That's it, I'm done.

I bend at the knees, lean into her belly, and throw her over my shoulder.

She lets out a screech.

I give her butt a hard swat.

She opens her mouth to scream again.

"The police," I say, satisfied when I get no response.

"You can't keep using that," she warns with a hard pound to my back as I stride out of the room toward the back of the gallery.

Maybe not, but it worked, and that's all I care about right now.

She wiggles in my hold as I carry her through another gallery room, down a hall flanked with offices, and out the back exit. The back alley is a patch of bare concrete surrounded by buildings. Black iron fire escapes crawl up the sides of the buildings, which carve a square frame of dark sky above.

I carefully slide Star down to her feet, but before she can get her bearing, I corral her against a brick wall until I've got her where I want her.

I tower over her, my arms resting on either side of her head, hemming her in. She trembles slightly and tries to hide it by scowling up at me, but I'm not fooled. I can practically smell her rising desire, and I plan to use it to teach her a lesson.

I gently run my knuckles down her cheek and order softly, "Turn around and hike up your skirt."

Her eyes flare. They flash from left to right, scanning the dead alley, but I already know there's no one out here. After all, it's where I parked my car, lining it up so it's in equal distance from the buildings on either side of it.

"Are you out of your mind?"

My knuckles drop to the dip where her throat meets her collarbone. Delicate like butterfly winds, the two fine clavicle bones serve to connect her shoulders to her breastbone. Their perfect symmetry gives me a moment of rest until I notice the faded slash from Roxie's attack. Seeing that blemish on her flawless skin and I'm possessed with a sudden rage.

Swallowing my self-disgust, I skim my knuckles down the deep V of her evening dress. It's a classy bronze number with a sheen to it. Silk, maybe. I don't know, but I know it makes her look older by a few years. Which I don't like.

My teeth clench at the thought of men looking at her, thinking she's of age and lusting after her. Technically, she is, but the idea of her being propositioned by another man makes me crazed.

The fabric of her dress clings to her generous curves. I want to tear it off her and lay her bare before me. My knuckles push the silk aside and edge the scalloped lace of her bra encasing a beautiful pair of tits. Big enough to spill over my hands. I lick my lips with the anticipation of tasting her again.

I trace the edge of her lacy bra and she goes to slap my hand away.

I grab her hand, tap it against the brick wall, and growl in warning.

She freezes but her chest fills and empties rapidly, betraying her desire.

Since catching her blatantly escaping from her house, my control is frayed. Hovering over her, I wrap my fingers around her jaw and grip it, pressing until it pops open. I crush my mouth against hers. My tongue sweeps in like a marauder. I'm not going for skillful or patient. This is an attack. A lesson. I spread my large hand wide across her chest. Her strong, rapid heartbeat thumps hard beneath it.

Despite her anger and hurt, I know Star wants me. It's the only advantage I can count on, and she doesn't make me wait long for her surrender.

First, she moans. Then her tongue advances hesitantly.

I soften my movements, pulling back to allow her the space to get bolder. She pushes in, getting more confident by the moment, and soon our tongues are entangled together.

I greedily swallow her soft mewl.

"Good girl," I purr.

My fingers slide from her jaw and drive into her hair, pulling her head back to get access to her throat. I press my hard cock against her belly and she sways toward me.

Fuck, yeah.

I slink my hand down to the part in her dress and cup her pussy. Her heat scorches me. Greedy for more, I slip a finger beneath the waistband of her panties and hit the jackpot.

Hot and wet.

Not gonna lie, but I've dreamt about this moment for weeks.

Okay, let's be real. I've dreamt about if for years.

Still devouring her mouth, I tease her opening. Her pliant, moist flesh easily parts for me, urging me to probe farther, push in deeper.

I feel the proof of her virginity and fuck if I don't have the urge to thrust my fingers hard and burst that red cherry. I want to be the man to take it. But not with my fingers. No, I want to feel her tight flesh wrapped around my thick cock. And I don't just want to be the first. I want to be the one and only man to thrust into her wet heat.

"You're mine. You were always mine," I murmur in her ear.

Her pussy clenches around my fingers.

"Fuck, you like that, dirty girl. You like when I get possessive over you."

She tosses her head in denial, but I'm determined to prove her wrong. I toy with her clit as I thrust my fingers in, careful to preserve her innocence. Her fingers clutch my shirt, yanking me closer. She starts riding my hand like the dirty angel she is. But I need her coming on my mouth. I need to feel and taste her as she succumbs to me.

I drop to my knees, yank her panties down, and duck my head until I've got an eyeful of her pretty pink cunt. The bare light bulb swaying above the door to our right illuminates more than enough, and I see everything.

I lean in and take a nice, long lick. She gasps and her fingers twist in my hair. I push into her sweet heat and her malty flavor explodes on my tongue.

I let out a desperate moan and she yelps at the vibration.

She pushes at my shoulders. "Please, Lucian. Don't do this. You don't have to."

I cut off my licking long enough to scowl up at her. "I want to."

She continues her useless effort to shove me off. If embarrassment is motivating her, that's not going to budge me. Instead, I loop one of her legs over my shoulder to give me better access. The fact that she lets me tells me all I need to know.

With my fingers playing her, I go back to licking and sucking, interspersing it with words. "Try denying it all you want." *Lick.*

"Try hating me all you want." *Nip.*

"You won't succeed 'cause you're addicted to being my..." *Suckle.*

I pull away and demand, "My what, Star?"

"G-Good g-girl," she says in a rasp.

"Damn right you are," I praise. "And I'm gonna brand my good girl with my cock. Mold you until your tight cunt is stretched to take it any way I give it to you." *Lick, nip. Gentle suck.*

"You've got a fresh, untouched pussy begging to be taken, and I will be the first and only man you let inside," I predict, almost out of my mind with the frantic urge to make her mine. To keep her.

"You want to walk out of here with messy hair and a puffed-up pussy, don't you? You want everyone to know what I do to you. Show everyone who you are."

I keep up the exact rhythm of tongue until I'm ready for her to explode.

Then, I switch it up. *Twirl clit, suck hard.*

And drive her over the edge with one last, "Good girl."

Her fingernails drive into my shoulders as her scream bounces off the buildings.

She drags her fingers through my hair, yanking, twisting, and pulling as she spins out of control.

"Oh my God, oh my God," she repeats in a mantra. Mouth open on an O, she stares down at me blindly.

I think this might be her first.

And I feel vindicated.

My cock may be as hard as a rock and my balls heavy

with seed, but the pain is worth it because she's a dirty slut and a good girl wrapped up in one. And I just proved it to her.

I gentle my licking as she comes down from her high. She drops her leg and goes back to pushing at my shoulders, hopping from foot to foot when it gets to be too sensitive. I finally relent and turn my face away, rasping my bristled cheek against her inner thigh.

I lick my lips, greedy for her essence, and then bite down on the downy flesh of her thigh.

She yelps, then groans.

Ahh, so she likes a bite of pain. My heart soars with satisfaction.

She raises a shaky hand to her forehead and asks, "What happened? What did we just do?"

She glares down accusingly. "Why did you do that?"

"To prove a point, of course."

Suddenly, she's in motion. She pushes off and squirms away from me. With shaky hands, she yanks her panties up and rights her dress.

Once she's sufficiently covered, she hisses, "I can't believe you."

I rise to my feet.

"Me?"

"Yes, you!"

"I don't recall you fighting my tongue once your sweet pussy was creaming on my face."

"Oh my God, you did not just say that. You're unbelievable, you know that. You don't like me. You find me disgusting." She points down to her pussy. "*That* was surely disgusting for you. I don't know what you were trying to prove, but whatever it was, you've gone too far."

My brows bunch together. Instead of acknowledging her attraction to me, she's...upset? "What the hell are you talking about? Why would licking your pussy be disgusting?"

Dismissing me, she huffs impatiently as her head swings around, checking for the quickest escape route.

Before she can run, I snatch her around the waist and point to my Mercedes. "I'm taking you home."

She whips out her phone, shakes it in my face, and threatens, "No, I'm taking an Uber."

The tension that had been siphoned off by having my tongue on her cunt returns tenfold.

"Like hell you are," I grind out. "It's not safe. Why do I have to explain this again? It should be obvious."

"What's obvious is that you're an overbearing brute. I don't need your so-called help. You sure as hell didn't help me in the cafeteria. That's when I needed you."

She wiggles out of my grasp, turns to face me, and taps her front tooth. "This broke when I got pushed to the ground by your fiancée. Trust me, the last thing I need in my life is your kind of help."

She sniffs as if she's about to cry and my heart tightens in response.

Tensing her shoulders, she grimaces as she forcibly fights back her sob, and announces, "I'm going home. *On my own.*"

She's frustrated, I get it, but why can't she understand what I'm saying. Taking a deep breath, I try to calm my temper. "Will you stop? Okay, I didn't come to your aid in the cafeteria, but this is different. This isn't about saving a bruised ego; this is about safety."

"You don't get to tell me what I feel," she replies mulishly. "I don't need your help. I needed you back then, and you let me down, so I reject your offer. I will go home *alone.*"

"Is this your way of getting back at me?" I ask incredulously. "I've already explained myself."

Temper flaring once again, I wrap my fingers around her wrist and yank her toward the car. I lay down the law. "You're coming with me. Inside. Now."

She tries to break free, but I pin her against my car. She grips the lapels of my jacket, tearing at them violently.

Face to the sky, she screams out, "No one cares! I made it here on my own perfectly fine. Don't give me some lame excuse about the Bratva and make me repeat myself a hundred times." She shakes me in frustration, tears falling from her eyes. "Why won't you get it? No one cares. No. One. Cares."

A shout comes from one of the lofts above us. "If no one cares then shut the fuck up!"

My head snaps in the direction of the disembodied voice and a snarl emanates from my chest.

I cover her, crushing her fingers to my chest, and whisper in her ear, "I care."

She pushes against me, struggling until there's a bit of space between us.

The corners of her mouth sag into a deep frown. "Lucky for me, your opinion doesn't count."

Angry words push against the back of my front teeth, desperate to leave my mouth, but I clamp my jaws shut.

There's no point in arguing.

I'm not leaving her here. I just had my tongue in her sweet pussy and she's lost her damn mind if she thinks I'm going to abandon her in the deserted back alley of a Chelsea gallery in the middle of the night. She's angry because she thinks I betrayed her in the cafeteria, but high school drama is nothing compared to the real dangers out here.

And the dangers are real. She doesn't know what I

know. Her brother, along with the brothers of her *şef*, killed the Russian boss and his second-in-command. Why her brother abandoned her and left her vulnerable, I do not know, but I'm the one who took advantage of their weakened state to attack the drug distribution of the Jersey shore and wrangle it into our hands. It's what tipped me over Dinu as the next in line for *consilier*.

Her brother, and now I, are responsible for what's coming next. The Bratva may still be regrouping, but revenge against our clans is imminent. Of course, I can't relay any of this information to her and dispel this crazy-ass theory she has that no one cares.

Tamping my anger down, I cup her breast and warn her with a squeeze.

Her eyelids dip.

Fuck, that small reaction is almost too much, what with my hard cock and my heated blood from all of this arguing.

Fighting to keep focused on the issue at hand, I reply, "My opinion's the only one that matters right now."

I push a knee between her thighs and press into her so she can feel the ten hard inches I have packed for her. "There will be rules for you to follow, and by God you will follow them."

"And if I don't?" she taunts me, glaring up at me with defiance.

Quickly, I drag her skirt up, yank her panties down, and give her ass a sharp slap.

"Ow!"

Ignoring her protest, I spin her around, flattening her against the car. I ache to give her a series of swift, painful smacks. God knows, she deserves a good spanking.

I've watched Star for years. I've seen how she leans into the attention I give her, even negative attention.

Especially negative attention.

She enjoys the bite of pain; she unconsciously understands the pleasure-pain of teetering on the razor's edge of humiliation. It's a bully's best-kept secret, the subtle push and pull we maintain. Bullies get a bad rap, but it takes two to tango. I may have made a miscalculation and broken our unspoken pact in the cafeteria, but I swear, I will do everything in my power to repair that trust. And when its restored, she will feel the full wrath of my hand.

I grit my teeth and hold back my raging instinct to correct her.

Instead, I lean in and make a shushing sound near the curve of her outer ear. "You will not roam around the city alone. You are mine. Under my protection."

"No," she refutes.

"Yes," I shout.

I squeeze my eyes shut as I fight to regain control.

Breathing out a long breath, I continue, "You don't know what's going on, but trust me when I say it's about your safety. When I say, no more, I mean no more."

I grip her ass cheek, which I see is a sweet shade of pink from the lightbulb above the gallery exit and a few lighted windows from the building across the way.

One cheek resting against my car, I watch tears slide down the side of her face.

"What's going on?" she asks.

I let out a sigh as I smooth my hand over her burning ass cheek, remaining silent.

She sniffs. "You won't tell me."

I've already said too much. I gave her a hint because she needs to understand the level of danger involved. We haven't yet established the kind of trust where a smack to her ass will prompt her to behave. I'm hoping that the few choice words of warning I gave her will do the trick.

I pull her off the car and into my chest. She instinctually cuddles a little into my larger frame and I pray it's more than just the slight chill of the spring night. I hope it's because she feels safe with me. With her slight body nestled into me, it hits me. I may have fucked a lot of women, but this is the first time I've held one in my arms.

Star feels like a bundle of warmth and softness and I tighten my embrace around her. In this moment, I realize that my words to Cristo about her being under my protection were prophetic, because I will do whatever is necessary to keep her safe.

Her eyelids drop to half-mast as she settles her cheek against my chest. She lets out a sigh that sounds suspiciously like relief.

"Come on," I urge gently. "Let's get in the car."

Maybe it's because she's tired, but for once, she does what I say without giving me lip.

I place my hand on the crown of her head when she bends down to get in. I close the car door, grateful to shut her inside. Relief surges through me knowing she's enclosed in a bubble that I control. In my car. Under my guard.

The words I spoke to Cristo echo in my mind, *she's mine.* They settle like a truth, a rightness in my heart. Star is mine. Maybe she always was.

CHAPTER 12

LUCIAN

Two days after my confrontation with Star, I've ordered her to meet at my house to study.

Cristo has given me a rare day off. I suppose I should be grateful for his "understanding," but he's just afraid I'll randomly shoot someone who speaks to me sideways today. He wouldn't be wrong. On this day—on this specific day every year—I'm righteously pissed off.

Pissed off…and soul-crushingly sad.

Lying on the bed, I cover my eyes with my arm. The warm late afternoon sunlight from the open window slants across my body. I take in a breath and let the melancholic strain of piano emanating from the speakers wash over me as I wait, like a predator in its lair.

I hear the creaking of the floorboards above me. Star has arrived through the front door. Either Mama or Zoe answered, forcing Star to talk to them for a bit before being pointed toward the staircase to the basement.

I imagine her lightly tripping down the basement steps.

I fantasize of one day being there to greet her. I'll sweep her into my arms and carry her to bed. I'll carefully lay her down and spread her creamy thighs so I can delve into her sweet nectar, smear her scent across my mouth and jaw like I did in the back alley of the gallery. Even shrouded in darkness, I reveled in her blush when she fell apart, her onyx eyes flashing, saying, *I can't believe I'm letting you do this to me in public.*

Oh, she's a dirty girl underneath that studious, oh-so-serious demeanor. Her confusion was adorable when I dropped to my knees. She thought teenage boys notoriously want girls to do it. She thought we're not interested in reciprocating, much less initiating on our own. I loved proving her wrong.

And I'll prove her wrong again because I'm certain she's more determined than ever to throw up a wall between us after what happened the other night.

A trumpet riff brings me back to the present, the cello and piano slowly unravel the smoky melody around the rapid trumpet. Only music and Star can save me on a day like today, and I need as many saviors as I can get.

I hear a light tap on the door, but I can't move to answer it. The music has taken over, inundating me with memories. Memories of sitting beside him in this very room, turning the pages of the score he's playing until he goes off script and improvises, spontaneously composing on the spot. That memory morphs into a darker scene of him gripped with delusions—of him beating me with a stick.

My brilliant, terrible father.

Today, on the day he finally took his own life.

The knob twists open. The swooshing sound of the opening door is followed by a cool breeze over my skin.

The music grows louder, the trumpet riffing fast and swirling in my head.

I hear Star moving quietly, not wanting to interrupt my reverie, and I love her more for it.

The music, it hurts to listen to. A lump in my throat squeezes. It aches so bad...so I hum. I hum to ease the anguish, to distract from it. It's a soft sound, almost drowned out by the volume of the music coming from the speakers.

But I hear Star's little gasp. She's heard my humming.

Eyes still closed, I tilt my head to the side.

I hear a tiny giggle.

I move my arm off my face.

My eyes pop open.

Startled, Star steps to the side too quickly and bumps into a low bookcase. It wobbles a little. She puts her hand out to steady it.

Her eyes clash with mine and whatever she sees sobers her. My nostrils burn from unshed tears.

I'm glad she's here, today of all days. Her presence soothes me. It always has, even on the days I went to school after the horrid nights when my father paced the living room, jazz music blasting through the house with the windows open for the entire neighborhood to hear.

Lulled by her presence, my heartbeat slows down, the choking sensation of a rope wrapped around my throat eases. It's not totally gone, but it's bearable. I close my eyes and fall back into the world of sound. Listening is a task of its own, like meditating. My father taught me that. It was the only thing that would calm him, listening to music and playing his trumpet.

I hear Star dragging a chair beside me and sitting down.

I know the piece by heart and the moment after its swelling crescendo and finale, my eyes flicker open.

I rise onto my elbow and say, "Nice."

"Nice?" One side of her mouth ticks up. "Not exactly the words I'd use to describe it."

I suppose there are parts where it seems like a runaway train going off the rails.

"Thelonious Monk is one of my favorites."

Intrigued, she leans forward. "Who?"

"Thelonious Monk. The composer. The guy playing the piano. He's something of a genius."

"I don't know…at times, it sounded like he was attacking the piano, not playing it," she replies.

My eyes crinkle with mirth. My lips twitch. That's a really accurate description. So apt. So like my father when he was well. It's funny—funny in a painful way. I can't help but throw my head back and laugh.

Star jolts a little in her seat, mesmerized by the thick column of my throat.

She jerks her gaze away from me. It bounces off the walls while her fingers flutter in front of her, looking like butterflies seeking a place to land. Flustered, she grabs her backpack and drags it toward her, practically hugging it to her chest. She opens it and digs around, ducking her head to hide the way I affect her.

It's mutual, baby girl. Believe me, it's mutual.

My eyelids grow heavy. With Star here, when I'm beating back a flood of memories like the birds in that Hitchcock movie my dad once made me watch with him, I feel unhinged. Gone is the posturing. Gone is my anger toward her. Gone is my frustration at school.

In this moment, as the music weaves a spell around us, nothing matters. I crook my finger at her and command in a lazy voice, "Come here."

She points a finger at her chest, her brows raised high.

"Who me?" she squeaks out, sounding winded. Goose bumps skitter down her arms.

I chuckle, soft and low. "Yeah, you."

I lean over, reach around the table, and grab the back-pack off her lap. She puts up a nominal fight, but eventually releases the bag and lets it fall to the ground.

I grasp her wrist—I love manhandling her—and gently tug her onto my lap. It's like the crazy music broke the fourth wall inside me. My hard control is gone. I'm relaxed, my face smoothed out, my movements mellow.

She comes to me.

Hmm, I should've been gentle with her before because she has no defenses against the gentle me. I can't describe what it's like to have her willingly come to me, to let me wrap my arms around her. Her warm skin, combined with the soft weight of her body in the tight band of my arms, is a blessing on a day like today.

I lean in and kiss her languidly, sinking my questing tongue into her mouth, tasting her. This time, I'm not proving a point or exacting a punishment. I'm just exploring.

I break our kiss only long enough to drag off my shirt. Her eyes drop and my heart stops. She lets out a loud yelp. My men are used to my chest. They never react to the gashes crisscrossing my chest.

My chest twists sharply as I watch the realization of what she's looking at wash over her.

She peers closer…

"Whipping marks," she breathes out.

That's right.

As if speaking to herself, she murmurs, "Some clans whip their inductees on their backs, but the Popescus only use a blood pact with a simple nick to the thumb. These look like bullwhip marks, like someone went after you without mercy…"

The more she speaks, the more I stiffen beneath her.

She lifts a finger to my chest.

I flinch, bracing myself.

Undeterred, she presses her index finger to the top of one particularly long, thick scar and slowly traces it to its end.

Drilling into her with my eyes, I answer her unspoken question. "My father."

She gulps. "Your father. Your *dead* father."

"Yes, my brilliant, broken, dead father."

Her eyes redden, but she struggles to keep the tears from falling.

"I don't tolerate pity."

"I don't pity you," she cries out. "You know I don't." Her bottom lip trembles. Tears fall. "But I can't help feeling sad. It's not right. It's not—" She pauses and gulps. "Right."

"He didn't know what he was doing," I explain.

Her lips twist into a grimace. "It doesn't matter."

"It *does* matter," I reply harshly.

I hate her tears, but I hate the truth even more. I don't want her weeping for the boy who had to deal with an insane father, who had to deal with violence, but the worse still—who tried to save his father but lost him anyway. "It's the only thing that makes it bearable. Don't cry."

She nods her head but can't speak as she fights the tears for me.

And that breaks me. It breaks something inside me.

"Baby girl…I need you," I says hoarsely.

She answers by spreading her hand over my old wounds. I return her touch. My hand threads through her hair. My lips are on hers once again and I'm lost.

I push her onto the bed. Her white-blonde hair fans out

over the knobby red knit of the embroidered bedspread. I drink her in greedily, memorizing every inch. I unbutton her shirt and spread it open for my perusal. I run a finger down the center of her chest, gliding over the pink silk rose in the center before undoing the front clasp.

Her chest quivers. I should stop it, I know I should, but I won't. This has been a long time coming, at least for me. For her? Star stares up at me conflicted and that alone should check me, but like Monk's music rising to its inevitable crescendo, nothing can stop me now.

Sensing her agitation, I make a tsking sound to bring her focus back on me. On us. In our world, a woman doesn't lose her virginity lightly. I'm slated to marry Roxie and Star has plans to run away. My heart clenches at the thought. At both thoughts. But this can only happen precisely because we can never be together.

I place my hand over her heart, silently urging her to calm down. I caress her hair and run my knuckles down her cheekbone until her fluttering chest steadies. Once her heartbeat settles, I help her out of her shirt and bra, and then efficiently attack the side buttons of her skirt. I toss it to the floor, leaving her in her panties.

She shifts in place nervously, her fingers twitching at her sides as if she's desperate to cover herself. Sweet Jesus, but why? I'm enthralled by her beauty. She's fucking gorgeous with her plump, high tits beaded with perfect raspberry nipples. Her belly slopes down, accentuating the lovely curve of her hipbones on either side. I can't tear my eyes away from her and she arches her back just a tiny bit, lifting her breasts and offering them to me like a tribute.

My nostrils flare.

I reach for the band of her panties and peel them off, leaving her bare to my gaze. I drag my fingertips over the light dusting of hair.

"Christ, that's pretty fluff."

Her cheeks burst into flames.

I slip a finger down her slit. "Wet."

Smacking my lips, I press a finger in. "For me."

I pop the finger in my mouth and slurp it. "Tastes as good as it did the other night."

A violent shiver racks through her.

"I didn't get a chance to taste these," I muse with a frown as I lean over and lap at a jutting nipple, curling my tongue around it before sucking it into my mouth. I expertly roll the nub around until she lifts off the bed, crying out raggedly.

My tongue may be wrapped around her nipple, but I bet she feels it in her pussy. I suckle one nipple and then the other, repeating it over and over until her breath is hitching and hiccupping, her hips twitching and writhing for more.

"Goood…" I drag the word out in a dark, satisfied tone, leaving it hanging for her to complete in her thoughts…*girl*.

I can't wait to wind her up till she's begging to do whatever I ask— anything to be my *good girl*. Little does she know, she already is. Everything this girl does is fucking perfection.

I move up, and press into her, planting my elbows on either side of her head. Abruptly, I bury my head in the crook of her neck and take in deep breaths. A guttural sound rises from the back of my throat. A breath rattles out.

My naked torso warms her, but the rough material of my jeans makes her cry out as I push my thick thigh between her legs and rub against her sensitive clit.

At this point, I can't take it anymore. I want every inch of her against me. I want my cock inside her wet heat. I want to feel her flesh wrapped around my shaft for the first time, without a barrier. She's impatient too because she claws at my button fly, tugging my jeans down. I chuckle indulgently. That only motivates her to speed up, but I stop her and draw away.

Sitting up, I spread my legs wide, and command, "Precious, come over here and get on your knees."

Precious?

It's such an old-school endearment and yet it feels right. Must feel right for her as well because she closes her eyes and another shudder ripples through her.

A terrible thought occurs to me. I know Star's a nerd and a virgin. Hell, my crew was ordered to never approach her, but who knows what kind of experience she's had. I mean, she clearly roams the city at all hours of the day and night.

"Star, have you done this before?"

I stiffen and my face turns hard, tension rippling through my muscles as I brace for her answer. I shouldn't be jealous. I have no right to be, but I'm greedy and possessive. Rabidly so.

She nervously licks her lips and bites into the bottom one—a sudden awkwardness descends upon her. Strands of blonde hair are stuck to her cheek, such a contrast to her dark eyes. She looks so fucking hot, I could watch her forever.

She shakes her head.

Tension rushes out of me and the vital need to mark her surges in its wake. I want to beat my chest and crow at the top of my lungs. Virgins are a dime a dozen in my world, but Star's different. She's always been special. Beyond the purity that men like me covet in a wife, she fits me like a key in a lock.

My eyes rise to the ceiling, and I let out a little silent

prayer and a relieved *thank fuck*. I return my gaze to her and point to the floor, the corners of my lips turning upward into a wicked smile.

She scoots to the side of the bed and slides down to her knees. In that moment, there's no doubt in my mind that even if I'm her first in everything, she's the one who will run away with my heart.

Impatience pounds inside me as I unzip my pants and release my painful, aching cock.

"Open wide."

CHAPTER 13

STAR

He's not turned off, thank God.

Wives should be virgins, but that's not what I am to Lucian.

I thought my inexperience was obvious the other night, but maybe he thought I just hadn't had a man go down on me before. Maybe he assumed I wasn't a virgin and expected someone with more experience. But no, I love the possessive gleam that entered his eyes in response to my confession. It makes my insides turn into chocolatey goo.

On my knees, I'm riveted by his large hand, languidly dragging up and down his thick cock from balls to crown. My hands twitch on my knees, antsy to touch him.

I drop my jaw open, panting, and my hot breath coasts over the fingers wrapped around his cock. I lean in and take a deep whiff.

Good God, it's unfair to smell this good. I'm hit with the scent of crushing pine needles beneath one's shoes in the quiet hush of the forest, punctuated only by the hum of insects or the call of a bird. It reminds me of summer in the Poconos, where we would go to Romanian camp for a week. The sparking bonfires with the *hoot hoot* of owls and the erratic swooping of bats in the break of the pines above us.

I lick my lips in anticipation.

Watching me, Lucian groans and his eyes almost roll back in his head.

"Fuck me, is this the first cock you're going to suck?"

His dirty words crash through me.

Not only is it the first cock I'm going to suck, but it's the first cock I've seen in real life.

My patience snaps and I slap his hand away, stick out my tongue, and lick his shaft from root to tip.

"Filthy girl, licking it like a popsicle."

I close my eyes, let out a long, desperate moan and take another thorough lick.

"Take your time and go slow. Otherwise, my cock will end up deep in your throat."

That puts a fire under me.

With another groan, I wrap my lips around the tip and suck harder, swishing my tongue back and forth over the thick vein running up the underside. His abdomen clenches. He grasps the covers and clenches them, wrestling with himself to give me space to explore.

Confident that he won't interfere, I take my time exploring and wrap my fingers around the base to stroke while slurping up and down his shaft.

"Fuck, if it's like this when you're just beginning, you'll kill me once you get a bit of experience."

He cups the back of my head and thrusts lightly toward my throat.

"I want to see your nose touch my belly," he challenges me. "You're going to have to open your throat for me to fit."

My eyes shoot to his and I nod. *Challenge accepted.*

I push farther down. His shaft disappears between my lips until I go so far that I gag. I pull back and inhale deep, grounding myself and focusing. Then I push back down as I prompt him to push in slowly. He goes deeper and deeper until the tip of my nose grazes his stomach.

Lucian pulls out, letting me take in a harsh breath, and then comes back in.

"I should give you a break, but my restraint is slipping fast. I've had my cock sucked many a time but having your beautiful dark eyes on me as I thrust inside your throat—"

He breaks and takes over, fucking my mouth forcefully a few times. I moan around his shaft, reveling in his dominance, when he abruptly withdraws.

I look up at him with questioning eyes.

"Gotta pull out before I come all over your pretty face," he explains. "I want the first spray to coat your womb, not your throat."

My pretty face? I preen inside, but then give myself an internal smack. Those are just empty compliments men give when they're in bed with a woman. They mean nothing.

I sit back on my haunches, delighting in the way my mouth feels roughed up and used. One corner of my glistening lips dribbles saliva mixed with pre-come. My tongue darts out, captures the drool, and sweeps it into my mouth.

Hmmm...so good.

A choked, guttural sound rises from deep within his chest.

"On the bed," he demands, pointing to where he wants me.

Eyes glued to his cock as he yanks off his jeans, I warn, "I don't think that's gonna fit."

He grins at me. "It fit in your throat."

I touch my neck. "And that hurt."

"Oh, precious, you shouldn't say things like that to a man like me. It'll only drive me to fuck you harder. Now get up here so I can prep you for my dick. I promise you, I'll make it fit."

It doesn't look like it will fit, but then again, this isn't Lucian's first rodeo. Most definitely not his first virgin. I have to trust that he knows what he's doing.

Crawling onto the bed, I drop to my back. An instant later, he falls ravenously between my thighs, licking and whipping his face from side to side, smearing my juices over his cheeks and jaw.

I grimace. He'll be smelling and tasting me for days.

Why would he want that?

I lick my lips and taste his musky pine taste. Hmm, oh yeah, things make more sense now. If he tastes good to me, then I have to believe that I taste good to him.

Wow, what just a little experience can teach you.

Between licks that rile me up, I feel a finger push inside me. It's not so bad, but the second finger is a much tighter fit. I wince from the stretch and he shushes me against my mons, making me twitch from the vibration. Before I know it, he's doing a slow and gentle scissoring motion *inside* me. He laps me with his tongue, stroking my clit, interspersing the laps with suckles and nips. I reach down, yanking and twisting his short curls as an orgasm sweeps over me abruptly.

Through blurred vision, I see him rise above me, triumphant.

His shoulders seem even broader, each clavicle like a dash of calligraphy just below his thick throat. His chest puffs up and he smacks it proudly as if he wishes everyone could see him in this state, his mouth and lower face covered in my slick.

"You look so damn proud of yourself. Do you have a virgin thing?"

He bursts out into a laugh. "No, I don't have a virgin thing. I have a you thing."

"Don't be silly," I reply instantly. He doesn't have to give me empty platitudes just because we're having sex.

His face turns serious. He looks devastatingly handsome in this moment. His high cheekbones slope sharply into hollow cheeks, his chiseled jaw rigid. "I'm going to take you now, baby girl. You ready?"

My eyes go soft.

Despite the tug-of-war between us over the years, he's giving me a chance to back out. But that question, in this pivotal moment, suddenly freezes me. I'm a good girl. Always have been. Sure, I want to assert myself in the world with my bucket list, but this virgin thing is a big deal. If I do this now, I will never be able to offer this gift to my husband. I know it's stupid and anti-feminist, but I'm *mafie* to the core and this is a core value.

At the same time, I'm not leaving here with my hymen intact. I love the way Lucian takes control. I've seen more than a few glimpses of it, and I've had more fantasies about him than I can count. I want this, and for him to take it from me would be the cherry on top.

So what do I do to resolve this inner tussle? I gaze up at him and demand, "I want you to force me."

His hips punch forward and he grips his cock hard to get a hold of himself. Okaaay...clearly this has been a running fantasy for him, too.

"Oh, I see," he replies. "You want dirty sex with a bad *mafie* dude and still stay the good girl. And continue denying how much you want me."

I gulp.

Yeah, that about sums it up.

I brace for his rejection.

Instead, he huffs out a little chuckle, leans over, and murmurs in my ear, "I have no qualms popping your cherry, precious, any way you want it."

I exhale a breath of relief.

Almost as an afterthought, he adds, "And who knows, maybe one day, I will end up as your husband."

My insides explode at his offhanded comment, but I stifle it viciously.

This is the sex talking. He doesn't really mean it.

He knows how much this moment means and he's just trying to soften the impact of it. It's almost sweet really, his attempt to comfort me. But a man like Lucian would never give up a perfect *mafie* wife like Roxie for a girl like me. I might have long harbored a fantasy of Lucian choosing little ole me over his fiancée, his family, and his clan, but that will never be reality.

He eyes me up and down carefully. "If you're gonna be my dirty, filthy girl, then that's how you'll be treated, understand?"

I nod excitedly.

Yes. Yes, please.

"Hold your knees open for me."

I hesitate for a moment.

"You gonna be a good slut for me, Star, or am I gonna have to hold you down to bust through that untouched cherry and make you bleed?"

Breath accelerating, my gaze is glued to him. Slowly, I

bend my knees and grip the back of them, spreading wide for him.

He wraps a hand around my throat. I almost swoon.

"What will it be? Tell me, what are you going to be?" he prompts.

Oh, he wants me to concede, to own how much I want this. But I won't play his game. No, this time, I'm calling the shots of how this goes.

I snap my legs shut and grip his hand, but instead of pulling it off, I press it tighter against my throat. "I'm *not* your good little slut."

He gives a vicious laugh. "You want to play with me? You have no idea how that gets my blood pumping..."

His hold on my throat tightens. He tips my chin up and brushes a soft kiss against my lips. "Test me, baby girl. I'm going to tame you yet."

In the blink of an eye, he grabs my wrists and loops them above my head. Snagging my bra, he expertly ties my hands.

Oh my God.

Pushing my bent leg to one side, he gives me a hard smack on the ass. Exalted, I shunt out a harsh exhale. Moisture gushes from between my thighs, coating them. I peek over my shoulder and see his handprint blossom against my pale skin.

"Open your legs," he demands.

"No," I snarl back.

His steel-gray eyes spark with bloodlust and determination.

He pries my legs open, but I fight him. Raising his hand, Lucian repeatedly smacks my butt until I'm straining to get away from him and screaming *ouch, ouch, ouch.* He grabs me by the thigh and pins me to the mattress, shoving my other leg open and locking it down with his knee.

He takes a hard swat at my pussy and warns me, "Be still or I take out my belt."

Nostrils flaring, I stop fighting him. My senses are heightened and everything inside me is vibrating like a tuning fork. I heave in long draughts of air as I relax my legs, letting them fall open inch by inch.

I can feel his control deserting him as he fists his cock and rubs it against my clit and then down my slit.

He groans. "Fuck Christ, my dirty girl is drenched."

My juices slather the crown of his cock. His lips part as he watches one bead catch, drip, and roll down his shaft. Proof of what our scuffle has done to me.

Eyes hard and determined, Lucian notches his cock to my opening and presses in. I squirm beneath him, the girth of him uncomfortably stretching my unused cunt.

This is nothing like his fingers.

My eyes widen. I curl my fingers into his shoulders, drag them down his chest and draw blood. The hard jut of his jaw above me tells me nothing's going to stop him. And when he hits a thin layer of resistance, he simply bursts through it.

Fuck! It burns and feels like I'm being stretched to the breaking point. I hiss and slap him twice on the chest. "Oh God, it hurts."

He takes my mouth and laps at my tongue to distract me from the pain, but he doesn't stop pushing until he's bottomed out.

Good God, he's in.

Finally.

"Relax, precious, relax," he croons, pulling out of my slippery, tight sheath and then pushing back in.

Despite the traces of pain, I shudder at the slow drag of his cock. He's kissing me again, and that helps, too. Soon, the pain subsides and if I rock my hips ever so slightly, it even feels good. I try again, a little harder. He drops his head and groans into the crook of my neck. A few more deep kisses, a few more slow and steady thrusts, and I'm urging my hips to meet his. We repeat it over and over again until we're swaying in a defined rhythm.

"Look at you, taking this fucking like a good girl. Red pussy stretched to take my cock, the way you were meant to."

My inner muscles flex around his shaft. Now that the pain is gone, I kinda want him to go harder. And that inner clenching must signal to him that I'm ready because his thrusts increase.

He hits a special spot and stars explode in my vision. I kick at his back for more, mewling and keening loudly, but he keeps his pace steady.

Frustrated, I beg, "More. More."

Thank God, he gives it to me, thrusting hard enough for his balls to slap against my ass. Intense pleasure overtakes me. My legs wrap tightly around his hips as he pounds into me, hitting the same crazy spot. Each time, I get carried deeper until I spiral headlong into a screaming, writhing climax.

My limbs thrash in ecstasy as my inner walls grip and milk his cock.

He buries his face in my mane and ruts into me, grunting and growling. Then he floods me, just like he said he would.

My body goes limp and he collapses on top of me. He's heavy but I wouldn't have it any other way. Eventually he shifts off me slightly and I mourn the loss. He gently eases his cock out. Come oozes out, painting both of our thighs.

He wraps an arm around my waist, pulls me in close to him, and swings a leg over my legs. Laying his head on my breast, he lets out a satisfied sigh like he's put in a good day's work.

In awe, I whisper, "I came. Even though it was my first time, I came on…"

I swallow and open my mouth to finish the phrase, but he answers for me. "My cock."

"Yeah," I reply.

He lifts his head and looks up at me with a wink. "Did you doubt my skills?"

"No. Maybe," I reply with a grin. "Crina said the first time hurts."

His brows crease together. "How would she know?"

I tense beside him, shutting down, but he murmurs, "I'm not going to get Crina in trouble. I don't care about Crina. She's Marku's problem, not mine."

Retreating from the subject, he teases me, "You were doomed from the start."

My muscles loosen and I relax into his big frame. His arms tighten around me.

"Oh, is that right?" I tease right back.

"It was inevitable that you'd come on my cock. First time." He drops a kiss on the tip of my nose. "And every time from now on."

"Is it always like this?"

I hold still, the words slipped out of my mouth despite my better judgement. *Shit, why did I say that? Making it sound like it's something special.*

I shake my head ruefully. "Of course, it is for you. You're a man, and anyway, women are interchangeable. Fuckable pawns used to elevate one's status, I think were your exact words."

He flinches.

Reaching down, he brushes the soft down of my pussy with the back of his knuckles, making me twitch. "No, it's not."

"You lie."

He rises on his forearm and frowns down on me. "Lying is for the weak. I have no need to lie. Not to anyone. Especially not to you."

Especially not to you, he says, making the point that I matter to him. Which is ridiculous. Either that or he's trying to bolster his silly argument that I'm somehow on the Bratva's radar, which is also absurd.

That last phrase breaks the spell he's woven around me. There can't be anything special between us. Of course, in a moment of weakness, I want to indulge in that fantasy, but that's not real. No way am I falling for Lucian Popescu again. That's never gotten me anywhere, and if I ever needed further proof, I got it in the cafeteria.

What we just had was sex, nothing more.

Suddenly feeling suffocated, I shove his arm and leg off me, and scramble away while protesting, "There won't be a next time."

"*What?* Like hell there won't."

I put more distance between us. He goes to grab for me, but I hop away from him, grab my shirt, and whip it on, tugging the sides together to cover myself.

Lucian's eyes snap with fury at me. He rises to his feet. Buck naked, with his legs spread apart, he looks like an avenging god. Furious and utterly gorgeous. He opens his mouth to argue but happens to glance down.

I follow his gaze.

Red blood streaks his semi-hard cock. It jerks and grows under my attention and I snap my eyes up to his.

Instead of seeing the anger or lust that I expect, he's giving me a shit-eating grin. A grin that confirms, *like hell there won't be a second time.*

I narrow my eyes at him. For a split second, I think to

argue but that won't get me anywhere. Instead, I do what any self-respecting deflowered woman at risk of falling in love with her tormentor does.

I run.

CHAPTER 14

LUCIAN

Riding up the elevator to Cristo's loft, I know what I must do, and I'm feeling surprisingly light-hearted about it.

My whole world is upended, but there it is. I am nothing, if not adaptable.

I've fucked many women, but none of them were like Star. Not an hour ago, I was thrusting mindlessly, desperate to empty every single drop of semen in her. To breed her. I pounded away at her untouched cunt ruthlessly and filled her to the brim with my seed—Christ, I'm descending into the crazy.

But I grab the crazy by the horns and run with it.

I came to a few conclusions after her declaration that we would never be together again.

First, I want this woman as my own and I want the world to know it. I want a fat diamond on her ring finger. I want her big and round, carrying my child. I want the

Popescu eagle tatted on her breast, like every good Popescu wife has.

My chest seizes.

She's truly mine and I will do whatever is necessary to lock her down. I *will* marry her.

I grin, thinking back on what we just did. She's not shy now, is she? I did that. I made her wild. Broke down the last wall separating us.

Then she asked if it was normal to feel this way and brought up what I said about fuckable pawns. I rarely regret anything I say or do, but remorse hit me like a punch in the gut. I remember saying it during one of our early tutoring sessions. I was talking like an idiot.

And when she said there wouldn't be a next time, I wanted to yank her back in bed and prove how very wrong she was. I was straining not to grab her when I glanced down at her blood on my dick, and everything clicked into place.

It was like a fucking vision the old saints used to have.

Suddenly the clouds of anger and frustration parted, and I saw my future as clear as light.

My future is Star.

She may not see it yet, but that's my truth.

And I'm here at Cristo's to fight for what's mine.

I stride out of the elevator into Cristo's loft. He's by the wall of windows overlooking downtown. I walk over to him and casually listen to his conversation as I stare off into the skyline with the Freedom Tower. Not gonna lie, it's a nice view.

He finishes his call and turns to me. "What couldn't wait, runt?" he asks indulgently.

He may be one of the biggest assholes I know, but he's been like a second father to me. Instead of throwing my family out of our house to install his father's current *consilier*, he fought for us. He gave me time to grow up and prove my worth. He didn't give me any favors beyond that, and he sure as hell never coddled me, but he roots for me in the background. That does something to a man— knowing someone sees your worth when everyone expects you to follow in your father's footsteps.

"Thanks for meeting me, *şef*." Leaning against a white column, I say, "I have a proposal to make. It benefits our clan, it benefits you, and it benefits me."

Interest—the greedy kind—sparks in his eyes.

Turning toward me fully, he says, "You've got my attention." He gestures with his hand for me to continue.

I take a moment to gather my strength, drape it around me like a fucking cloak of invincibility, and declare, "I want to marry Star. I've fucked her and I'm claiming her."

Crossing his arms over his chest, he leans back against the windowsill and lets out a soft, disbelieving chuckle. "I should've known... All that talk about how you don't want to be tutored by her."

"I didn't," I admit.

"And the fuckup in the cafeteria? You still managed to get her in your bed after that? Impressive."

"Never underestimate me."

His eyes harden. "There's Roxie to consider."

I knew this would be the sticking point.

"I've considered it and after reviewing the pros and cons, Star still wins out by a mile."

"Explain."

I clear my throat, suddenly nervous.

"Well, first and foremost, I've fucked her. She's mine."

One eyebrow rises. "And..."

"You were saving her for Simon, but I'm worth ten

times what he is on a good day. This will make the alliance with the Lupu clan even more significant. It will show the Bratva how united we are."

"I could have you marry Roxie as arranged, have Star marry Simon, and still get enough of what I want. Now I'll have to contend with an offended Popescu family that has serious clout. I'll have to appease her father. I'll have to rearrange things to get her married to another important made man. It's a headache really…"

"You can marry her to Dinu. He's the second most powerful after me and he's always had a hard-on for her, if for no other reason than that she was mine. Her father wouldn't dare argue with his rank and you can put it on the Lupu boss. Say Alex insisted I marry Star. That he made it worth your time. He already has a reputation for being a pain in the ass. Let the hatred fall on him."

"Devious…I like it," he concedes.

"And Star is at a high risk right now. If the Bratva are spying on me, they already know we're together. If they didn't consider her a valuable target before, they sure as hell do now."

"Simon can protect her."

A surge of violent emotion swells inside me. My hands curl into balls at my sides. I look off into the distance, focusing on the lines of the jagged red strokes in the huge paintings hanging on his wall until I get hold of my temper.

"Like hell he will," I reply roughly. "She's mine to protect and I protect what's mine. No one touches her but me. Ever."

"Hmm…touchy." murmurs Cristo. He eyes me knowingly. "If I didn't know better, I'd say you love her."

I stiffen beside him. My heart is pounding a mile a minute.

"Of course, I fucking love her," I admit.

My head jerks back. Fuck, did I just say that?

But I *do* love her. I've fallen in love with Star. I love everything about her. I love the way she gushes over books and gets angry at me for hauling her out of a gallery before she's gotten a chance to check out the exhibition. I love the taste of her pussy. I love the way her eyes follow me in a room, anointing me like a fucking god. But most of all, I just love her. I always have, but I wasn't ready to admit it. Now I am and, by God, she'd better be ready for me, 'cause I'm coming for her.

Cristo shrugs his shoulders. "Far be it from me to get in between a couple that loves each other," he says with an almost wistful tone.

He sure as hell did everything in his power to keep his sister Cat away from Luca. Hell, he tried to get him killed. Fuck me, but if I didn't know Cristo was a cold-hearted, brutal man, I'd venture to say that he loved someone.

I shake my head slightly. *Nah.*

"So does that mean I have your support?"

Cristo gives me a chin lift. "Yeah, runt. You've convinced me. Now you're gonna need a helluva lot of luck to convince that fucker, Alex."

My heart sinks, but I blow out an exhale and rally my determination. I've convinced Cristo. I can face Alex. Hell, I just won now and no one's a harder adversary than Cristo.

* * *

"No," replies Alex tightly on the video chat.

Exasperation fills my chest. I run my hands through my hair and lean forward on the couch to give Alex a hard stare through the computer placed on the table of Cristo's living room.

This is not going well.

"She could be carrying my son as we speak," I shout, throwing my hands up.

Goddamn, but he's a stubborn old bastard. I expected the Lupu boss to explode at my bombshell, but then to acknowledge that he has no other choice but to agree.

Instead, there's a long pause.

He finally responds with a drawl, "*Could* is the optimal word here."

Oh, for fuck's sake.

"If she's not yet, she will be soon," I throw back.

"If you can get her in bed again," he returns just as quickly.

Cristo chuckles. "We're not like you Lupu fuckers. No woman can say no to a Popescu's big dick."

Christ, the way these old men talk.

Alex rolls his eyes. "Believe what you will about Popescu dick, but I can forbid her from seeing you."

Addressing me, he goes on, "I can't imagine how you got a girl like her into your bed after what happened in the cafeteria. Regardless, Tatum's gone and it's my duty to protect her."

I give a derisive snort. "Oh, like you've done such a great job protecting her so far. Look what kind of protection you have on her? None, that's what. Tatum killed the Bratva boss and you have no one watching her."

"Don't question the way I rule, boy," growls Alex. "You're no *şef*. Hell, you're not even a *consilier*, so shut your damn mouth."

"Look how forbidding anyone to do anything worked for you, Alex," Cristo interjects, bringing up his marriage to an outsider, which had been the scandal of the year.

"Or Luca and Cat. How did that end up? If Lucian and Star wanna fuck, they're gonna fuck regardless of what you or I say. If they want to be together, let them be together. We were already discussing another alliance. I suggested Simon, but Lucian is a far better choice."

"Oh, and are you finally going to make him your *consilier*? Because that might change my mind."

"It's in the works," Cristo replies vaguely. "It's a Popescu clan decision without Lupu interference. Don't push."

"Don't pretend it's anyone's decision but yours, Cristo. And who's pushing? I don't give a fuck what you do. I'm only asking because it might influence my decision."

Cristo hates being questioned. He curls his lip and opens his mouth to insult Alex, but I step in and say, "The Bratva will know what she means to me. I bet they already know. That puts a target on her back. They may have dismissed her as not valuable since Tatum's fallen from grace, but now—"

"Now she's fucking bait," Cristo finishes. "The sooner she's married to Lucian, the safer she'll be."

"Or she'll be in more danger," Alex argues.

"That's a given, which is why her protection is vital. Once they know she could be carrying my son, her value skyrockets. They hate Tatum for the assassination and they hate me for invading their distribution routes on the Jersey Shore. She's the perfect target. How will it look when she gets kidnapped, hmm? People will either think that you sacrificed her because you actually hate her brother or…"

"Or that we can't protect what's ours," concludes Cristo. "And there's no way in hell I'll allow that to happen. If Lucian doesn't claim her, it suggests that I either don't know what's happening in my own clan or that I'm so incompetent that I can't do simple math. It's a given that if they're fucking, they should marry."

"And under the blood oath, we're practically married anyway," I insert.

"We've done away with that barbaric tradition," Alex counters.

"Technically, yes," Cristo replies. "But it still holds power in the minds of every Romanian *mafie*, especially the older generation."

"Fuck, why are you fighting this?" I demand through clenched teeth.

If I have to kidnap her myself, I goddamn will.

"Fuck, why do you want her so bad?" Alex throws back at me.

Silence.

"Why, Lucian? Tell me why you want Star?" he pushes.

"Because I fucking love her," I bellow. "There. I said it. Are you satisfied?"

A smug smile spreads over his face. "Yes, motherfucker, yes."

Bastard.

"Just for the record, I wasn't going to let her go for anything less."

"Don't pretend you care about her, Alex," I snap.

"Fuck you, Lucian. I've known that girl since she was in diapers. Her brother was my *consilier* for ten fucking years. She's close to almost every female in my clan. Yes, she's slipped in the ranks since her brother's—" he pauses ominously, shakes his head, and continues, "I may not have paid attention to her as I should have of late, but have no fear, there's no way I'd force her to marry you if she was nothing more than a stepping stone on your climb to the top."

Ouch.

"She deserves better than that," he adds. "Honestly, if I hadn't tested you and you hadn't fought for her, there's no way I'd allow this alliance to proceed. You barely deserve her as it is."

"But you were going to just hand her over to Simon," I say incredulously.

"Simon's a good man…underneath it all."

"He kills people for a living," I roar.

"We all have blood on our hands, but he's a good man. You're a heartless bastard. Ambition is everything to you. Honestly, I didn't think you had it in you to love anyone as much as you love yourself or your clan."

I'm simmering with rage. Why does that sound like a fucking insult when I would've proudly waved that flag in the past?

Then a thought pops into my head. My eyes narrow. "You sure your opposition doesn't have to do with my father?"

If that's the real reason behind his pushback, I don't even know how I'm going to hold back from going to his house and strangling him with my bare hands.

"What? That I don't want her marrying you because he went crazy so you will, too?" He shakes his head. "Nah, I don't believe in that old superstitious nonsense."

He leans forward, his brows raised. "Do you?"

"Fuck no," I reply.

"Alright then. That's all I need to know." He slaps his knees and turns to Cristo, "It's settled, then. He marries Star. Good luck with Roxie's father. I'd like to be a fly on the wall and watch you try to worm your way out of that shit show. He's gonna be pissed."

Giving Alex a sly smile, he replies, "Don't worry about me, you asshole…"

I tune out their bickering and wipe my brow as I let out a whoosh of relief.

Hopefully, being *consilier* isn't as stressful as this was. Jesus.

I take in a deep breath and allow pride to sweep into my chest. *I fucking did it.*

My chest deflates.

Now I just need to convince Star to marry me.

CHAPTER 15

STAR

"*D*umb, broken lock," I mutter, bending my head and trying the combination again. I'm running late for class, yet here I am, rattling the lock on my locker.

I hear the click and let out a little yip of triumph.

Ducking my head, I rifle around for my math book and quickly thrust it into my backpack.

I close the locker door and let out a screech.

Lucian is leaning against the locker next to mine, arms crossed over his chest. His broad shoulders block my view of the hallway, making me very aware of his size. A frisson of awareness skitters down my spine. *Ugh.* Man, I'm praying it's only a normal reaction to a guy I've just had sex with and that it will fade naturally. And quickly. I really need a quick end to this intense awareness of him.

He looks like he's been up all night, his hair tousled like he didn't have the time to drag a comb through it before he came to school. I'm irritated with myself for noticing that tiny detail. I told him we'd never hook up again, yet his tired eyes gaze softly down on me, making me squirmy on the inside.

I feel eyes on me. On us.

The first bell has already rung and the hallway is mostly empty, but there are still a few people rushing around. I crane my neck past him and my eyes dart around, tracking how many people might have noticed us together.

"What are you doing?" I mutter in a low voice.

He leans into me and takes hold of my hip. I wheeze out a surprised breath and slap his hand away, trying not to bring attention to the fact that he's touching me. *In public.* Is he delirious or what?

My voice raises a fraction above a harsh whisper. "What the hell are you doing?"

His concerned eyes zero in on me. "I wanted to see you. See how you're feeling." His voice turns to gravel. "Are you sore, baby girl?"

Oh my God. I shut down another inconvenient shiver and close my eyes in pure mortification. Why does his stupid voice have to affect me so? And what is he doing coming up to me in broad daylight? What kind of trickery is this?

"You could've texted me if you were so concerned," I hiss. "People are staring, wondering why you're talking to me."

His expression hardens. "Let them stare. I don't give a fuck."

"W-what are you talking about?" I stammer. "You don't want anyone seeing us together. You don't want anyone knowing I tutor you. Remember the cafeteria." I widen my eyes, nodding my head in hopes that the encouragement will joggle his head back to normal because he's clearly got some loose bolts in there.

"Fuck the cafeteria. I don't give a shit what people think."

My mouth drops. "Since when?"

His hand returns to my waist, secured hard enough that I can't dislodge it with a wiggle of my hips.

Dear God, the gravel is back in his tone. "Since now."

This won't do. I'm not sure what the hell is going on, but it won't do one bit.

I smack his hand again, but it only prompts him to tighten his hold on me. I'm out of my depth here. The idea that one bout of sex is behind his sudden change in behavior is preposterous, but it feels like the ground beneath my feet is shifting like sand. This must be what an earthquake feels like.

I let out an irritated sigh. "Well, I care. I don't need people knowing we...you know." I flap my hand in his direction, then mine, then his again.

He looks down at me stubbornly.

Hoping to appeal to his ever-important ambition, I ask, "How would this look to Roxie?" His expression darkens quickly so I add, "Or how will it look when I go missing and they come around to question you about where I've disappeared to? Being linked to me will sabotage your plans."

God knows, it will sabotage *my* plans, and honestly, that's the greater worry. More than ever, it's imperative that I disappear. I can't stand by and watch Lucian marry Roxie. Just the thought of a ring on her finger or, even worse, an eagle tattoo over her heart makes my stomach clench and bile rise in my throat.

"Tell me," he insists, his palm caressing my cheek.

I pretend I don't know what he's talking about. "Tell you what?"

I can't begin to imagine why he'd bring this up in

public, where anyone could guess what we're talking about or, even worse, overhear us.

"What are you doing?" I ask, feeling itchy and hot under the collar.

"There was blood, as you well know," he goes on. "And don't think I'm not mad at you for running away, for not letting me take care of you. I would've gotten a warm washcloth and wiped away any traces of blood on your pussy and inner thighs. Then, I would've made it all better with my tongue. But you took that away from me so the least you can do is tell me if you're still sore. Either that, or I drag you into an empty classroom and find out for myself."

Oh, God, no.

My entire face bursts into flames, imagining the things he'd said. Refusing to let me go until he took care of me. Images flash in my mind of Lucian pushing me back onto the bed, dropping to his knees, and meticulously taking care of me. With a warm, wet towel. With his tongue.

Just thinking back on his naked body, looking *fucking* glorious with his semi-erect cock swinging in front of him, I want to lick every inch of him.

Despite my harsh words and running like a coward, a part of me had ached to stay longer. I'd felt so warm and gooey when he laid his head on my chest, his arm securely draped around my waist. I hadn't felt that safe since Tatum left but feeding those kinds of feelings are scary. Lucian fucked the virgin out of me, and then he went ahead and snatched my heart as well.

I don't regret losing my virginity to him, but my heart is another matter entirely.

I'm fixed on the spot where I'm standing, blinking up at him, my heart stuttering in my chest when I see something coming at me from the side.

Roxie charges at me, shoving a hand into my chest.

I jump back.

"What the fuck, bitch? Can't you leave another woman's man *alone*?"

"Hey," snaps Lucian, placing a hand on my shoulder to steady me and his other hand keeping her at bay. Blinking at his hand, I feel the numbness spread over my body like it's the cafeteria all over again.

I recoil, ready to back away and get the hell out of there before another disastrous scene unfolds, when Lucian growls, "Don't speak to her that way."

Roxie's jaw drops open, but she quickly rallies. Her tone morphs into something sickly sweet as she explains, "I was in class and Luminita texted me that *she's* in the hall, bothering you again. I just came to rescue you, baby."

She lays a hand on his arm. He shakes it off. "This is none of your business, Roxie. This is between me and Star."

Her eyes narrow dangerously. Oh, Roxie doesn't like that one bit. "What exactly is going on between you and this...this," she waves her hand at me, "bitc—"

"Choose your next word carefully," he warns in a low, dangerous tone.

My eyes bulge. I've heard Lucian speak harshly, but I've never heard *that* tone before. A threatening energy shimmers in the air that makes me want to scurry away, and I'm not even the target of his ire.

I try taking a step back into the lockers, squinting down the hall to see where I can make my getaway, but his grip slides down my arm and tightens around it. There are only a few people around, but instead of going about their business and rushing to class like they're supposed to, they stop to watch The Cafeteria Scene 2.0 unfold.

As if summoned, Luminita and a couple of other

Popescu girls sidle up behind Roxie. With her gang behind her, Roxie must feel emboldened. Either that, or she's not aware of the tone in Lucian's voice.

"What the fuck, Lucian? You're taking her side. This girl, who you've called disgusting."

His head snaps her way. "Shut your mouth, I've never said that."

"Actually, you have," I blurt out softly.

His gaze swings back to me and I recoil against the lockers, as much as I can in his iron grip.

"Have not," he replies, but scanning my face, his brows lower ominously. "Have I? I don't remember."

Of course, he doesn't. It doesn't matter enough for him to remember. Not only did he say it, but it was overheard by everyone, including Roxie. My gaze drops to the floor, humiliation rushing more heat to my face.

In a whisper, I remind him, "When I was on the floor in the cafeteria with food all over me." I gulp before adding, "After I chipped my tooth."

His expression turns stormy, the flashes of silver stark against the flat gray of his eyes. "I don't remember," he repeats.

"Of course not," I mutter, trying to tug out of his clasp, but no luck. It's like a metal cuff around my bicep.

He looks pained. "And if I said it, I didn't mean it in that way." He exhales harshly. "I say things I don't mean, sometimes. Or it doesn't come out right. Like yesterday."

Before I can even think about his words—which sound suspiciously like an apology—Roxie demands, "What happened yesterday? What are you doing with this...this... girl? Because if you're fucking her, I won't have it."

Scorn curls her upper lip. She crosses her arms tightly over her chest and taps her pink bubblegum-colored Versace platform shoes on the carpeted floor of the hall.

Lucian's face morphs into a mask of rage.

Swinging me behind him as if to protect me, he turns on her. "What did you say to me? You have no power over me, Roxie. Not now. Not ever."

His head swings over his shoulder at me. Pointing to the spot where I stand, he commands, "Don't move a fucking inch."

Then he rounds on Roxie, pushing her back a step, and continues, "I'll do whatever the fuck I want."

He jabs a finger in my direction. "If I want to be with her, in any shape or form, I'll do it. If I want to fuck her, I'll fuck her. If I want to have her, I'll have her. Hell, if I want to marry her, I'll damn well marry her."

Roxie and I gasp in unison.

I shake my head. *No, no, he can't mean that.*

"What?" she shrieks. Her head swings back and forth to her friends on either side of her, looking for guidance.

"You can't mean that," she says, echoing my own thoughts.

"Like hell I can't," he sneers. "The only person who tells me what to do is my *şef*. And when it comes to my personal life, not even him. I'm a grown-ass man and you sure as hell have no say in what I do."

Roxie's face is flushed with fury, her jaw tight and the tendons in her neck popping out. At her sides, her hands flex and clench into fists.

Stamping her foot like a spoiled child, she says, "I won't have it. I won't!"

Lucian widens his stance as if he's going to go toe to toe with her, but then seems to change his mind. He pivots on his heel, showing her his back and swings an arm around my shoulder. Tugging me into his side, he orders, "Come on."

I'm too stunned to do anything but follow his lead.

Pausing in midstep, he turns around and, speaking in a suspiciously calm tone, he drops the bombshell of the century. "Oh, and one more thing. Star is under my protection. No one touches her."

His glare transfers to her friends, who cringe under his fierce expression. "If I hear that either you or one of your posse has fucked with her, you're fucking with me. And Roxie...you don't want to fuck with me and mine."

I'm rooted to my spot, speechless with shock.

The man put a target on my back, an even bigger one than I already had, and then he threw a cloak of invincibility over it. Why would he take my side over his future fiancée? I open my mouth to ask, but then snap it shut when he crushes me into his hard body and drags me down the hall with him. I hear a feminine screech behind me and cringe at the high-pitched sound.

My head is a jumbled mess, trying to make sense of what just happened. Maybe he publicly scolded Roxie because she'd overstepped. Yeah, that's it.

Before I can sift through my jumbled thoughts, Lucian deposits me in front of my classroom, opens the door, and shoves me through it with a relaxed "See you soon, baby girl."

Stunned, I let the door smack me in the ass.

"You're late," the math teacher says. "Take a seat, Star."

I shake the daze from my head, slink into my seat, and hunch down. I feel like a balloon full of helium floating high in the sky, untethered. Gripping the smooth laminated surface of my desk, I let out a shaky breath.

I can't read into what just happened. Squeezing my eyes shut, I rack my brain for explanations and the only rational one is that it was a power play between Lucian and Roxie. They're still very much a couple. This was simply a lover's spat and I was a pawn in their game of love. Yes, that makes much more sense. Anything else is a figment of my imagination.

My heart squeezes in pain, but I nod my head firmly as I open my backpack to take out my laptop and math book.

Nothing's changed.

I repeat, nothing's changed.

CHAPTER 16

LUCIAN

I'd rather spend the evening with Star, preferably in bed, but no clan member would dare miss Nelu's sixtieth birthday/retirement party, a black-tie reception at the Metropolitan Museum of Art.

It's being hosted in one of the reception rooms of the Egyptian Wing. One wall is lined with paintings on papyrus while another side captures a view overlooking Central Park. In the twilight, there isn't much to see beyond a few flickering lights and the pyramid top of the obelisk, Cleopatra's Needle, poking out above the treetops.

At least I'm confident Star will show up.

Not for me or Nelu, of course. I didn't bother asking her, knowing she'd never attend if I did. No, I've guaranteed she'll be here via Marku's mother, who invited Crina's family. Crina's mother is a stickler for rules, and if Crina is here, there's no doubt she'll guilt Star and Gabby into joining her. With every clan, big and small, present, this is my chance to put everything to rights with her and claim her as I should.

I'm in the middle of a conversation with Marku when Star enters the room alongside Crina's entire family.

For a black-tie event, she doesn't disappoint.

She's wearing a black taffeta cocktail dress, showing off her toned, trim legs. The front plunges into a deep V, but it's lined with floppy ruffles that play peekaboo with her breasts. From where I'm standing halfway across the room it covers just enough of her gorgeous tits. Fuck me, but my woman is stunning.

I may not be able to acknowledge her publicly quite yet, but that doesn't mean I can take my eyes off her either. I'm whisking another champagne flute off the tray of a passing waiter when I clock Roxie from the corner of my eye. She's sauntering up to me with an exaggerated sway of her hips. I let out a sigh.

This is going to be a long night.

Determined to ignore her, I dive into an animated discussion with Marku. Roxie stops beside me and drags a finger down the sleeve of my tux. I tense at her territorial move. Irritation simmers in my gut. I'm not her fucking property.

Instead of taking the hint, she bats her eyelashes at me.

Roxie's no fool. She senses the tide turning away from her, and whether she cares for me or not, I imagine her mother has given her a lesson on how to seduce me back by her side. Not gonna work. I only have eyes for one adorable book nerd who happens to be dressed in a once-in-a-lifetime sexy cocktail dress.

But that doesn't mean I can put Roxie in her place like I did at school. Not here. And knowing that, she's taking advantage of the fact that there are power players here, and she's trying to stake her claim on me.

My snub only encourages her to plaster herself to my side, cooing some nonsense or other in my ear. I grind down on my back teeth and play nice, giving her as little attention as possible without insulting her parents. I discreetly watch Star and catch her dashing tears from the corners of her eyes. Crina is forcefully whispering in her ear, gesticulating in my direction with slashing motions.

Aww, fuck.

Star shakes her head. Crina wraps her arm around her friend and, shielding her, guides her out of the reception room.

Fury snaps at my heels. I pluck Roxie's hand off my chest, place her away from me with a mumbled excuse, and stalk up to Cristo, who's in the middle of a circle of men.

"Cristo," I interrupt.

He smirks at me meaningfully. Knowing him, he's seen everything that's happened from Roxie's excessive flirting to Star's sudden departure. That guy doesn't miss a thing.

The men part to give me space.

I step into the inner circle and declare, "I'm going to marry Star."

Cristo cups his ear and commands, "Sorry, didn't hear that. What'd you say?"

I grit my teeth. This guy. I respect him, but he likes to work my last nerve.

His eyes shift to his left, toward Alex, who's standing a couple of feet away. I see what's happening here. He wants a performance.

After all, it's not every day a Popescu gets engaged to a Lupu.

Loud and clear, I pronounce loudly, "I'm going to marry the Lupu girl, Star."

This time, everything stops. The conversation, the clinking of glasses and silverware. Even the catering staff seem frozen in place. I hear a feminine gasp to my right, most likely Roxie or her mother.

Alex's head snaps in my direction. He arches an eyebrow like this is the first he's heard of it. Jesus, the fake-ass acting is ridiculous. His eyes sweep me up and down, taking stock of me as if for the first time, as if we hadn't battled each other like two gladiators in a Roman arena.

He suavely glides in our direction, stops beside Cristo, and claps a hand on his shoulder.

Cristo stiffens. His little sister might be married to Alex's brother, but there's still no love lost between these two.

"What's this I hear? A Lupu becomes a Popescu this time, I see." He nods in approval. "Congratulations are in order. The timing couldn't be better."

Alex raises his voice for everyone to hear. "It will strengthen our ties and show the Bratva we are united in the oncoming war." He winks at Cristo. Cristo's jaw muscle pops. "I always knew you'd eventually be as conniving as your father."

"Yes, it's a good alliance at the right time," Cristo agrees between gritted teeth, ignoring the last dig. His eyes flare with pure hatred. "But not for a war I started," he says pointedly.

Dismissing his comment, Alex looks at me critically and asks, "And who is this? Seems a bit young."

For fuck's sake, he damn well knows who I am. My fists clench momentarily, but this is the kind of games they like to play, so I wipe any emotion off my face.

"My new *consilier*," Cristo replies with a slight uptick of one side of his mouth.

I suck in a breath. Beside me, Anton chokes on his drink.

Cristo flashes me a white grin full of teeth. He

could've told me this the other day, but it's typical of him to wait to announce it where it'll make the biggest splash.

This time though, I'm too fucking elated to be angry.

"Assuming you graduate," he murmurs softly for my ears only.

That little poke bounces off me. Nothing can kill my buzz. After what happened to my family, after losing my father, after toiling for years and doing every dirty job demanded on me, *I fucking made it.*

Anton grasps me by the arms and kisses me on both cheeks. Marku rushes toward me and takes his turn, gripping my hand and giving me a chest bump. The men, Lupu and Popescu, take turns congratulating me and making ribald jokes about new brides. Even Alex pats me on the back. Everyone knows how hard I've worked for this, the grueling hours I've put into this clan, and it's finally come to fruition.

There's the *chink chink* sound of Cristo tapping a fork on his glass.

He raises a toast, "To my *consilier*, Lucian, and to his fiancée, Star. Welcome back to the top."

Every man and woman raise a glass to me with shouts of "*Noroc*," and "Good luck."

My gaze swings around the room. Star is still missing.

After much handshaking, back-clapping, and cheek-kissing, I break away from the crowd and stalk to the exit in search of my fiancée.

Crina steps into my path, a grim expression on her face. "You have no idea what you've done. You're an idiot if you think she's going to marry you."

I give her a hard look. She may be Marku's, whether he's willing to acknowledge it or not, but no one confronts me like this.

"Oh, she's going to marry me alright, and there's nothing you can do to stop it."

Gabby slips in from behind Crina, laying a hand on her arm, and murmurs in a shaky voice, "It's done, Crina. There's nothing we can do."

I lean in close and say, "She may be carrying my child as we speak so you'd better damn well step aside and let me get my fiancée."

Staring me down, Crina spits out, "If that's true, then you'd better not hurt her, because I swear if you do…"

I hear a sharp intake of breath from behind me.

Suddenly, Zoe is standing in front of me, shielding me from the angry female. "He'd never hurt any woman. He'd never hurt Star."

I'm touched that my little sister is coming to my defense, but it's not necessary.

Crina's razor-sharp eyes descend on my sister with fury. "What the hell do you know? He's bullied her for years. You say he'd never hurt a woman, that he'd never hurt her, but he's *already* hurt her."

"But he chose her over Roxie because he loves her," Zoe injects.

Crina snorts. "Loves her," she says in a tone dripping with sarcasm. "Ask him if she even knows about this so-called engagement. Ask him if he's bothered to propose to her. Does that sound like love to you, Zoe?"

Zoe's face wobbles with uncertainty. She glances over her shoulder at me. "It's not true, is it, Lucian?"

I swipe a hand over my eyes. "It's complicated, but no, of course, I'd never hurt her."

"But you already have," Crina insists, her voice gaining traction.

Gabby's gaze darts around and she cautions, "Shhh, people are looking."

Lowering her voice, Crina leans forward and threatens me. "I'm warning you, if you ever hurt her again, I'm going to hurt *you*."

"Ach," I say. "You always were a hothead, Crina, and if it wasn't for Marku spoiling you, someone would've already put you in your place by now."

Crina gasps in indignation.

I take a step closer.

Alarmed, Zoe puts a hand on my chest, but then swiftly takes it off as if she's been scalded. The reminder of my scars always upsets her.

Unrelenting, I place Zoe behind me and get in Crina's face. "I respect the fact that you're defending your girl, but don't ever threaten me again and don't ever get between me and my woman. Now I'm going to go look for her and make this right. Don't come after me," I warn and storm out of room.

* * *

CROSSING a deserted hall flanked by large statutes of kneeling pharaohs, I hunt one empty gallery after another. *Where the hell is she?* I skirt around a huge black sarcophagus and enter the Sackler Wing, the enormous gallery with a slanted wall of glass on one side looking out into Central Park. The stone Temple of Dendur is in the center, surrounded by a shallow moat and flanked by two large black-stoned guards.

Relief whooshes out of me when I find her standing near the monumental gate of the temple. The dramatic lighting casts stark shadows around her. Her head is bent down, staring down at the calm water surrounding her. Her shoulders droop as she lets out a heaving sigh. My stomach clenches.

"Star," I call out.

Her name echoes in the deep silence of the massive empty gallery.

Her head snaps up as I stride toward her. She backs away, looking to her left and right. I'm still far away, but I'm not above breaking into a run to catch her. And I *will* catch her.

My hand shoots out in warning. "Don't you dare run."

Poised to sprint, she freezes.

Her gaze shoots around for the fastest way out, but I repeat, "Dammit, Star, if you make me run you down, I'll give you the spanking of your life."

That makes her pause long enough for me to make it around the moat and bear down on her. She backs up a few steps until she's directly underneath the arch of the sandstone gate, casting her in a dark shadow.

I stop near her and reach out to her.

"Hey, hey, easy," I say gently.

She frowns over at me, her fingers twisting in the tulle of her skirt.

Her eyes dip to the ground.

I take a small step closer, like I would with a startled animal. I know she's upset about Roxie's hands all over me. The thought makes my own chest burn, but that's over with. From now on, no one will touch me but her.

"Why did you leave?"

"I only came for Crina and I regretted it almost the minute I arrived," she grumbles miserably.

Just as I thought. "You missed my announcement."

"I don't want to hear your stupid announcement," she sneers.

I grin inwardly. She's glorious with her black eyes snapping fire. She thinks I've announced my engagement to Roxie.

She wrinkles her nose. "Why are you here, Lucian? What can you possibly want with me?"

That's a loaded question and I'm on her in an instant, backing her into the pillar of the arch. My hand slaps the sandstone beside her cheek with a resounding thud in the silence of the cavernous space.

"You think you know what I said back there." I take a strand of her hair and curl it with my forefinger. "Hmm… you couldn't be more wrong."

She sucks in a breath, instinctively pushing her breasts into my chest.

I lean in and burrow my face into the side of her neck, scenting her. My tongue comes out and trails a line up her exposed throat. "You taste fucking delicious."

She arches her neck, letting out a guttural sound of pain and longing.

Her hand smacks me in the chest, trying to push me away. "Fuck you, Lucian. You're engaged now. It was one thing when you weren't, but you can't touch me anymore. It's wrong. It's just wrong and I can't do it."

I shove her hand out of the way and palm her plump tit.

"Don't ever keep me from mine," I snarl at her.

An infuriated puff escapes her lips. "I'm not yours."

"Oh, but you are. You're mine in every way that counts."

I open my mouth to say more, but the distinctive clomp of a heavy tread interrupts me.

Star's head ticks up in the direction of the sound.

A guard is making his rounds.

I grab her hand and tow her past two columns in the shape of lilies and into the narrow corridor of the Egyptian temple. We circumvent a white headless torso on a pedestal, pass yet another room, and then enter the inner sanctum of the ancient temple.

While the outer chambers are strongly lit, the sanctuary

is intimate and dark. We're surrounded by four smooth pale walls covered in reliefs of gods and hieroglyphics. Soft beams of light are coming from two small horizontal openings at the top.

I press back against the farthest wall and pull Star into my embrace. She buries her head in my shoulder as the guard outside methodically circles the huge gallery, his footfall ominous in the profound silence.

I could tell her about our engagement, but I first want her to admit that she cares for me. She's fought me every step of the way. Granted, for good reason. I likely don't deserve her confession, but I've never pretended to be anything but a selfish bastard.

"You don't get to hate fuck me anymore," I whisper low in her ear. "Admit it, you were jealous when you saw Roxie's hands all over me."

Perhaps it's our illicit presence in the ethereal space of the sacred temple, hiding from the guard, that loosens her tongue. "Fine, I admit it. I'm jealous, but this will be the last time we're together. After tonight, I'm sure Roxie won't even let me tutor you."

"See, it wasn't that hard to admit," I reply, ignoring her second sentence. "I'd be jealous AF if any man laid a hand on you. I'd rip his arm out of its socket and he wouldn't live to see the dawn."

We're shrouded in the subdued light of the temple, ghostly stone relief figures and hieroglyphs dancing around us. She's in my arms, smelling of berries and vanilla. Her tits are pressed against my chest and she rubs them against me slowly.

I want more than her confessional words. I want her coming to me on her own. Before she learns about our engagement. Before we return to the world. I want raw honesty.

"If you want something from me, I want to hear you say it."

She remains stubbornly silent, avoiding my gaze.

"Come on, say it," I prod.

Star lets out an irritated huff. "Yes, okay, I want you."

She grasps the lapel of my tux, goes on her toes, and nuzzles the side of my throat just above the starched collar of my shirt. I tug my black silk tie off, toss it to the floor, and unfasten the buttons of my shirt. With each inch exposed, she moans and dips her head to pepper my skin with feather-light kisses.

It's so different this time. While everything we did yesterday was un-fucking-believable, her unmasked desire for me is a victory.

Or so I think until she opens her pretty lips and says, "This changes nothing between us, Lucian. Just because I like to fuck you, doesn't mean I like you. You're still a puppet. You always will be."

I grab her jaw, pressing on both sides. Not enough to hurt her, but enough to express my displeasure.

"No one disrespects to me like that. You're about to get a spanking and then a fucking, in that order," I warn her. "Now get on your fucking knees."

Her eyes are molten onyx, glittering in the beam of light hitting us from above. She licks her lips once. First the top, then the bottom one. And then, dear God, she slowly falls to her knees.

Staring up at me, she tilts forward and her hands gently slap the smooth marble floor. She looks fucking sublime from where I'm standing. My cock strains at my trousers, but I'm not rushing this. I'm going to savor every moment of it.

Pulling my jacket off, I demand, "Unbuckle my belt."

Her hands reach for the buckle of my belt. She fumbles

with it in her haste, the dirty girl.

"Give it to me."

She slides it out from the loops.

I extend my hand. She bends it in half and lays it reverently over my open palm.

"Good girl. Now flip your skirt up and pull your panties down."

She pulls up her skirt and shimmies her simple white panties—Good Lord, help me *please*—right below the gentle curve of her ass cheeks. Her skin is luminous in the eerie lighting.

"Lower," I growl, as I smack the belt lightly on my palm, careful not to make any loud sounds.

Her body jerks as the slap of leather hitting my skin echoes in the tight confines of the sanctuary.

Inclining my head, I listen carefully. Faintly, I make out the sound of footsteps fading in the distance.

I turn my attention fully on her. "You're at my mercy now."

A shiver runs through her.

I grab the gusset of her panties, twist once, and wrench them off her.

"Spread those legs."

She hesitates for one second too long so I slap her pussy from the back.

She lets out a gasp and does as I say.

"You've been a bad girl, running out of the reception. Not staying to listen to my announcement. Throwing insults my way. You've been begging for a correction and I'm the man who's going to give it to you."

I place a hand on one buttock, caressing it lovingly, and then I strike, slashing the belt across her other ass cheek. The shaft of light from the narrow window near the ceiling beams down to highlight the blossom of hot pink sliced across her skin. She pitches forward, but I tighten my grip to keep her in place and let my belt fly again.

She lets out a gargled cry.

I slip my fingers down to test her pussy, and yep, my bad girl likes the kind of correction only I can give.

"You filthy angel, you like a good spanking before you get the fucking you deserve."

I wallop her ass again and again until I get the nice shade uniform pink I'm looking for. Once I'm satisfied, I plunge two fingers into her sopping wet cunt. She's utterly primed for me and the animal inside can't hold back any longer.

I toss the belt away.

It hits the floor with a clang.

I tear at my zipper, fist my cock, and position myself behind her. I land hard on my knees and spear my fingers coated in her juices into her hair, tangling in it and tugging her head back.

I give her another firm slap as I thrust into her inviting heat, plunging hard and deep until I'm buried to the hilt.

As I wait for her to adjust to my invasion, to relax and soften her cunt around my shaft, I lean over and tear at the opening of her dress, shredding off the flappy material hiding her tits from me. I fling it away. It hits the wall of hieroglyphics and flutters to the floor.

Thrusting from behind, I grasp her luscious breast and swear, "I will see the Popescu eagle right fucking here, over your heart. I will see the head peek out when you wear a dress showing off your tits."

With one hand still tangled in her hair, I slide the other hand up and around her throat, squeezing it closed as I feel her cunt clamping down on me.

"Put your cheek on the floor and get your fingers on your clit," I command.

I slow down so she can follow my instructions.

The instant her cheek touched the marble swirl on the floor, I let go of her hair.

Using my hand to smack her ass, I praise her, "What a hot, wet cunt my good girl has for me. You'll make a stunning Popescu wife."

I release my grip, allowing her to inhale a deep, stunned breath and then cut it off again with the words, "I will be the envy of the Popescu made men with you at my side."

Her core gushes around me, her inner walls lock around my shaft, letting me know she's close.

And the image of her in a luxurious gown, long slit up the side to showcase her gorgeous thigh, and a low-plunging neckline that will flash every man with my clan tat suffuses my vision.

I release her throat and she comes on my cock, shaking beneath me. "Oh, God, Lucian. More!"

I take hold of her hips and pump deep. Her cunt cinches down on my cock, milking me like a hundred tiny fingers. My balls tighten, and I have seconds before I climax. My balls slap against her pussy as I rut into her. Again, the primal urge to breed grips me by the throat.

As every nerve ending in my body fires, time slows down. I snap my head back and bellow into the low ceiling, "Oh, fuck. Fuck!" as I spill my seed into her once again, hoping against hope it plants a baby in her.

Panting, I tangle my fingers back in her hair, pull her head back to expose her throat, and bite down hard, marking her. She lets out a yelp and struggles to get away, but it's not done till I say it is. I hang on long enough to ensure that everyone sees my brand on her.

Unclenching my teeth, I give it a long lick.

Whether she likes it or not, she's mine.

And from now on, there's no hiding it.

CHAPTER 17

STAR

*L*ucian pulls out of me slowly, being as careful as he was the first time, and he must accidently hit my G-spot because my vision lights up for a moment. When he's finally out, I settle back on my haunches. Hissing with pain, I lift my butt off my calves.

My torn panties lay discarded on the floor beside me and I snatch them, clenching them in my fist. Dear God, what have I done?

He's engaged.

I cover my eyes, groaning. I just fucked an engaged man and I enjoyed it far too much. Honestly, I don't know how I'll ever have another orgasm without his firm hand. His dark intensity calls to me, drawing emotions deep from the pit of my soul.

But he's not mine.

And there's no way I'd stoop to being a sidepiece for a *mafie* prince. That is never going to happen. I may not want to remain here, I might not want him as a husband (I stoutly ignore the pang in my chest), but I can never touch him again.

If for no other reason, it's a matter of self-respect.

Lucian wraps his hand tightly around my fist, and gently pries my panties out of my grip. I snap my eyes open and gaze up at him as he savors them for a moment before tucking them into the pocket of his trousers. I groan.

Oh, God, he's weaving his spell around me again.

I wipe the glistening dots of perspiration off my forehead. It's unbelievably steamy in this tiny chamber. Guess that's what happens when you have kinky taboo sex in a place that's forbidden.

Damn him for fucking me the way he does. Not only did he use his belt, but he took me from behind. I was still sore from yesterday, but it felt so good when he went in deep.

Without protection.

I suck in a harsh breath.

Again.

I'm going to have to take care of that right away. No way am I going to have a married man as a baby daddy. I shudder at the thought of Roxie in a white wedding gown standing beside Lucian looking much like he does now in a tux, with crowns suspended over their heads.

I slowly and gently lower my butt down again. Damn, that hurts, but at this point, what the hell. My life is a mess.

Spearing him with an accusing look, I say, "We shouldn't have done that."

"We're going to be doing it again very soon," he replies as he shrugs his jacket back on.

I look at him aghast.

"Never," I growl.

Looking impeccable in his tux, even with his missing

tie, he extends his hand for me to take. With my butt burning like the fires in hell, I begrudgingly take his outstretched hand.

"You're going to be married soon." I clench my lips together to hide their tremor and lift my chin high.

I might not be as tall as him and, granted, I'm feeling vulnerable as hell with my ass on fire, a stinging bite on my neck, and him looming over me, but I gather the scraps of my self-respect and repeat, "This can never happen again."

He moves closer, so close I inhale the musky pine scent of him.

"It can and it will. With my wife." He pauses a beat. His hand reaches for my chin. Shaking it a little, he finishes, "That will be *you.*"

I frown up at him. "W-what are you talking about?"

"My announcement? You know, the one you so rudely missed? I told the entire gathering that I will marry you. I went to Cristo yesterday and asked for his approval. It took a bit of convincing, but he's on board. Even Alex congratulated me. Roxie and her parents will be disappointed, of course, but that's to be expected. I will handle it, I promise. She won't bother you again. You're under my protection. *You're mine*, period. In front of the world, and soon, in front of God."

"The fuck—"

He makes a little tsking sound. "Watch your tongue. It's not befitting of the wife of the Popescu *consilier*," he scolds. He gives my tummy a meaningful look. "It's not good for the children."

My head is swimming. Ignoring the last bit about children—*because hello, has he lost his damn mind or what?*—I ask, "Wait? He made you *consilier* without you marrying Roxie? I don't get it."

"It's not for you to understand the intricacy of our

plans. There are forces at work you don't know about, but our engagement comes at a perfect time," he says smugly.

My hand shoots out and I smack him across the cheek. The crack reverberates in the small space. His head snaps back.

"No," I refute. "I'm not going to be part of your *plan* to conquer the world."

He takes a step forward, the buttons of his shirt scape against my chest. "I understand it's a shock, so I'll let that one go, but if you ever do hit me again, I swear you won't be able to sit on your ass for a week, understand?"

Caressing my cheek with the back of his hand, he cants his head to the side. "I don't understand why you're fighting this. What's so wrong with marrying me?"

I throw my hands in the air. "Because I'm not a pawn! And because I have plan, remember. I have a life."

"After everything that's happened between us, you can't possibly believe I'm marrying you only to get ahead. That's preposterous." His voice drops. "And as for leaving, get that notion out of your head. You can't leave. You're mine. We *will* marry. Now that I'm not marrying Roxie, I must marry you."

I jab a finger into his chest. "See, right there! You just admitted that you have to marry me because I somehow fit better into your grand master plan. Well, guess what? We're not interchangeable, Roxie and I."

"That's not what I meant—

"Let me tell you," I bulldoze on. "It will be a cold day in hell before I marry the likes of you."

A vein throbs in his temple. Anger ripples off him in waves, but I don't care. He completely dismissed my plans, which he damn well knew about. And did I even get a proposal? Nope. I'm not even worthy of that.

He arches one brow. "I could evoke the blood oath."

I clutch my chest in horror. I can't believe he'd stoop so low as to revive that dying tradition. My left eye ticks, fury rampaging its way through my body. "Like hell you will. I'll deny it's you who took my virginity till my dying breath."

"That's dishonorable."

I toss my head in frustration. "You're unbelievable, you know that? What's dishonorable is forcing me to get married and stay in this godforsaken backward society, that's what's dishonorable. But you have zero qualms about doing that. Don't talk to me about honor. I told you about my plan from the beginning. How about honoring the pact we have, because I only agreed to tutor you in exchange for your help to *leave*, not to get coerced into marrying you."

"I didn't think you were crazy enough to go through with it." Pointing to the entrance leading out into another chamber, he roars, "There are dangers out there that you have no inkling about."

"Dangers, shmangers," I retort. "What about the danger of my soul shriveling up if I stay here?"

"And what about me?"

I pause at the strain of vulnerability in his voice, but then I pull myself together. Screw that, marriage is nothing more than a business matter to him. Love isn't even on the table. Hell, I'm not even sure the guy likes me. Either way, I'm certain he didn't consider either of those things when he came up with his nutty plan.

"Oh, please, I didn't hear a marriage proposal come out of your mouth. You've presented it to me as a done deal. You don't even have the good sense to pretend to want me. You only chose me because, for some reason, I now happen to make a better wife than Roxie. I'm nothing but a clan transaction to you and you know it."

He opens his mouth to argue, but I hold up my hand. "You can't ignore me for years and then just up and decide that I'm going to be your wife, Lucian. And before you even bring it up, no, good sex won't replace true love."

He runs his hand through his hair.

His voice is low and controlled, as if he's struggling to hold on to his temper. "What we have is a helluva lot more than good sex. I just used my belt on your ass. You think I do that with just anyone?"

I wave a hand dismissively. "Oh please, don't even."

His hand shoots out and firmly takes hold of my jaw. Drawing me toward him, I have no choice but to follow.

Eyes bleeding with something that looks close to regret, he says, "I'm sorry for the years I didn't treat you right. I'm sorry I didn't come to your aid in the cafeteria, and I'm sorry I said anything to make you think I don't want you. You've been mine for a long time, long before I was man enough to admit it. I've denied us for years, but that's over with. I want to marry you. I *will* marry you. And yes, it happens to help our clans and my career, but those are secondary reasons."

It's a once-in-a-lifetime event when a man like Lucian apologizes for anything, much less three things in a row. In the past, I might have accepted it. Let's be frank, I would've been all in before the cafeteria incident. But things have changed irrevocably, and there's no way I can accept his offer.

I lick my lips slowly, considering my words.

"It's too late," I reply gently, almost tenderly because I understand his struggle.

His ambition means everything to him, and in this moment, I'm tied up in that ambition. I can appreciate the role reversal, but that doesn't mean I'm going to buckle because he's desperate to have me. My life has been dictated by men with their own best interests at heart, not mine. Lucian is just a repeat of the same pattern, and I'm done being a pawn in their games.

"It's not," he insists.

"Even if I wanted you, I don't want this life."

I do not want to be a *mafie* wife, a woman who puts her husband's needs above her own, who's meant to breed children and nothing more, who has no identity of her own. I don't want to end up like my mom, a woman drowning in grief over the loss of her husband and son because that's all she has.

His fingers tighten around my chin. They glide down and grasp my throat and damn if that doesn't melt my insides. I love his power moves; I crave them. He backs me up against the wall. The bas relief of the engravings on the wall scratches against my shoulders and upper back.

He pushes his thumb between my lips, pulls it out and then twists it, getting it nice and wet. He caresses my bottom lip a few times before he dips his head and kisses the corner of my mouth. So gentle for such a rough, intense guy.

"What we have is more than great fucking sex and you know it. Don't deny what's between us, Star."

I close my eyes as he kisses me again, pressing deft fingers around my jaw, opening my mouth for the invasion of his tongue. He sucks and nips at my lips, breaking down my resistance. It would be so easy to slip into the spell he always manages to weave around me.

Then I feel his seed trickle out of my pussy and drip down my inner thigh. It jolts me back to reality.

What if I'm with child?

I'd be as tied to him as any marriage vow.

I break off our kiss and demand, "Did you purposely not use a condom?"

A gleam of light from the roof hits his face and I have

my answer. If I hadn't been watching carefully or if he'd been in shadow, I would've missed it. Damn him!

I twist my face away from him. "I won't be manipulated or bullied into marrying you, Lucian."

His hand slaps the sandstone wall beside my head. He breathes raggedly into my neck. "I want you. I'll do whatever it takes to have you."

I shove at his chest. "Get it through your thick head, it's not up to you. It's *my* decision and if you try to take it away from me, I'll never forgive you."

"I don't need your forgiveness," he growls. "I need *you.*"

"Try forcing me into this and I swear, I'll make your life a living hell. I'll make it my job to punish you. Every. Single. Day. Are you willing to risk both our happiness? For the rest of our lives? Because there's no such thing as divorce in our world."

I look past him to the carvings on the wall, ancient hieroglyphs overlaid with graffiti carved in stone. The newer large Latin words clash against the older, worn Egyptian engraving. Our story is like that—what started out as mutual, childlike wonder has been marred by his obstinance.

I always admired Lucian for his ferocious determination—but I won't be forced into this. A part of me might resent Tatum for leaving me, but his disappearance gave me more than one lesson. He didn't only leave because Alex excommunicated him for our father's crimes. He left for true love. Clara never demanded it of him. He gave it freely. Even without the punishment, he intended to leave everything—his family, his clan, his entire world—for her.

Lucian would never make such a sacrifice for me. I glance down at the part in his open shirt, the whipping scars visible like dark shadows on his olive skin. His suffering has made him strong and driven, but also borderline obsessed about restoring his family's name. When I say his family name, I mean *his* name. *His* reputation. His ambition supersedes everything. Just because it was bred in pain doesn't make it any less selfish, any less ruthless.

He expects me to renounce my plans for him, but he would never reciprocate. He didn't stand up for me in the cafeteria. He might have stuck up for me yesterday, but he didn't lose anything by it. He'd already made up his mind about Roxie. He has done nothing to earn my trust.

Trying to make him understand one last time, I say, "We have nothing to build a marriage on. There's no trust. No love. No sacrifice. What do you have to offer me to stay for you?"

I pause before answering the question myself. "Nothing, Lucian. Nothing."

CHAPTER 18

STAR

*I*n the end, he lets me go.

I'm sure it's a calculated move on his part. He's a tactician, if nothing else, and this is a retreat-to-fight-another-day situation if I ever saw one.

He carefully arranges my clothes until I'm decent. He picks up the ruffled fabric he ripped off my dress earlier and tucks it into his pocket, his vow about the Popescu eagle tat on my breast reverberating in my mind.

Before I have a chance to escape, he takes firm hold of my elbow and doesn't leave my side until we're back at the reception.

From the corner of my eye, I see him murmuring low into Anton's ear as I approach Crina and Gabby and tell them that Lucian is escorting me home. Their eyes betray their concern for me, but now is not the time to discuss the marriage announcement.

"It's going to be okay," I whisper to Crina as Lucian returns to my side and wraps a proprietary arm around my shoulder, making my teeth grind and my stomach flip at the same time.

As he leads me away, I glance over my shoulder and Crina makes a gesture of holding a phone to her ear, indicating she will call later.

In the museum parking lot, he opens the passenger door to his sleek, black Maserati coupe. I drop into the cool leather seat. My hips instantly shoot up—my bottom's sizzling. Heat blazes across my cheeks. Even my ears go red at the memory of how he took a belt to my ass.

Sweet Jesus, what was I thinking?

Beneath his smirking face, I slowly lower my butt onto the smooth leather and yank at the seatbelt. He taps my hand away, takes hold of the rayon belt, and smoothly buckles me in.

Warmth spreads through my chest at his gesture, but that only adds to the churn of chaotic feelings inside me.

"I could have done that," I rebuff him. Why is he so calm when I'm still thrown after everything that happened in the temple. The punishment, the hot sex, the marriage *what's-it-called...* I can't exactly call it a proposal. A marriage demand, maybe?

I wipe my brow. Good grief, that's not even a thing.

He doesn't react to my snub. He simply closes the car door and goes around to the driver's seat.

We speed up the ramp of the museum's underground parking, passing the illuminated fountains on the plaza in front of The Met before turning onto Fifth Avenue. It's well past ten o'clock, but the city streets are hopping.

As we wait at a red light, I peek at his profile, outlined by the light cascading down from the streetlamps. His sensual bottom lip protrudes, much fuller than his top, and I lick my own lips remembering his kisses. His kisses on my lips, on my breasts, on my pussy. The last memory has me squeezing my legs together.

Noticing the movement, Lucian shifts slightly beside me. His gaze moves to my pressed thighs, his eyes a molten sheen like two silver coins. I recognize that look. He's aroused, and dammit, so am I, even after his attempt to ruin my life. God, it just makes me want to smack him.

I snap my head in the other direction and concentrate on the people walking along Central Park. The leaves of the great elm trees lining the park create a canopy of bright spring green.

He smoothly drives in and out of traffic, the only sound penetrating the tense silence between us is a passing car blasting hip-hop. We stop at another light on 59th Street, in front of The Strand Bookstore kiosk, with its booths and rows of long tables piled high with used books and other quirky mementos.

His composure puts my teeth on edge, and I ache to rattle him. I only pull myself off the ledge because I still need his cooperation. He has got to abandon this ridiculous marriage business and allow me to escape.

Once I'm gone, I can take care of myself. I have money from the trust fund Tatum left me and Mama, which I've controlled since I turned eighteen years old. I haven't told Tatum about my plans. He was the Lupu *consilier* for ten years so I can't imagine he'd act any differently than Lucian. He'd only try to persuade me to stay. For my own safety, of course. As the saying goes, it's better to ask for forgiveness than permission.

We speed over the East River into Queens. The crisscross of steel bars from the Queensboro Bridge slashes light and dark over Lucian's features, making him look more devil than human.

Fitting, to be sure.

I spot one of my favorite retro landmarks on the Queens side, the Pepsi Cola sign. It warms my heart to see the huge neon cursive letters, reminding me of being in the back seat of the car when my father or Tatum would drive us home from a party or wedding in the city.

After what feels like an interminable drive, we finally pull up to my house. The instant Lucian puts the car into park, I unsnap the seat belt, throw the door open, and plant my foot on the sidewalk.

"Don't you dare," comes a gruff warning. "Close the door, and don't move until I say so."

With a long string of muttered complaints, I do what he says. It's bad enough that I'm wearing a short mini dress that barely covers my smarting butt, but now I must stay put until Lucian gets out of the driver's seat, rounds the car, and opens my door.

He extends his hand, helping me out. I grudgingly take it, but instead of letting me go, he crowds me against the car.

He slaps a hand on either side of me, and says, "I don't know who taught you your manners, but from now on, you wait for me to open the door for you."

He dips his head until we're eye-to-eye. "Understand?"

"Yeah, okay," I mutter resentfully. I try to slip out from underneath his arm and rush away, but he backs me up against the car again.

With a brittle smile, he says, "In what world do you think I'm not going to walk you to your door?"

I hear the resolve in his tone of voice and panic rises up my throat. Good God, does he intend to meet my mother? "It's not necessary."

"And I will introduce myself to your mother."

"No," I cry out in horror, and then rush to temper it with an excuse. "It's late. She's already asleep."

He smirks at me. "Come now, who do you take me for? No *mafie* mama is going to sleep before her unmarried daughter is locked up tight for the night."

I wince at his remark. My mom hasn't been a normal *mafie* mom for a while now. Truth is, I don't know what state I'll find her at this time of night, but there's no way can I have Lucian in my house.

Trying a different tactic, I place a hand on his chest and give him pleading eyes. "Please, Lucian, it's late. Why don't you walk me up to my door and come by tomorrow afternoon to speak with her."

I try to school my expression. He looks like he's about to agree, but then sees something he doesn't like on my face. Most likely it's the panic I can't hide.

A muscle in his temple jumps and he replies, "No, we're doing this tonight."

"Please," I whine, frustration and fear beating against my chest bone.

His eyes narrow at me. "You're hiding something."

"I'm not," I deny indignantly.

Of course, I am.

God only knows what I'll find in there. I wasn't home to watch Mama this evening. I left for Crina's house in the afternoon to have her do my makeup and hair since I'm hopeless with that kind of stuff. Who knows how much Mama's been drinking. She may be peacefully sleeping in her bed—*pray God*—or she might be sprawled out on the living room couch or, God forbid, in the hallway leading up to her bedroom.

Anything is possible and I can't have him witnessing it.

I grab his arms, which flex under my touch, and kiss him hard on the mouth. Normally, I wouldn't dare touch him, especially in public. It's dangerous to kiss him again, he's so addictive, but I have to distract him.

Lucian opens instantly, groaning as he takes my mouth. Shoving me against the car, he grinds into me. His cock is getting stiff and damn but that feels good. I can't help but rub against him. I clasp the lapels of his jacket and drag him closer, but he breaks off the kiss and steps away.

Smoothing down his jacket, he says, "Nice try, but I'm never distracted from my goal. Might want to keep that in mind, precious."

Dazed, I let him take my arm. He peels me off the car and frog-marches me up the stoop to my door. Assuming my mother won't hear the bell, I push him aside, flip the doormat up, and pluck up the key.

He shudders out a breath of disbelief. "You did not just take the front door key from underneath the *doormat*. That's…that's…" He looks positively enraged.

"Yeah, yeah, a security breach, I know." I shove the key into the lock and explain, "It's not a big deal, Lucian. Alex's family lives down the street. The security is insane, and anyway, no one's looking to break into our house."

Lucian claps his hand over his mouth, rubbing it back and forth. "Jesus, I should give you a spanking for that. We've talked about this."

I swing the door open and spear him with a vicious look. "Yes, we've talked about it, and I've explained to you time and again that I'm not in danger. No one wants me, not even you despite your ridiculous engagement. Get that through your thick skull already."

With that parting shot, I take a step into the house and call out softly, "Mama, are you up?"

Lucian closes and locks the door behind me as I take the stairs two steps at a time. When my head is high enough to see into the landing, I stretch my neck and check the hallway floor. No one's lying on it. I release the breath clogging up my throat.

Hoping she's in her bedroom sleeping off her drunken stupor, I scurry back downstairs to get ahead of Lucian before he goes roaming around by himself.

Kicking off my shoes beside the front entrance, I fast walk in front of him and get into the living room a step before he does. My eyes go straight to the couch. Another sigh of relief.

Hands on my hips, I turn around to face Lucian, who's doggedly followed me.

"See, I told you, she went to sleep. She's an early sleeper." *Total lie.* "Now can you come back tomorrow?" *Or preferably, never.* "It's not right for you to be here with me without a chaperone." *A little too late for that, but whatever.*

Lucian's head snaps to the side. His eyes widen. A sick feeling washes over me as I sneak a look.

My gaze sweeps to the floor and I wince.

On the floor, two bare feet stick out from where the second sofa ends.

Hands fluttering in front of me, I hop from foot to foot. "Fuck, fuck, fuck."

Rushing to my mother, I kneel to check on her. She's lying on her side, vomit spreading out beside her open mouth onto the hardwood floor.

She lets out a short little snore. I scramble back on my haunches with a screech. Clutching my chest, I let out great gusts of breath.

I hear the rustle of clothing behind me.

Shit, I forgot about him.

I glance left and Lucian is crouched beside me.

"Is she okay?"

His voice is concerned.

Tears spring to my eyes.

I smack him in the chest and say, "Why do you have to be so pushy? Why can't you mind your own business and come back tomorrow like I asked instead of forcing your way into my home. Now look at her. *Look at her.*"

I shouldn't shout at him. It's not his fault, but I don't care. I'm so angry.

My nostrils burn as I swipe at my falling tears. "Happy now? Are you fucking happy?"

He grabs hold of my nape and pulls me into his embrace, pushing my face into his shoulder.

His voice cracks when he says, "I'm so sorry, precious."

His sympathy only fuels my fury and self-loathing. My sobs come out hard and loud.

"How long has this been going on?" he murmurs near my ear.

I cling to his jacket, leaving wet spots on the fine wool fabric of his tux. "It's been bad since Tatum left."

"Why didn't you tell me?" he asks gently.

"Oh please, don't act like I should have come to you."

I lift my head and fling my hand out in her direction. "Look at her, she's disgusting. When she's like this." I sigh as I stare down at her surprisingly peaceful face and repeat, "Disgusting."

"Don't say that," he croaks. "She's not disgusting, she's sick. She has an illness and it's called alcoholism."

He swallows and then confesses, "I never meant it, you know. When I called you 'disgusting' in the cafeteria. I remember saying it. I wanted to throw Anton and the others off my scent. He's long suspected I had feelings for you, and I couldn't look weak."

My mother chooses that moment to make a snuffling sound and mumble something unintelligible before settling back into oblivion. I don't have the bandwidth to take care of her and unpack the baggage in Lucian's declaration.

Staring down at her, I swallow the painful lump in my throat, wipe my nose, and try to stand up to help her.

Lucian bands an arm around my waist and swoops me into his lap. Rocking me gently in his arms, he strokes my hair. Thankfully, he doesn't give me empty platitudes. He doesn't pity me, which I would hate. He *knows*. From deep in his bones, he knows what I'm going through.

Even though he accused me of not telling him, he implicitly recognizes why I kept it a secret. The horror of anyone finding out is worth any sacrifice. I can't even tell Tatum, and he's my flesh and blood. When he calls and asks me to hand the phone to her, I make up excuses to cover for the fact that she's drunk.

What choice do I have? It's not like he can help us. She's one of the main reasons I want to leave, and at the same time, she's the single most terrifying reason why I'm afraid of leaving. If I go, what will happen to her?

My sniffles and hiccups settle, and I dry my tears.

Hugging me tight, he says, "Come on, let's clean this up and get her upstairs to bed."

I gape at him. "No, you leave. Y-you can't help me. It's m-messy. You leave."

He chuckles sadly and my heart breaks with the sound of it. "This isn't the first mess I've cleaned up and it won't be the last."

Crack. That's my heart fissuring for the little boy who had to clean up messes. I place a hand on his sleeve. "It's sweet of you to want to help, really it is, but it's better if I deal with this alone."

His eyes turn steely and he adds hotly, "That's never going to happen. I'm not leaving you to take care of this alone. You'll never be alone again."

Okaaay, most people would jump at the chance to avoid

cleaning up vomit and lugging a half-comatose woman up a flight of stairs to her bed.

He gives me a light slap on the butt, and continues, "After we clean her up, I'm sleeping here. We need to check on her throughout the night."

My heart does a little pitter-patter.

I slide off his lap and get to my feet. I bend down to check on my mother and I'm immediately grateful for two things. One, she's not hurt. Miracle of miracles, she turned on her side when she vomited so she didn't choke and die.

Although much less important, I'm grateful she missed hurling over her precious rug. She brought it back from Romania and she'd feel horrible in the morning if she saw what she did. Plus, it's easier to clean vomit off a wood floor than a handwoven wool rug.

While I clean her up and roll her to her other side, Lucian not only finds the kitchen but he returns with a bucket of soapy water and a mop.

I go to take the mop from him, but he places it out of my reach.

"I don't want you doing that." I'm so dejected, I don't have the energy for much more of an objection.

"That's not how a partnership works."

"Since when are we partners," I scoff.

"Marriage is a partnership," he replies evenly as the wet mop hits the wooden floor with a plopping sound.

He gestures to my mother, and instructs, "Try waking her up. Call her name, shake her, pinch her if you must. Once I'm done, we'll get her upstairs together."

I do as he says. I call her name and shake her shoulders. Nothing seems to work and my anxiety ratchets up. I'm bracing myself to pinch her when she groans and wakes up. She might have blacked out from excessive drinking, but after vomiting the excess alcohol, I think she simply fell into a deep sleep.

Groaning, she clutches her head. Confusion clouds her eyes. Her gaze roams around and she eventually focuses on me. "Where am I?"

"You fell," I lie. "You must have hit your head and knocked yourself out."

Lucian finishes cleaning up and turns toward the kitchen, not wanting my mother to freak out upon seeing a strange man in the house.

Hearing noise, she looks briskly to the side. "Oww." She clutches her head. "Is someone here? Who is that?"

"That's Lucian. He's a Popescu who drove me home from Nelu's retirement party at the Met."

"Oh, yesss," she slurs. "How was the party? Nelu, that old fox. I don't think he'll stop working. What's he going to do with his time, eh?"

"Yes, Mama," I reply as I help her to sitting.

Lucian returns to my side, crouches down, and introduces himself. "*Bună seara*, I'm Lucian."

"*Bună seara*," she replies politely, as if she isn't on the floor, legs sprawled out indecorously from her nightgown.

She looks at him critically. "A Popescu, huh?"

He'd taken off his jacket and tossed it over the sofa. His tie is long gone and his hair's disheveled, but he still looks ruggedly handsome. "Ever since Cat married Luca, these Popescu boys have been sniffing around here."

Lucian's brows crash together, a deep slash etched on the bridge of his nose.

Over my mother's head, I tap my temple to say that she doesn't know what she's talking about.

"Come on," I say as I struggle to guide her to her feet.

Lucian comes to my aid, and together we make slow progress across the living room, into the foyer, and up the stairs. In her stupor, she rambles on about boyfriends that don't exist, and then veers into a soliloquy about Lucian being my boyfriend.

With each wavering step, her incoherent blathering ratchets up my frustration. Ugh, she knows full well that *mafie* girls don't have boyfriends. It's either abstinence or marriage, at least officially.

Increasingly embarrassed, I mutter, "He's just a friend, Mama."

"Friend, harrumph. He better put a ring on it," slurs my mother.

Help me, Lord.

Lucian swoops in to distract my mother with random pleasantries and easy questions while we maneuver her down the hall and into the bedroom. Once she's on the bed, I sprint downstairs for a tall glass of water. We turn her to her side, and Lucian props a couple of pillows against her spine so she won't accidently turn on her back, in case she vomits again.

I dim the lamp on the nightstand and drape a light blanket over her. Her eyes flutter closed. Her face softens with sleep, her clasped hands tucked beneath her cheek. She looks so serene in that moment.

I tiptoe out of the bedroom and softly close the door behind me with a sigh of relief. At least, that's done. Craning my neck, I glimpse Lucian through the open door of my bedroom.

Ballsy of him to waltz right into my bedroom, I'll give him that.

An inquisitive expression crosses his face. Something has caught his eye on the opposite side of my room and he moves toward it, out of my line of sight.

I approach my room cautiously and slowly push the door open wider.

His strong back is to me, perfectly encased in his tailored dress shirt, which creates a sharp angled line from his broad shoulders to his tapered waist. He's staring at the map of the world I have tacked on the wall facing my bed. Big round colored pushpins poke through the cities I intend to visit. There's a corresponding bucket list I have tucked away in the drawer of my night table.

He must sense my presence because, without turning, he says, "This is where you want to travel."

I shift from one bare foot to the other and hedge, "At some point…"

I feel awkward with him in my private space. It's neat enough, but I still have remnants of my childhood like my matching furniture set. I also haven't gotten around to throwing out the ruffled bed skirt. In my defense, I never thought I'd have to host a guy in my bedroom.

Thankfully, he isn't focused on anything other than the map in front of him. He traces a finger from one push pin to the other in the boot of Italy. "So many in Italy…"

Feeling exposed, I stay mute.

"Why?"

"Why Italy?" I ask, stalling.

"Yeah, why Italy?"

Realizing I can't get out of answering without being rude, I grimace slightly and reply, "Because it's the cradle of the Renaissance."

He motions with his hand impatiently. "And?"

I shrug self-consciously. "And that's one of my favorite periods of art history."

He finally turns around to face me. Head tilted to the side, he considers me carefully. "But when I followed you to the gallery in Chelsea, the exhibition was of modern photos."

I nod. "I do love modern art, but you asked me why

Italy, and Italy has the largest concentration of Renaissance art and architecture. Modern art can be found anywhere."

"Huh," he replies, as if I've described something fascinating. I thought a map with pushpins on the wall was pretty cliché for a nerdy, sheltered girl like me.

Picking at his white dress shirt, he asks, "This is filthy. Do you have extra clothing laying around that I can change into?"

I breathe out in relief as his attention moves off me, even if the idea of Lucian taking off his shirt makes my tummy flutter in a way I'd rather not dwell on.

"Sure, I'm sure there's something in Tatum's room that will fit you," I explain, pointing toward his bedroom down the hall. "Take anything you want."

I take advantage of his absence to change out of the torn cocktail dress into a pair of oversized gray joggers and a crop top, a variation of my usual out-of-school outfit. Waiting cross-legged on the bed, I'm in the middle of forcing my thick hair into an elastic band when he returns.

He halts at the door. His silvery gaze sweeps over me as if I'm wearing something sexy, which is absolutely *not* the case.

He, on the other hand, looks devastating in sweats that ride low on his hips and one of Tatum's favorite Italian soccer team jerseys. I'm not especially surprised by his choice since his clan is notorious for fixing matches high up on the international stage, or so I've heard.

He idly scratches his belly, pulling the rayon material up to flash me a hipbone and one side of the V demarcating his taut abs. I even spy a bulging vein.

I swallow. *Damn.*

By the look on his face as he stalks toward me, I don't think he'd accept my suggestion to sleep in another room.

He crawls onto the bed and keeps going until he's forced me down to my back.

Looming over me, his eyes snap, the normally slate color blazing with heat. He presses his knee between my legs, spreading them, and settles between my thighs.

I give him a little huff. "Presumptuous."

He nibbles in the dip of my crop top, his hot breath scorching my skin. "You wore this knowing what it would do to me."

I snort out a nervous laugh. "I did not. This is what I wear around the house."

Tugging at my top, he lazily swipes at one exposed nipple and moans around it. I think he says something like, "Then I can't wait to live with you."

It's hard to focus when he's doing that to my breast. I half-heartedly push at his shoulder because we really shouldn't be doing this, but he ignores me. Pulling himself up, he parts my lips with his tongue. He gives no quarter, taking my mouth like it's his right. I taste remnants of alcohol, the tang of champagne.

His kisses are relentless, all-consuming affairs that leave my brain scrambled.

The rough bristles of his five o'clock shadow scrape against my cheek and jaw.

I tear myself away from his mouth before completely losing my wits. "W-we shouldn't do this."

"We're way past that," he replies casually, rasping his chin against the upper swell of my breast.

I shift my hips beneath him, already wet from his rigid length rubbing against my mound. Regardless of how good he smells, tastes, feels...I'm determined to resist him. I don't know why I'm most comfortable pushing back against his wishes. Even though I gave up my virginity to him, even though we've had sex more than once, I can't give up the fight. If I give in, even a little bit, I'll get dragged down into the brutal undertow that is Lucian Popescu. All my hopes and dreams will fall apart in his world, and I can never allow that to happen.

He reaches out and brushes his thumb over my bottom lip. Unexpectedly, my wrists are wrapped in his grip and stretched above my head. "You've proven how stubborn you can be, but I'm ten times worse than you on a good day. You want me to prove it to you, I will. As many times as you need. But mark my words, Star, in the end, you will be mine."

LUCIAN

Fuck, I love when she pushes back and fights me.

And how do I respond?

With brutality.

After I viciously crush her resistance with a hard fuck, I'll mark her with my semen and bite marks until she submits and *finally* acknowledges who she belongs to.

With one hand manacling her wrists, I yank my sweats down enough to fist my cock, hard and ready. Shaft in hand, I lead it to her mouth. "Open up for me, precious. I want to see those pink lips stretched around my cock."

She stares at it, her brain ticking away, registering every ridge and vein as if memorizing it for an exam. I grab her sexy high ponytail, wrap it around my fist a couple of times, and drag her until the smooth head of my crown parts her lips. The corners of her mouth stretch around my shaft, and fuck if I don't come right then and there.

Her gorgeous eyes snap up to me, and my hips punch forward of their own accord, making her gag at the sudden movement. I pull out, and dear God, her saliva has slicked a perfect ring around my cock.

She fists the base, stroking up and down. She wraps her lips around the tip and lathers it up, her mouth warm and wet and everything good in the world. I push her top farther down and catch the weight of one of her heavy tits in the palm of my hand, thumbing her nipple in rhythm with my short thrusts.

Star arches her back, giving me deeper access into her throat, and moans. The vibrations rumble down my shaft, and I see stars. She groans again, and I shoot out a string of come.

"I want my cock in your throat, baby. Think you can do that for me?"

With her sparkling jet-black eyes on me, she nods. Her hand glides down her sweatpants and I nearly lose it, imagining her slim fingers in her wet cunt. The sight of her getting aroused by the idea of choking on my cock is almost too much.

Growling, I thrust harder until my balls slap off her chin. She gags again and I instruct her, "Relax your throat, baby girl. Breathe through your nose."

She does as I say, elongating her neck. I hit the back and her throat muscles clutch around my cock. My knees almost buckle. It feels fucking glorious.

Her mouth is too hot, her throat too tight. I pull out, stroking roughly. With my other hand, I tear her top clear off and come a second later, spraying across her chest. Pleasure crashes through me. I slap a hand on the headboard of her bed, gripping the top to keep myself upright as I empty over her pristine skin. Droplets fly up and paint her beautiful throat.

She looks down, eyes glazed over. The corners of her mouth lift. "Just like a Pollack painting."

Heaving in deep breathes, I watch as she arches her back for me, her legs spread wider and her hand works furiously.

I shove her pants down and grin wide. "Looky there, no panties. What a pretty little slut you are. Painted in my seed and begging for me to watch you come."

She writhes beneath me. "I need… I need…"

I know exactly what she needs, and it makes me high knowing she can't come without it. I add two fingers to her glistening, juicy pussy.

Hardening my tone, I give her the permission she seeks, "Now, be a good girl and come for me."

Then I fall on her like she's prey, licking and sucking her swollen bead. She lifts off the bed with a gasp, her hands clutching my hair for dear life as she comes.

"Good girl," I murmur. "You're my perfect, precious girl."

I've never said truer words in my life.

I stay between her legs until she drops back down. Her fingers go from yanking to pushing my head away as it gets too sensitive for her.

Chuckling with glee, I rise to my knees, lick her juices from my lips, and give her a hard kiss. A pang of regret hits me as I take the jersey and wipe the come from her tits.

Sinking down beside her, I gather her in my arms. She's too sated to fight me, and while I do love how she pushes me, I savor this rare moment, too. There's something about wrapping your arms around the woman you love, suffused with pleasure you've provided.

Earlier, as I changed in Tatum's room, I debriefed Anton on how it went with Star in the temple.

He gave me this advice: *Don't force her. It will only back-fire on you. Play it smart, Lucian. Seduce her.*

I texted back: *Already tried that. Didn't work.*

He replied: *Then give her what she wants.*

I think hard about what that is. I think back on Star throughout the years. She was either hiding in a corner, squashed between her two friends, or peeking out from behind her brother's back.

A light bulb goes off in my head.

More than anything, Star wants to be seen.

Her ambition is to be more than being a wife and mother, and I'm the last person to fault someone for their ambition. Fact is, I respect her for it. She's the smartest person I know. There's no reason she should stop striving simply because she'll be married. The image pops into my head of her lying on my bed after a good hard fuck, her laptop and books spread across the rumpled sheets. I won't have her wearing anything more than the crop tops she favors so I can see the long curve of her spine and the smooth globes of her ass jiggle as she shifts around.

Fuck, and now I'm getting hard again.

I'm not a natural at being magnanimous, at putting someone's needs above my own, but for Star, I'll try.

Stroking her hair, I start with an admission. "I regret what happened that day in the cafeteria."

Her brows draw together. "You didn't seem to have a problem with it. When Monica called you out, you said you don't get involved in cat fights. Don't change your tune now, Lucian, simply because you want something from me."

"I don't get involved," I growl. "But I should've stood up for you that day. Truth is, I wasn't ready to acknowledge what you mean to me. How was I going to admit it in front of everyone else? But that day changed everything. It was one thing when I used to bully you. This was not that."

Her fingernails unconsciously dig into my chest. "Don't make it sound like you were doing me a favor when you bullied me. You were awful."

"I stopped short of humiliation."

"Hmm, I don't know about that," she mused.

"But it was different," I insist, desperate for her to admit to the difference. There was one, dammit. I won't deny hurting her, but I controlled it. I knew how to modulate it.

She lets out a deep sigh. "I suppose…"

"I used to feel your eyes on me whenever I entered a room," I continue. "When that stopped…it didn't feel right. Only once it was gone did I realize what I'd lost."

Star purses her lips. "You only want to marry me because you've come up with this crazy notion that I'm yours."

"You *are* mine and I protect what's mine, but I realize that I had taken you for granted. I'd ruined what we had, and if anything should happen to you, if I lost you, too, I won't survive it. I don't ever want to find out what that'll be like. Even if you're a righteous pain in my ass."

I pause and then admit something aloud I've never admitted before. "My father was a pain in my ass, but I've never loved anyone more than him. He's gone and I'd give anything to have one more pain-in-the-ass day with him."

I look down at her, and she gazes up at me with an expression that's so sad. Her lips are turned down. Her eyes are luminous with unshed tears.

She lifts herself off me and rolls over to the edge of the bed. With her back to me, she says, "I'm going to check on my mom."

I place a hand on her forearm. Her skin is so cool to the touch. "I'll do it."

"No, she's my mom," she insists.

I give her a look to quell her protest and drag her back into the middle of the bed.

I put on sweats, pad across the hall, and softly open the door. Her mother's asleep, in the same position as we'd left her. I gently shake her awake and confirm that she's lucid. She's surprisingly blasé about the fact that there's a strange man waking her up in the middle of the night, but then again, when you've been found blacked out on your living room floor, you probably don't have enough in you to give a shit.

I give her a drink of water and wait until she falls back asleep. Returning to Star's bedroom, I notice her dejected profile, shoulders slumped forward and chin dropped to her chest. If anyone knows about the strain of taking care of a sick parent, it's me. I remember the trips my mother used to take with me and Zoe on, to skate at Rockefeller Center in the winter or out to Coney Island in the summer. Anything to shake off the melancholy.

"Come on, let's get out of here," I tell her.

Her eyes light up with excitement.

Sitting up on sprawled knees, she looks so damn innocent and sensual at the same time. I just want to topple her back into bed, but more sex is not the answer to our problems.

"Where are we going?" she asks, her hands clutching the bed sheets excitedly.

"There's a bar I go to in Brooklyn. A little hole-in-the-wall in Prospect Heights."

Her face drops. "I can't drink."

I place my knee on the bed, plant my fists in front of me, and lean in to say, "I've been a certified killer since the age of thirteen. Going to a bar for a few drinks isn't a problem."

Star gives a little squeak of excitement and rushes around her room, throwing on a crop top and tight black jeans that almost make me regret taking her out in public. I grab a pair of jeans and another shirt from her brother's closet and meet her on the landing.

We drive to the bar, which is still hopping on a Saturday night, and grab a table near the back. This bar is a little-known treasure, with a distinct vintage vibe. One wall, painted a crimson red, is occupied by a long bar made of dark wood and a dozen stools. The rest of the place looks like it was put together in a slapdash manner with old furniture and vintage pinball machines, but it's clean and the drinks are solid.

Star takes a seat in the booth and looks surprised when I slide in beside her, but I'm not about to give her the opportunity to put any space between us. I drape my arm over the back of the seat, playing with a few golden tresses of her high ponytail as we wait for the waitress. When she swings by, I order a couple of beers and then turn my attention back to Star.

She shifts under my perusal, but I let her take in her surroundings. My kitten's a curious one. Having run through every borough of this city since I was twelve years old, I sometimes forget just how sheltered *mafie* girls are.

"The first time I came here was with Cristo after hitting up a store under our protection down the street," I confide.

Those were back in the days before we solidified our power base exclusively in Queens. What I don't tell her is that while he stopped by for a brew, I played the pinball machines with bloodied knuckles from our so-called "visit" to the store.

The waitress returns, plopping mugs of beer on the old-school, blue floral Formica tabletop of our booth.

Liquid splashes over the top of the glasses and I glare up at her. She mumbles an apology before rushing away.

Star takes a dainty sip and wrinkles her nose. Guess Star isn't a beer girl.

"Want me to get you something else?"

"No, no," she rushes to say.

"You don't seem to be enjoying it."

"I have to get used to it. This is what American college students drink most, isn't it?"

Shrugging my shoulders, I take a sip and decide to go with a more neutral topic, "So tell me more about your plans."

"Why?" she asks suspiciously.

I twirl a lock of her hair around my index finger and tug it. "Because if I'm going to help you, then I deserve to know more about what you want to do once you're so-called free."

I don't know that I deserve anything from her, but that's the excuse I'm going with.

She raises a brow, but at least her gaze is back on me, where I like it. "So-called free, huh? I'm pretty sure it's just regular human free."

"And how do you see that playing out? When you're *regular* free, what will you do?"

Her face turns grave. "I want to go to college, obviously."

As if the mention of college reminds her of her beer, Star picks up her mug and tries again. She grimaces, but my stubborn girl goes for another gulp and then a third.

"Obviously," I reply, although I'm not going to lie, I'm surprised. If I were in her position, I'd sow my wild oats. At the very least, I figured she'd take advantage and travel the world. Hit the spots on her map or reunite with her brother.

"And then I'll need to get a masters in fine arts, either in art history or curatorial studies. Columbia University and NYU both have great programs, but they're too close for me to apply."

She's really thought this through. In fact, it seems like she's researched it in depth.

My brows rise. "Too close?"

"I'm running away, remember? Can't exactly do that and stay in the city for the six years it takes to complete undergrad and a graduate program."

"How are you going to pay for this?" I blurt out because, although I'm willing to pay for her schooling no matter what the cost, she's acting as if she can take care of it on her own.

"My brother set up a trust fund for me and my mother, which I've controlled since I turned eighteen." Her stubborn chin raises an inch. "See, I can take care of myself."

"I never doubted it," I lie with a tweak of her ponytail.

Damn, I'd completely doubted it.

I hadn't taken her scheme seriously whatsoever but learning that she has the funds to do whatever she wants dumps adrenaline into my bloodstream. I wipe all emotion from my face, retaining a calm mask on the outside while panicking on the inside.

For years, I've foolishly taken her presence and infatuation for granted. I wasn't lying when I said that when it stopped, I felt the wrongness of it in my bones. I've been trying to claw my way back into her good graces, but now I doubt whether there's enough time to succeed.

Even worse, she's plotting to leave at a time when she's most at risk. Once she's out of the city, she wouldn't be under my protection, not even under my watchful eye. She'll be vulnerable. If she's vulnerable, then that leaves me exposed.

"So have you applied yet?"

She laughs. "Oh my God, Lucian, of course I've applied. The deadlines were in December. I'm waiting for my acceptance letters. They should come any day now. Gabby has already been accepted."

I don't know how Anton feels about this turn of events. He acts as if she doesn't exist, but that doesn't fool me for a second. I'll be sure to alert him of this new development.

As if reading my mind, she jabs a finger into my chest and warns, "And don't you dare go telling Anton about this. This is none of his business."

"That's not how he sees it."

"It doesn't matter how he sees it," she shoots back. "I've told you this in confidence."

She narrows her eyes at me, as if daring me to test the little confidence she's put in me. Well fuck, I guess Anton's on his own.

I put my hands up and assure her, "It's certainly none of my business. I've got my hands full with you."

She gives a little harrumph. "It better stay that way."

Bingo. I feel the burn of that admission in my chest. My lips twist into a triumphant smirk.

Flustered, she says, "That's not what I meant. I don't care what you do or who you're with…o-or even who you marry."

Lie, lie, and triple lie. That had to be the most unconvincing series of lies I've heard to date.

To cover my grin, I drink my beer, and mutter, "Uh-huh."

Unable to stop myself from teasing her, I catch her hand and stroke the inside of her wrist. "It's okay, precious, you can admit you'd miss me just a bit."

She tries to pull her hand out of my grip, but I tighten

around it, soothingly caressing the skin with my thumb. She flounces in her seat with a cute little huff.

I lean in, nuzzling the curve of her throat just below her ear, and snag her earlobe for a quick bite. God, I love biting her.

Her breasts swell with her sharp intake of breath.

"Come on, precious, just admit it. You'd miss me—you'd miss *this*—just a little."

She shoves at my shoulder half-heartedly. "Fine, I might miss *this* just a little. Not you, just this."

Growling low against her ear, I feel her shiver beside me. I trace her erect nipple with my nail, and whisper, "See, that wasn't so hard to admit. The truth will set you free."

I pull back just far enough to ensnare her gaze. "Remember that."

Knowing how close I am to dragging her into a bathroom and fucking her against the wall, I throw myself away from her. The point of this outing is to do something relaxing, something other than fucking her.

Her glazed eyes follow me rapturously as I stand up and hold out my hand. God, I love when she watches me.

Perplexed, she asks, "Where are we going?"

"To play the pinball machines."

"I don't know how…"

I crook my finger. "It's about time you learned. You have no idea how addictive it is. But once I teach you, you won't be able to tear yourself away."

She relents and takes my outstretched hand.

"You'll see," I promise her.

I hold on to her hand as we walk to one of the machines. As I teach her how to play, I move in behind her and can't help but press close and feel her warm, curvy body against mine. Of course, my woman's a fast learner and soon she's squealing when she beats me at a game.

Before we know it, hours have passed and its last call. I pay our tab and I wrap my arm around her shoulder as we cross over the threshold into the street. A little tipsy, Star leans into me.

I revel the feel of her snuggling into my side when a man passing by bumps my shoulder.

WTF?

I glare at him, and he and his friend both turn around at the same time. *Fuck.* Bratva motherfuckers. I even recognize the two idiots. It's Vadim and Dimitri, two simple Bratva foot soldiers. They aren't related but look nearly identical in their Adidas tracksuits, cheap leather shoes, and fringe haircuts combed down the forehead over a shaved head.

Instinctually shielding Star from their intense scrutiny, I glare at them. "What the fuck, assholes? What the fuck are you doing here?"

No way is this a coincidence. Even if I'm in Brooklyn, this is nowhere near their territory. I don't know if they're following me or her, but if Star wasn't on their radar before, she sure as hell is now. I have my arms wrapped around her. There's no way they could construe this as anything but what it is. And right this moment, she's not my wife, she doesn't live under my roof, and she sure as fuck isn't in my bed every morning.

This is not good, not good at all.

I've been attempting to take my relationship with Star one day at a time, but that's not gonna last for much longer.

Dimitri, or Vadim, hell I can't tell, pats me patronizingly on my back.

A low growl emanates from deep in my chest.

"This is our fucking borough, yo."

"Like hell it is." Pointing down the street, I state, "Little Odessa is that way, motherfucker. You don't own the whole borough and you sure as hell would never be caught dead in this neighborhood."

Prospect Heights was technically Brooklyn, sure, but it was the definition of gentrification. No way would a Russian gangster randomly show up here. And D. or V. shows his hand again when his gaze returns to Star.

Feeling his gaze on her, she shrinks into me, clutching onto my shirt. I love that she instinctually seeks my protection, but I hate that she feels the need to. These bastards shouldn't know she exists.

The other gangster spits a sunflower shell from his mouth onto the concrete sidewalk, missing my shoe by an inch. That's a fucking provocation. If they're consuming sunflower seeds, it means they've been here a while, either staking us out while squatting against a wall or purposely pacing up and down the street to bump into us.

"We're in Brooklyn," he says doggedly. "You're in our borough."

I step up to him, yank the bag from his hand and toss it the ground. Seeds scatter everywhere. His gaze drops to the sidewalk. "My fucking sunflower seeds," he grumbles.

"Fuck your seeds, asshole, and fuck you," I spit out as I shove him in the chest.

He stumbles back a couple steps. Star whimpers behind me and it's her sound of panic that stops me from beating the hell out of them. They're bulky, but no match for me, and there's no way they would dare pull out their guns in the middle of this civilian neighborhood.

This isn't the kind of 'hood where people know to look the other way. As if to prove my point, a couple of bros stagger out of the bar, arms wrapped around each other.

They weave and bob as they stumble past us, singing at the top of their lungs.

"Crawl back into the hole you came from," I warn them as I grab hold of Star, corral her into my chest, and turn my back on the soldiers. If they wanted to kill me, they would've done it already. This little encounter is nothing more than a message and a threat.

For once, Star doesn't fight me. She hugs my middle and allows me to lead her back to my parked car. She doesn't have a snarky comment for me when I open the door. I place her inside and firmly shut the door, sealing her off from their gazes.

Glaring down the twins, I round the car and settle into the driver's seat.

I drive down the street, leaving them in my rearview mirror.

I need to fast track the timeframe for getting Star attached to me. Not only do I need to formulate a new plan, but it's gotta be foolproof.

Failure isn't an option.

CHAPTER 20

STAR

Time to accelerate my plan of escape.

Lucian pulls out a Glock from the console of his car and places it in reach as he races down the street.

Most women would freak out over something like this, but I'm not most woman. If anything, it's a relief because it confirms that he hadn't been lying to me. The danger is real. The only question is whether those Russian goons are interested in me because of Lucian or because I'm Tatum's sister.

Call me paranoid, but Tatum did explode the car bomb that killed their boss and second-in-command. Before he left, Tatum told me that no one knew who did it but me, my *şef*, and his two brothers, who were also involved. But what did he know? Maybe they weren't careful and the Bratva have known for a while.

I shrink back into the leather seat, panting out shallow breaths.

In that case, I'm lucky to be alive.

Either way, I'm in a precarious position and my best option is to get out of here. My brain scrambles to makes sense of this new reality. I have money and I'm a straight A student. I can finish high school anywhere. I can hide out in a boarding school in Switzerland. Surely, no one would find me there.

Lucian grips my thigh and squeezes reassuringly. There's a painful ache in my chest at the thought of never seeing him again. Even that one, harmless touch sends pulsing need between my thighs. This guy is like a drug for me, and I'm turning into an addict because the idea of escape doesn't fill me with excitement the way it used to— and it's not just because I could be hunted prey.

It's because of him.

Damn him for messing with my head.

"I'll take care of you, Star," he swears. "Nothing's going to happen to you. But now you understand why we need to get married. As my wife, you won't be considered Tatum Lupu's little sister. You'll be Lucian Popescu's wife, the new *consilier.*"

I glance at him in horror. "You must be kidding, right? That's what you got out of this?"

His slate-gray eyes turn brittle and he slams a black velvet box on the console between us. "Like hell I'm kidding and, yes, that's exactly what I got out of this. It's the only sane solution."

Such a tiny innocuous-looking object and yet it strikes terror in my heart. "I won't marry for protection. If anything, I'll move up my plans for leaving. The sooner I disappear, the better."

"The fuck," he snaps. "That will only make you more vulnerable."

He bares his teeth as his hands clench the steering wheel harder. He releases one hand and grasps my thigh again. "I couldn't save my father, but fuck if I let you die, even if I have to save you from yourself."

"Not if you don't find me first," I shoot back, trying to shove his hand off me. Like usual, any struggle on my part makes him double down. His fingers tighten around me.

"And what the hell do you mean, *save me from myself?* I'm eighteen years old, a grown woman. I control my own trust fund. I'll decide my future, not you and not my mother."

"Speaking of your mother, are you really going to abandon her?"

That accusation rocks me to my core. He just identified the one major stumbling block in my plan. Of course, I know she'll be alone, and I volley back and forth between leaving her in anger and trying to find a solution.

Before I can reply, he continues, "Will you stop being so damn stubborn and listen to reason? I may be a fuckup at school, but this is my area of expertise, and you're in serious danger."

The air in the car suddenly feels hot and oppressive. I roll down the window and shove my head halfway outside, letting a gust of wind off the Brooklyn-Queens Expressway cool me down. It's pitch-black outside, which means we're passing over the long stretch of the Calvary Cemetery, nestled between the two boroughs.

Despite my flushed skin, a shiver whispers through me.

Staring out over the dark expanse, I have to admit that it's time to listen to him. I'm just a high-school student without a made man to protect me and my mother. I'm trying to patch this Bratva story together from bits and pieces, but it's hopeless. If I'm going to survive, I need to concede that he's right. But damn him, I'm not going down without a fight.

Pulling my head back in, I reply, "You accuse me of

being unreasonable, but you haven't given me a motive to be reasonable. You intimidate me with threats of danger, and you order me around like I'm a child, but I refuse to be anything less than an equal. I'll do what you say…on one condition. You've got to tell me what's going on."

"Why do you ask for the impossible? You know I can't do that," he replies instantly.

It's a big ask, but I don't care. Information is strictly controlled, even among made men, but he either gives me the information I want or I do this on my own. I'm done being treated like I'm less than.

"Then, I'll run away. You may be my fake fiancé, but you're not my husband. You have no real authority over me. You can't force me to do anything. I know you've put a tracker on my phone since the night you found me in the gallery. I'll ditch it and run away. I'll be long gone before you can get me to the alter."

His face twists into a scowl. I've got him and he knows it. It's not like he can hustle me in front of a magistrate and *ta-da*, we're married. A political marriage like ours requires a showy Romanian wedding. Both clans will want to pull out all the stops. If anything, it'll become a contest of who can outdo who.

He slams the palm of his hand on his steering wheel. "Damn it, Star."

"I already know what Tatum did," I divulge. "If they're not after me because of you, then it's because of that."

His eyes flash to me, surprise lighting them a silvery hue in the semidarkness of the car interior. He scrubs his jaw for a moment, grimacing as he tussles with himself.

"Fuck, alright, I'll tell you what I know. But swear to God, Star, if you fuck me over, I will hunt you down across every continent of this godforsaken earth. Try running as fast and far as you can, but I *will* catch you. And when I do,

I will tan your hide. You'll scream for mercy, but I won't give it." His sharp eyes flicker over to me. "Feel me?"

I nod, gulping over the lump in my throat.

It's official: I'm sick, because the vision of him running after me in the dark and catching me has me squirming in my seat, trying to distract myself from a flood of arousal.

He blows out a long breath and starts. "Tatum, along with Alex's brothers, Luca and Nicu, blew up the Russian boss as revenge for killing their father, your old Lupu *şef*."

My mouth drops open but I quickly snap it closed.

"Yes, that's right. Your old *şef*. Alex, Luca, and Nicu's father."

He lets out a belabored sigh. "From the intel Cristo received, your father turned against your clan, aligned himself with the Bratva, and helped kill Alex's father. After the assassination, the Bratva turned on your father and killed him. Tatum somehow found out and hid everything from Alex. As you well know, nothing remains secret in the *mafie*. Eventually Alex found out. He spared Tatum's life on the condition that he kill the Bratva boss and then disappear."

I swallow around what feels like a lump of coal in my throat. Of course, Tatum already confessed this to me. I just didn't realize that everyone else knows. With my family's tainted past, it's a testament to Lucian's determination that he wants to marry me instead of Roxie. Even if a Lupu-Popescu alliance is necessary right now, it makes no sense that Lucian would want to marry me, instead of staying with Roxie. Maybe it's the final sacrifice Cristo demanded of him...but why me?

"If Luca and Nicu were involved, why would the Bratva focus on me? Luca and Nicu are Lupu royalty, with wives and children. Compared to them, I'm nothing."

"They may be better targets, but the Lupu brothers

have their women—their *wives*—under strict protection. And anyway, killing any one of them will guarantee a full-scale war. You're the low hanging fruit that can satisfy the Russians' thirst for blood while possibly avoiding an apocalypse of gang warfare on the city streets." He swallows. "It's the plan I would pick if I were them."

I lean forward to read his reaction as I ask, "Since when did I become important?"

Frustration is what I see.

"Woman, you've always been important. You're your father's daughter and Tatum's sister."

"But they're both traitors."

"If nothing else, traitors wield power in people's minds. Your father was a powerful man and Tatum is married to the queen of the Hagi clan in Los Angeles. You're under the protection of Lupu clan. Alex could have exiled you and your mother, but he didn't. That's very telling. It means you're valuable to him."

"Why haven't they killed me yet?"

"I don't know. Maybe they were focused on the Lupu brothers and their families but then decided that it's not possible or not worth killing them. It doesn't matter. For whatever reason, they're focused on you."

Another question nags me. "Why would they show their hand in public like that?"

He scratches his chin thoughtfully.

"It's a smart tactic," he muses to himself. "The whole point of declaring our engagement at Nelu's party was to make it public. They might have chosen you but killing the fiancée of a Popescu *consilier*—and they do not have a direct beef with us—is a risky proposition. Yet taking out a fiancée is not like taking out an actual wife. They tested my interest in you. Whether it's to kidnap you or outright kill you, they want to see whether this another loveless arranged marriage or whether you matter to me."

I sputter in stunned disbelief. This new information changes everything. I want to leave, sure, but I don't want to die. At the same time, it won't change my mind about marrying Lucian.

"What do I need to do to stay alive?" I hurry to add, "Other than marrying you. That's still off the table."

His cheek muscles flexes in frustration. "We need to make them believe that the engagement is real. That we're in love. If they believe you'll be my wife, and that you matter to me as much as Luca's and Nicu's wives matter to them, then you'll have a chance of surviving." His gaze sears into mine. "But we need to eliminate any opportunity of them getting to you. You stay by my side 24/7. I mean it, Star. Every minute. I either sleep at your house or you sleep at mine. It's the only thing that will prevent them from killing you in cold blood."

The breeze coming from the window chills my skin. My teeth chatter slightly. I wrap my arms around my chest. The window instantly rolls up.

I glance over at Lucian; his finger is still pressed on the control button for the car windows.

I gently lay a hand on his arm and say, "Thank you."

The muscle of his forearm jumps. His gaze lands on my hand, his eyes turning to liquid silver again. I suppose this is the first time I've willingly laid a hand on him, if you don't count being in bed with him or clutching his shirt when those two thugs came up on us.

We're back in the neighborhood. Lucian swerves into a spot and grabs the engagement ring box. He pops it open, and I shy away from him, shaking my head in denial.

"You've gotta wear this."

Lucian removes the huge diamond ring from the

surrounding black velvet and holds it out for me to inspect. My breath hitches. I can't help but lean forward to inspect it. It's an opulent round-cut diamond centered over three thick bands encrusted with yellow diamonds. Even in the dim light of the cab of the car, it throws out ferocious sparks of light.

It's massive. Ginormous. And…utterly gorgeous. I bite my bottom lip. My fingers twitch and I clasp my hands together to stop myself from lunging for it.

"It's a Buccellati. I chose the most iconic one I could find."

He cants his head to the side, frowning as he examines it critically. The way he speaks, one would think he'd taken his time and looked over many rings before he chose this one.

A ridiculous notion, I know.

"It's the closest to Renaissance I could find," he continues. "I figured you wouldn't want to go modern on something like this."

My mouth is agape; I'm speechless. He's right, and I have no idea how he could possibly know something so personal about me. My head is spinning. It was only tonight that he stared at the map on my wall and asked me why I loved Italy. Yet, he got me the perfect ring, as if he already knew my taste.

But that's not possible…

Too distracted to continue with that line of thought, I greedily pluck the ring from between his fingers.

The ring is outrageous…but it's stunning. It's hard to express the jumble of emotions battling inside me. No, I can't marry him, but I was brought up *mafie,* and no *mafie* girl who has spent half her life dreaming about her big wedding could resist an engagement ring like this one.

Then there's the pure artistry and uniqueness of it. If nothing else, I can gush over that.

Let's face it, it's the only silver lining in this whole debacle.

"I'm not marrying you," I insist again because there's something unmistakably grave about this moment. Not only have I fantasized about it for years, but I've fantasized it specifically *with this man.*

My chest hurts when he draws my hand toward him and reverently slips the ring over the last knuckle of my finger. His head is bent as if in prayer, as if he's immersed in a sanctified act. He lifts my hand to his mouth and kisses the ring on my finger. The soft, dry touch of his lips jolts me like an electric shock.

Rattled, I snatch my hand back and cradle it against my chest.

Sizzling heat hangs in the air between us.

Sheesh, why do I feel like we went through a ceremony or something? Why do I feel like something passed between us from his simple act of placing the ring on my finger? It's not like he even proposed, I remind myself firmly. This means nothing. It's nothing more than a way of protecting me until the danger passes. Then, I'll go back to plotting my escape.

I wrap my hand around the ring and promise, "It's a stunning piece. I'll make sure to keep it safe for you so you will have a chance to give it to your…real wife."

Hurt and confusion crosses his face, but it quickly morphs into defiance. Dammit, that's not good. He slams the steering wheel hard, grabs his Glock, and swings out of the car. Scanning the street carefully, he comes around to my side and opens the door for me. He blocks me and wraps a hand around my throat.

Tilting my head up until our eyes clash, he declares, "Precious, you are my real wife. My only wife."

"I am not," I rasp.

As if I hadn't said a word, he goes on to warn me, "And don't you dare twist the ring around on your finger and hide it when we're at school." He points to it threateningly. "To make this convincing to the Bratva, it must be convincing to everyone. Remember that."

With that final warning, he releases my throat and gestures for me to get inside the house.

* * *

SINCE OUR FAKE ENGAGEMENT, my life has changed quite a bit. In many ways, I grew up like an only child. With Tatum being so much older than I am and working so much, I've had lots of alone time to study and feed my growing obsession with art.

But in one day—*poof!*—all that privacy vanished like a puff of smoke.

Sunday was calm enough. Lucian took me with him to work and to visit his mother and explain why he was temporarily moving in with me.

But come Monday, everything changed. First, I woke up to Lucian's tongue on my clit.

Waking up to an organism is a definite perk, but then there are the not-so-great moments. Like no more subway rides with Crina and Gabby. Instead, Lucian drives me to school. And the hovering doesn't stop there. He seems to think he should flaunt our engagement like it's a billboard in Times Square. You know the one? The one that stands twenty-two stories tall with a series of high-def LED screens.

He drapes his arm around my shoulder as he frog-marches me through the front entrance of the school. Who knew I'd be pining for the days I was ignored by the three kings as they guarded the door? Then, he walks me to my locker. I immediately shove him off me, but instead of taking a hint, he pushes me against the locker door, wraps my hand brandishing the engagement ring around his nape, and kisses me in front of everyone. Even in the middle of chaotic morning traffic, I'm helpless to resist succumbing to his talented tongue.

With a squeeze of my butt, he leans in and warns, "Be a good girl for me, precious."

I roll my eyes, even if my tummy flutters like it's been invaded by a squadron of butterflies. I shouldn't like this, but truth be told, it leaves me giddy. How could it not when it's the fulfillment of girlhood fantasies I've had of Lucian for years? I may have moved past those silly daydreams, but they run deep. There's no denying that it's a powerful, heady thing to have your dreams realized after so many years of neglect.

He continues this strategy throughout the day, seeking me out during lunch and dragging me over to the infamous table, where he attempts to feed me himself. I refuse, but he still dares to reach over and brush a crumb off the corner of my mouth. I stomp on his foot to put a stop to this scandalous behavior. We're in public, for God's sake. Afterward, when he insists on walking me to my class, I ask him if Crina and Gabby can sit with us tomorrow. I can't put up with another day of being stared at like a specimen under a microscope.

After such a stressful day, all I want to do is head home and crawl into my bed for a nap. If this is what being popular is like, it's a big, fat *no* for me. But instead of going home, Lucian takes me to work with him.

Now his lack of good grades makes much more sense.

The guy's a boss. Not only does he coordinate and supervise a group of soldiers who do his bidding but he also attends meetings (of which I'm forced to wait outside the door) and drives to various hubs where they produce or hold or distribute drugs—I don't really know what's going on—and collects money.

We stop by his house and dine with his mother and sister, who break out a bottle of champagne to toast our fake engagement. By the time we reach home, it's past nine o'clock. As luck would have it, my mother is passed out, this time sprawled out on the living room sofa. Lucian helps me get her to her bedroom, where I press a glass of water to her lips and help her change into a nightgown before tucking her into bed.

Dead on my feet, I stumble into my bedroom.

"How do you do this every single day? There's no way I can do this again. I have exams to study for. I need to keep my grades up. There's absolutely no way I can waste the entire afternoon schlepping up and down half of New Jersey with you."

Lucian looks at me from his position on my bed, laid out with his hands behind his head. He changed into a suit before leaving school, but now he's dressed down with a loose pair of worn gray sweatpants and a tank top, showcasing the hefty bulge of his biceps. Jeez, he looks so good in my bed, relaxed in a way I rarely see with him.

I glance at my open closet, where half my clothes have been pushed aside to give way to a row of suits and pressed shirts. On top of my white dresser are neat piles of his school uniform pants.

Leaning against the doorjamb, I press a hand to my forehead. "This is too much for me…"

"You stressed out?" He crooks a finger at me, and demands, "Come here, baby."

I begrudgingly move toward him. He grabs me and swings me on top of him.

Wiggling to get away, he groans as he grabs hold of my hips and warns, "Stay still."

I freeze.

Then I press my pelvis down just a tad. His cock stiffens, hard and long against my belly.

"If you do that one more time, you're asking to be spanked or fucked. Your next move determines which one it'll be."

I wish.

"Neither, Lucian," I groan. "I don't have time. I need to finish my homework and get studying for a test in my Honors Chinese class in a couple days. I've already wasted away the weekend and today."

He claps a hand over one buttock, making me involuntarily twitch. "A spanking would relieve the tension of the day."

I narrow my eyes at him and shake my head. Exhausted, I drop my head on his chest and listen to the steady, solid pounding of his heart. "You do so much in one day. It's grueling. I'm used to being alone, either studying in the library or going home after school ends, but that's just the beginning for you."

"Hmm," he hums as he runs his hand down the length of my spine. "Maybe I shouldn't tell you that I stopped early today so we could have dinner with my mother and sister, or that I normally work past midnight."

I snuggle into his shirt, appreciating the soft weave of the cotton and inhaling the scent of laundry, cologne, and his natural musky fragrance. His hand squeezes my butt again, but even though there are ten stiff inches cradled between our bodies, he lifts his other hand and strokes my hair. I exhale deeply as I settle deeper into him.

The window near my bed is open, and I watch the littleleaf linden tree blossoms flutter as a cool April night breeze slips in and cascades over my back. Flashes of rainbow colors emanate from the diamonds on my ring hand, right beside my face.

If today was exhausting, it was also exhilarating. As irritating as he was, I can't deny that Lucian's attentiveness —one could almost say devotion—is enticing. I'd like to say he'd done it to convince everyone about our fake engagement, but that would be a lie.

And like him, I'm not a liar.

He's proven to be reliable, even before our arrangement, and he once admitted to loving me. Just cuddling against him, listening to the soothing thumps of his heart, is so comfortable. But something's holding me back.

I'm waiting for the other shoe to drop. He might *believe* he loves me at this moment, but what if he gets tired of me? The ghost of past humiliations creeps over me. Once I turn into his loyal puppy, nipping at his heels for crumbs of attention, he'll turn around and kick me again. That's what bullies do, and Lucian will always be my bully.

A hard swat comes down on my butt, startling me out of my reverie. I let out a little yelp.

"Stop it," he orders.

Pretending I don't know what he's talking about, I reply, "What?"

"You're thinking too hard with your big brain. No good comes of it for me. Stop plotting how to drive a wedge between us."

"I am not," I deny with a pout.

He stops stroking my hair and flips us until I'm beneath him and he's tucked between my open thighs with my skirt riding up to make way for his bulky torso.

"Don't lie to me." He strokes my hair again. "Precious,

I'm not going to hurt you again, I swear it on my father's grave."

"Even if I was stupid enough to believe you, you're still hurting me by not letting me go."

The silver luster in his eyes morph into a dark steely gray. "It's for your security. Nothing comes before your safety. *Nothing.*"

"Not even my happiness?" I throw back at him.

"Who the hell guaranteed us happiness? Do you think I'm happy waking up at the ass crack of dawn to go to a school I hate after working through the night to solidify my position in my clan? But I do it because I have no choice."

I shove at his chest until he lifts off me, although I can't help but miss his heat and the satisfying weight of him on me.

I scramble to a sitting position and tap my chest. "I want to be happy. I don't want to spend my life fulfilling other people's expectations of me, like I have up till now. I don't want to marry a man I didn't choose. Have kids way too early. Let my mind rot from disuse because I don't go to college."

His eyes lift upward. "You can go to college. I'd be thrilled to support you. I'd pay for it."

I point a finger at him. "Oh my God, that's what I'm talking about. I don't need your permission or your money. It shouldn't be your decision whether I go to college. That should be my prerogative and mine alone."

My chest is heaving from the rapid escalation between us. Frustration swirls within me like a maelstrom, a twisted ball of anger at him and resentment of the *mafie* culture I'm trapped in.

He scrubs the scruff around his jaw; his gaze pierces

me. "I was just trying to be supportive. Why does everything deteriorate so quickly with you?"

I break our staring contest and glance out the window, concentrating on the shivering blossoms on the branch outside my window. The creamy-white clusters of flowers look like delicate puffs of lace.

Once I've wrangled my emotions back under control, I take a deep breath and say, "Years of bullying can do that to a girl—"

He lets out a deep sigh. "Fuck, are you ever going to get over that?"

I glide my tongue over the front tooth that was bonded after being chipped.

"I don't know," I reply honestly.

There's always been a special bond between us, but our story is not like Marku and Crina's story. Everyone and their mother can see that he's loved her for years, whereas Lucian really was my bully. For whatever reason, he's decided he wants me. He might even care for me, but the truth is that I'll have to sacrifice everything for him. Tatum was my rock for nearly my whole life and look how that worked out for me. No, the only person I can depend on is myself.

"Regardless, I can't let you go."

His voice is soft. No longer angry, just tinged with frustration. He reaches out and brushes a strand of hair out of my eyes. He does that nowadays, leaving lingering touches here and there. His finger sweeps across my cheekbone before dropping away.

"One of the reasons I bullied you was because I couldn't admit how I felt about you, but I've finally accepted it and knowing you feel the same way—"

He holds up a palm to stop me as I open my mouth to argue and continues, "Whether you're willing to admit it or not, I can't let you go. I'd never forgive myself if anything should happen to you. I barely survived my father's death. I won't survive yours."

Ignoring the nonsense he spewed about not surviving my death, he's spoken some profound words. There's so much to examine, and my curiosity, my intense desire to dive deep, prods me to ask, *what do you mean you barely survived?* But I stop myself. He always gets me with his vulnerability. Those moments of tenderness between us weaken me.

Snap out of it, girl. You can't afford to fall for him.

Concentrating on my hands, which are clasped tightly together and thrust in the gap between my crisscrossed legs, I ask, "And once the danger has passed? Will you let me go then?"

There's a long, heavy pause.

The hair on my arms stands up on end.

Static energy crackles in the air between us like the pregnant moment before lightning strikes.

My fingers and toes tingle.

"Never."

CHAPTER 21

LUCIAN

*L*ast night did not go as planned.

Maybe I shouldn't have answered the way I did, but I'm not a liar and I'm not about to start now only to ease her feelings. She's torn, I get it. That's how I felt for so long.

After a tense morning, she's avoided me all day. Knowing she's safe in the school building, I'm giving her as much space as I can, but classes are done for the day and I need to take her with me on my rounds.

Leaning against Star's locker, I check the time on my phone. My brows lift. It's later than I thought. I have a meeting in half-an-hour in Queens. Fuck, I'm never going to be there on time. My gaze drifts down to the floor by her locker. I frown. Her cell phone is cradled up against the dark blue metal of her locker.

My gut churns.

What the fuck?

I text Anton to see if he's seen her around school and he

replies that he hasn't.

I text back to have him find out if her little friends are still in the building. He promptly replies that Gabby and Crina have left.

Something's wrong. I feel it in my bones. She knows better than to leave without me and yet my instinct tells me she's defied my order. Again. Fuck me, but without the geolocator, I have no idea where she is.

Abandoning my backpack, I sprint down the hall to the stairs and them two steps at a time. I fly across the lobby and out the door. Dashing down the street, I turn onto the avenue and search down that block.

She's nowhere to be seen.

It's too late for help. If anything's happened to her, I'm on my own. Hoping that I'm wrong, I dart down the street toward the subway station, texting my boys and muttering to myself that when I get a hold of her, I'm going to strip her ass with my belt. She will learn what happens when she pulls a stunt like this. No one gets the drop on me.

I reach the subway station and burst onto the platform just in time to see Star and her two friends laughing as they enter the subway car. A vaguely familiar-looking man in a suit with a shaved head enters right behind them.

I jump the turnstile and dash toward the silver-colored train.

The doors slam shut in my face.

I cup my hands over my eyes and peer into the car as it passes me; the man turns toward me, a malevolent smirk on his face.

My blood runs cold.

Bratva.

Fuck.

Panic attacks my throat like a hundred blades, choking me. No one hurts my woman. Once I get my hands on him,

I'm going to carve this fucker up from limb to limb. It's going to be the most excruciating death the world has ever known.

But first, I need to get on. The subway picks up speed, whooshing past me on the platform. With no other choice, I grab the stainless-steel chain on the back landing of the caboose and swing onto the floorboard of the car. The doors between cars are always open, except for the door of the last car—the one I'm hanging onto.

I glance up as we whistle through the dark tunnel. There isn't much light, but I can discern at least several feet of headroom between the top of the roof and the top of the tunnel. My first thought is to climb onto the roof, crawl across it, and drop back down to get into the next car, but then I remember that I'm on a local train. It will pull into the next station before I've accomplished that kind of next-level acrobatics.

I grit my teeth and hang on, praying that Star hasn't been kidnapped or outright murdered as I wait. The instant the train reaches the platform, I hop off and rush into the opening doors of the subway car.

Once inside, I fly from car to car until I get to hers. Before busting into the car where I last saw her, I squint through the grimy window of the door to see what's waiting for me.

Good thing I do because the thug is holding Star by the hair. Her head is yanked back, a gleaming knife at her throat. My stomach convulses. She's kicking back, trying to dislodge him without success. He says something and she stills, her eyes wild with fear.

Seeing the terror etched on her face guts me.

The civilians, mostly teens, huddle together in a shivering mass in a corner.

Good. I don't need a dumbass Good Samaritan getting in my way.

Crina boldly faces the Russian. Hands out in front of her, she's talking fast, probably trying to distract him as Gabby edges farther and farther away.

Guessing that she's trying to reach the emergency brake, the thug snaps at Gabby and she freezes in place. The Bratva dude drags Star near the door. My blood runs cold. I can't let him leave with her.

I pull out my Glock, praying Crina ducks 'cause I have one shot to get this guy before he escapes with Star. For whatever reason, Star must sense my presence because her gaze surveys the interior of the car before sweeping past the door and then snapping back to me.

I lift my index finger to my mouth. Her eyes scamper away, as if she's afraid of bringing attention to me.

I don't give a fuck. Let him see me. He's going to die, regardless. Slowly, I squeeze the safety on my gun until it's flush with the grip, disengaging it.

Star stares straight at Crina, who's gesturing slowly as she keeps talking to the thug and blinks her eyes rapidly as some sort of signal. Hopefully, that's enough to alert her because I won't have time to shout at her to get down. Pray to God, she drops to the floor. Marku will never forgive me if she gets hurt.

The subway slows as it screeches into the 68th Street station. The conductor announces the next station. I slam the door open, aim steadily for his head, and pull the trigger.

Clear hit to the head.

His hand jerks as he goes down, slicing across Star's collarbone, through her shirt, and down her chest before he topples to the ground.

Star goes down with him, entangled with his heavy body.

Her soft whimper cuts through the screams of the passengers as I run to her and haul the dead Russian off her. Time slows down. A rusty metallic odor fills the air. Gabby pulls the emergency brake and the train shudders to a complete halt. The intercom crackles. The conductor's garbled voice blares through the speakers.

I heave Star to her feet.

Wrap her in my arms.

Nuzzle my nose into her warm hair.

Breathe in her comforting cherry vanilla scent.

Jesus, she's safe.

Turning her toward the exit, my shoes squelch in a pool of blood spreading beneath the dead man's head.

The doors slide open.

Anton is efficiently jostling people away from the train, gawkers staring down at the dead man before moving on. Only in New York do people not run away at the sight of a corpse. Marku blocks the doors from closing with his shoulders.

In stunned silence, Crina stares up at him.

He crooks his finger at her.

Awed, she asks, "How did you know?"

"The tracking device on your phone. Now come here, you pain in my ass."

She jumps into his arms, clasping him hard and crying into his shoulder.

I gently move out of the train with Star in my arms, murmuring a thanks to my friends as I pass. Blood from the cut across her chest soaks the sides of her slashed white shirt and trickles onto my knuckles.

A woman shrieks "Oh, my God!" as she passes by, seeing the cut oozing blood.

Cursing under my breath, I turn Star into my chest, covering her head with my hand as I walk her to the exit. I buzz the button for the station master to open the emergency door because I don't see Star getting through the turnstile.

Once we pass through, she steps out of her booth and waves me over.

"Sir, wait for the police," she orders.

I ignore her as I move Star toward the stairs leading up to the street.

She approaches me, lays a hand on my shoulder, and repeats her command.

I shrug off her hand and growl, "Don't fucking touch me. My fiancée needs to get home. No way in hell we're waiting for the police. I just killed a man." I glare at her. "You wanna make it two?"

Smart woman, she backs off with her hands up in the air.

"Thought so."

I turn my attention back to Star, who begins shaking in my arms.

I curse under my breath. The shock is settling in. I half carry her up the steep, narrow flight of stairs. Her knuckles turn white as she clutches my shirt tightly.

I coax her toward the curb, crooning low about what a good girl she is.

A lie, for sure.

She's been a very bad girl, and once she's safe, she'll be punished accordingly. I've been lackadaisical and look what happened. I almost lost her. A wave of impotent fury rampages through me, but I lock it down. This isn't the time or place, but damn if I ever let this happen again. Strict rules will be imposed and enforced, and I will give her a taste of what happens if she ever breaks them again.

At the corner, I flag down a yellow cab and bundle her inside. I wrap her in my arms as I shoot off a text to Cristo, alerting him to what has just happened. He instantly replies that Marku and Anton explained the situation and backup is coming to get them out of the clutches of the police.

And then…we get stuck in midtown traffic. I roll down the taxi windows to let in some air. The loud drilling from a construction site and smog from standstill traffic permeate the car. Stroking Star's hair, I lift her chin gently from where she's hunched into my chest. The vinyl of the back seat squeaks at my slight movement.

She peeks up. Her eyes bleed terror. She licks her dry lips. I get it, she saw me kill a man point-blank. She may have been raised in the *mafie*, but this was clearly the first time she's witnessed what's an average day for me.

I send out a prayer of thanks. Tatum had done right by her. My lips turn downward. Until he left her. She's been exposed, and if I hadn't been obsessively watching over her, God only knows what would've happened.

Hugging her closely, I swear to her, "Precious, you're safe."

She shakes her head and says between chattering teeth. "I'll n-never be…safe."

Her eyes speed past my shoulder to whatever is outside the taxi window.

I wrap my hand around her nape and squeeze.

"Look at me," I demand. "You're safe. I will kill every last one of them, you hear. I won't rest until there's scorched earth beneath your feet. Death to them and everyone they love."

She bursts into tears, and I curse myself for letting my anger loose. She's frightened, and here I am, talking about killing more people. I tug her back into my chest, letting her weep in the protection of my embrace. It breaks my heart to hear her.

The release will help, I tell myself, even if I feel like a complete asshole. No, I didn't create this world of brutality, but I won't allow her to escape it either. One can argue that I should give her a new identity and help her disappear, but even if I thought it was feasible, I'm not that kind of man. This incident only makes me want to envelop her in bubble wrap and keep her away from the world, not free her into it.

As difficult as it was to take care of my father—and there were days when it was hell—I never abandoned him, never gave up on him. I loved him. After surviving his loss, I can never willingly abandon Star. She's the first person I've loved since him. It might have started long before, but now that I've accepted how much I love her, there's no un-knowing it.

I glance down at Star, whose sobs have receded to a steady sniffle.

And the frenzied panic I endured when I didn't know whether she was alive or not... I can't go through that again. I refuse to.

But there's no denying that I've failed her, and it's urgent that I redeem myself. Over Star's back, I shoot a text to Cristo, telling him that I'm taking her home, and that I'll stay with her until she falls asleep before joining him. They're likely meeting at this very moment to begin strategizing our counterattack. They will be expecting my immediate presence, but there's no way I'm leaving her.

Cristo's response comes quickly.

Cristo: Are you fucking serious?

Me: Yeah

Cristo: I need you here. Now.

Me: Gotta stay with her. Her brother's gone. Her mother's drunk. Her friends are on lockdown.

Cristo: This isn't a good look for you. You're my *consilier*.

Me: Give me a few hours. She's family now. She's my priority.

Cristo: Fuck me, since when do you put anything before the clan?

Since Star.

Me: Since now.

Me: I'll be there as soon as I can.

The taxi pulls up to her house. I throw a couple hundred-dollar bills at the driver and help Star out of the car. We get into the house and up the stairs into her room. I sit her on the bed and slowly ease her shirt off, letting out a soft curse as I get a better look at the damage.

Gazing into her eyes, seeing the pain, and knowing I'm about to add to it, I grind down on my back teeth. "Baby girl, you're going to need stitches."

She glances down, whispering harshly, "No."

I take her clammy hands in mine and pull her up to her feet. "Yes."

Back down we go, past the foyer and the living room where we found her mother, which feels like ages ago now, and into their kitchen. The light-yellow walls are decorated with rows of antique, handmade folk plates. It feels lived-in and cozy. Afternoon light streams in through a set of three windows just above a windowsill lined with pots of different herbs and a wooden container with cooking utensils sticking out of it.

"Where's the first aid kit?" I ask her.

She points to a large farmhouse sink. I crouch down and grab the kit, propping it open to check for a suturing kit. Considering this was a *mafie* household, I wasn't too worried.

Star slips onto a stool by the kitchen island, watching me nervously. She's only wearing her bra, which has a nick in the strap from the thug's knife, and her school kilt. She looks so achingly young and vulnerable sitting there. My heart jumps to my throat and I force the ache down with a hard, audible swallow.

The gash cut across her collarbone and down her left breast—crossing over her heart. The canvas of her pristine skin is brutally marred.

A swell of rage surges through me, making me want to howl at the sky and tear the cheerful kitchen apart.

The gash may have stopped bleeding, but it needs suturing. This is going to sting.

Her eyes widen in panic. "Can't we call someone?"

This is the first full sentence Star has spoken since the subway, which is telling.

"It's a quick patching. I can handle it."

Her shoulders sag. She was hoping I'd get the doctor we have on call for this kind of stuff, but I can take care of it. And funny enough, I don't want anyone seeing her like this. This gash is my shame. It's my responsibility. She's my responsibility.

"Where's the liquor?"

She points out the doorway to a credenza in the dining room, which is a dark and ponderous affair in comparison to the light and homey kitchen.

I stalk over to it, and ask over my shoulder, "What's your preference?"

Her answer drifts over to me from the kitchen. "*Țuică.*"

"Really?"

It's our traditional spirit, made from fermented plums, but to say it's an acquired taste is an understatement.

She gives a little shrug and winces when the movement pulls at her wound. "It's what we always drink on holidays. Guess I'm used to it."

I shoot her a wry smile. "You don't like the taste of beer, but you can handle this."

"*Țuică* it is," I murmur, pouring her a couple of fingers.

We usually drink it in shot glasses, but this might require a bit more.

I place it in her hand and watch her take a gulp. She sputters a little but swallows it down. I drop the kit on the island and lay out the instruments. Turning toward the sink, I scrub my hands thoroughly and don a pair of gloves. Hearing the snap of the latex against my skin, Star hurries to take another gulp of the liquor. I tear open alcohol wipes and clean off as much blood as possible between her hisses and mumbled curses.

Grabbing the sanitized needle, I take the needle driver and pull the thread out of the suture kit.

"I've done this many times, baby, so you have nothing to fear," I say, using my most soothing tone as I press the edges of the deepest section of her wound together to test them. Blood oozes out and Star whimpers.

"You're so brave, you know that?"

Staring into her eyes, I say, "I need you to pick a spot off my left shoulder and focus on it, precious. Think you can do that for me?"

"Yeah," she replies hoarsely as she does what I ask.

"Good, baby, good. I'm going in," I warn her as I push the needle through the skin at a 90-degree angle, stopping just short of the fatty layer of flesh. She takes in a sharp breath but holds herself still.

"Everything's going to heal just fine," I say, talking to distract her. "No scar, apart from this small section. Just gonna stitch this up fast..." I twist the needle counterclockwise so the needle comes out straight across on the other side of the wound.

I pull it out and say, "One down."

Despite her initial anxiety, the way she's handling this proves that she's perfect *mafie* wife material. I may want to protect her from the violence embedded in my life, but at least I won't have to hide it the way I know some men do from their wives.

"How is it you're not angry with me?" she asks with a long shuddering exhale as I pull the needle through again. "I thought you'd be furious."

"I am furious, but my anger is of no use here." I hit my chest a couple times. "It's locked up tight, to be taken out and used later. After you're all sewed up and healed." My eyes gleam as they skate over her. "Then we're going to have a good little session for your disobedience."

A shudder ripples through her and she bites down on her plump bottom lip.

"There's going to be a war, isn't there?" she asks, tears welling up in her eyes.

Her bottom lip trembles. "Because of me."

I poke another hole in her skin. "No baby girl, not only because of you."

"You're lying."

I pull the needle out, loop it in again, piercing her skin a third time. She pants beside me, bravely absorbing the pain.

"Told you already, I don't lie. A war was brewing. The Bratva were planning to take someone out. Luca, Nicu, you, one of their wives... You know the honor code. Revenge upon revenge." I shrug lightly. "It's a never-ending cycle."

I finish a couple more stitches, then wrap the thread around the tip of the needle holder twice, tie a simple overhand knot, and flatten the knot against her skin before doing a second and third knot to make certain its secure. I snip off the excess thread. It drifts down to the terracotta-tiled floor.

"There," I say, taking out an adhesive bandage to cover her wound. "It's done. Let me clean this up and we'll go back upstairs."

Once upstairs, I help her dress in a pair of sweats and one of my tank tops, since it's looser and won't rub against her covered wound. Tucking her in, I sit down on the edge of the bed and hand her a glass of water and a painkiller.

"Thank you," she says. "For this. For sewing my up." Her voice lowers. "For saving me. I know you're mad at me for leaving. I was angry and acting out, but more than anything I guess I just wanted things the way they used to be. To go home with my friends on the subway like I did every day."

"Those days were over, even if we weren't engaged. You openly defied me, Star. That can't stand."

Tears well up in her eyes again. I know she's overwhelmed, but I need her to understand.

"Can't you just let me go?" She grabs my hand and presses the back against her cheek. Her eyes look at me pleadingly. "Pleeease."

I take her chin in my hand, tilt it up to me so she can see my eyes. Staring deep into her melted chocolate-colored eyes, I give her a resounding, "Over my dead body."

CHAPTER 22

STAR

I knew the answer, but I had to try again. This life is a fucking nightmare. I can't stay cooped up like a bird in a cage. Like a prisoner.

As if an afterthought, he adds, "You can't leave alone. It's too dangerous."

Alone?

I lift up on my elbow, wincing when the movement tugs at my wound. "You mean you'll let me leave with a bodyguard?"

Can't say I've ever heard of such a thing, but if he thinks it's a possible option, then I guess I can make it work. I'll have to evade the bodyguard once I'm out of here, but that's a problem for another day.

He chuckles softly. "Sure, if you want to call me a body-guard, have at it."

My brows draw together in confusion. "You? What are you talking about?"

I might be a little tipsy from the liqueur, but I'm by no means drunk, and he's not making any sense.

He turns fully toward me and clarifies, "If you really can't see yourself staying and trying to make a life with me here, then I'll leave."

My tummy flip-flops like a caught fish thrown on the deck of a ship.

"For you."

Goose bumps break out over my arms. I wrap them around my middle and plead with him, "Please, don't do this to me, Lucian. I need to leave. I *need* to. I can't stay and…and fall for you. You'll leave me or you'll die or you'll—"

Lucian leans closer, hanging on to my next words. The ones I've cut off, having already admitted too much.

I press back into the mattress to put distance between us, but he plants a hand on either side of my shoulders and bends forward. "Or what?"

I finish my thought. "Or you'll hurt me again."

Slapping a hand down on the mattress, he claims, "I won't die or leave. I'm not your father and I'm not your brother. I fucking love you, Star. I swear to you, I'll never hurt you again. Not by accident. Not out of callousness. Not like I've done so many times before. Today taught me a lesson I'll never forget."

His gaze sears into mine. "Haven't you learned yours yet? You can't do without me any more than I can do without you. Believe me, that realization was as much of a shock for me as it will be for you—the moment you have the courage to accept it."

I want to fight back, accuse him of not having anything to lose, but that's no longer true, damn him.

"My father and brother loved me," I retort, grasping for whatever argument I can come up with.

"Not like me they didn't," he retorts. "They loved you, but I'm *in* love with you. Have been for years, and if you were half as brave as your brother you'd admit you're in love with me, too."

I wince at the mention of Tatum and everything he gave up for Clara.

Lucian's hand shoots out and lovingly grasps my throat. He slides his lips against mine, bares his teeth, and warns, "I won't leave you because you are the single most important person in my life—more important than my clan, my ambitions, my family—ask me to burn it all for you and I will."

I shake my head, trying to dislodge it. "You don't know what you're saying. You wouldn't—"

"I would," he grinds out. "I'd leave it all for you because there's no way I'm leaving *you*."

"No," I gasp.

"We're getting married regardless," he threatens. "That will never change. The only thing that changes is our future afterward. You want to stay, we stay. You want to leave, we leave."

"But you've achieved what you've always wanted. You wouldn't give that up for me. You're *consilier*—"

"And I'll renounce it for you," he shouts. "In a mother-fucking heartbeat. What's the use if I lose you? Just say the word and I'll tell Cristo to find someone else, but don't you dare deny what's between us anymore."

He swipes my legs open, moves between them, and traps me underneath him. With one hand on my throat, he has me pinned like a butterfly on a mount.

"Listen carefully 'cause I'm done playing games. If you'd died back there, I would've died along with you. I didn't realize how empty my life was until I let you in, and I'm not going back there—to that obsessive black hole where the only thing that mattered was success. You were right when you accused me of having an empty life."

What he's offering is almost too scary to believe. In his arms, I feel the security I'd felt my entire life before Tatum left. And when he left, he stripped me of everything. Could I risk it with another man? Lucian, of all people?

Lucian is a lot of bad things—bully and killer at the top of the list—but a liar isn't one of them. If he says he'll give up his position and leave his clan and family for me, then he will. This is no simple sacrifice.

No, this is the ultimate sacrifice.

"I can't make you leave the people you care for."

His grip tightened around me for a moment, his face stormy with frustration. "You're not making me do anything. If you want to leave, I'll renounce it all, but the one thing I won't fucking do is give you up."

"You can't mean it," I say, staring down at the drops of dried blood marring his white shirt. I pick at it, trying to scrape it off without success.

He releases me and gently flips me so that I'm on top of him. My hands slam down and clutch his shoulders as I straddle him.

"I'm dead serious, Star. I've tried to show you in a hundred different ways how I've changed since my fuckup in the cafeteria, but you refuse to see it." He stares me dead in the eyes and says it again, "I fucking love you, and one day, you'll admit to yourself that you love me, too."

I crush his shirt in my fists, screw my eyes shut, and cry out in frustration, "I do love you."

I hear a deep exhale and then a relieved, "Thank fuck. Finally."

I snap my eyes open.

"Come here," he cajoles.

I'm straddling his thick thighs. He bends his knees,

pushing me up until I slide onto his jean-clad cock. I feel him harden beneath my rapidly heating core. I swivel my hips a little because really, how can I help myself?

He lifts his hand and gently nudges a strand of hair off my cheek and then thinks better of it and rubs it between his fingers. "So fucking fair. For someone with such dark eyes, I never understood how you ended up with fine light hair."

It's a bit of a shock to hear him wax poetic about my hair. He's never shown himself to be a romantic. Far from it. Yet, he's seriously wondered about the color of my hair?

"I *do* love you," I admit. "But Cristo isn't going to let you go."

"You're right that we probably can't slip away tonight with a war on the horizon. Their first assumption would be that we'd been killed by the Bratva. We're safer here until the worst of it is over, anyway."

I recognize the expression on his face. Focused and determined. His brain ticking away making new plans to replace the lifelong plans he's just abandoned.

"Meanwhile, we can at least get you into a college in the city. Move near campus. Get you protection to take you to and from classes. I have years of practice waiting for my projects to come to fruition. If after the danger is over you still want to leave, then we'll make it happen."

"You assume I'll get into one of the schools here. It's not that easy."

His eyes light up and his lips morph into his signature smirk. It's a cocky expression I'm quite familiar with.

"You'll get in," he replies confidently. He shrugs a shoulder. "Who knows, I might audit a class with you."

I rolled my hips in a figure-eight and moan, "That has to be one of the sexiest things you've ever said to me."

His lids get heavy with desire. "So you agree to this? We stay until we can leave."

"It's a good compromise. I can still be close enough to watch over my mother. She was the main holdup in my plans."

"We'll find her help," he adds.

My breath catches. "You really think so?"

"I know so."

I arch my back, and a rumble shudders from his lungs and vibrates up the hands I have planted on his chest. "Once she's better and I graduate, then we can leave."

"And we marry. First and foremost, we marry."

My hands glide up to the top button of his shirt. I release it and spread it open, baring his bronzed skin to my eyes. I catch a brilliant flash from my ring, but this time, I don't wince or jerk in reaction. If he loves me so much that he's willing to relinquish everything for my happiness, then I can compromise.

I bring his hands to cup my breasts. He lets out a low groan. "Precious…"

"Don't hold back, Lucian, because nothing is going to hold me back."

His eyes turn wild. He inhales deeply, holds it for a moment, blows out a long breath, and says my two favorite words. "Good girl."

I have something to keep me here—Lucian, my soon-to-be husband. I have my friends. I have my studies. And if I still want to leave, I know he'll make it happen. This man is so capable, and if there's one thing I believe in, it's Lucian's ability to make *any*thing happen.

He's made me love him, and there were moments when I was so hurt I patched over my broken heart with hatred, but it wasn't my real heart. My real heart was always his.

And now that the patches have been set on fire, there's nothing—*nothing*—that can ever smother it again.

It's free. That love is free. Just like me. Because of him.

EPILOGUE

LUCIAN

I never wavered in my determination to leave everything behind for Star. I made her that promise and I was ready to do anything to stick by it. Never one to be caught unawares, I reached out to Tatum and explained our situation. He was overjoyed to have us join him in the Hagi clan in Los Angeles.

But then Star learned about Crina's marriage.

And then Gabby got hitched.

Just as important, Star's mother got better. After several stints in rehab, she's returned from the dead.

She lives with us now.

And we live in the West Village, which doesn't seem as far from Queens as one would think. Most days, I either walk down to Cristo's loft in Tribeca or I commute to Sunnyside. We found a brownstone on a private cobble-stoned street called the Washington Mews just north of Washington Park.

The road still looks like the row of stables it originally

was and we occupy a small two-story building that was renovated into an artist's studio. Most other buildings on the street are used by New York University as offices, which was our primary reason for moving there. Just as I'd suspected, Star got accepted into NYU. Her classes are a couple of blocks away and I have bodyguards with her wherever she goes.

The war is still raging, but my woman is safe.

It's what I make sure of every day.

Winning this war, eliminating any threats, and over-running the Bratva are my other, secondary goals.

I give thanks every night when I come home late and find Star asleep in our bed, her bright hair spread out around her like a halo. The soft sounds of her breathing put everything to rights. Whatever's happened that day, whatever death I have on my hands from the night's work disappears. It's like being cleansed. Like being reborn. Every day.

I straighten from my hunched position over the laptop just as Star enters the foyer. Her image popped up on my screen from the surveillance camera by the front door. I hear her call goodbye to one of my men who've trailed her from class to class. I hear her lock the door and then she's in my presence. My breath catches as it does every single day when she walks into our home.

She tosses her purple backpack onto the sofa in the living room, the diamond engagement ring on her finger flashes sparks around the room. There's a matching yellow diamond wedding band snuggly tucked beneath it. What I lacked in my non-proposal to her, I hope I made up for in the wedding of the century.

Star saunters over to me and I push my chair away from the desk and lift my arm for her to settle on my lap and cuddle into my side. She's soft and feminine and everything that I didn't know I needed in my life until I almost lost it all. I take in a deep breath and thank my lucky stars that I had the wherewithal to throw everything away for her. Just because I haven't had to yet doesn't mean I won't.

I drop a kiss on her crown.

And then, because I can't help myself, I drop another one on her brow and another on her nose and then another one when Star wraps her fingers around my nape and pulls me into a long, lingering kiss. Our tongues duel until it leaves us both panting for more.

Groaning, she plucks at the buttons of my dress shirt. "I missed you."

Fuck, how I love hearing those words. Words I'll never take for granted.

"How was class?" I ask as I strip out of my shirt.

"Good," she murmurs, looking at me from beneath her lashes. She licks her lips and my cock is stiff as a board and ready for her.

"Where's Mama?"

"Out at an AA meeting," I reply.

"Thank God. Not that I'm anything but ecstatic, but what are you doing home?" she asks as she stands up and pulls my arm to follow her. And I follow, Lord do I ever. I'll follow her anywhere.

"Waiting for you," I reply as I yank down my pants and take a seat on the couch.

Star is quick to whip the dress she's wearing up and off. The afternoon light from the back windows makes her hair shine bright. A gust of wind rattles the branches of the tree behind her sets off a cascade of yellow, orange, and red leaves like fall fireworks.

I want her straddling me, her ring-laden hand lying on my chest so I can have the pleasure of watching her tits heave as she grinds down on me and watch her diamonds sparkle with the bone-deep knowledge that she's mine.

She knows what I want, what I love, 'cause she lifts her hand and twists her wrist to show off her ring as she tears her panties down and places a knee on either side of me. I take hold of her hips, nuzzle into the slope of her belly, and breathe in the fragrant scent of her skin.

"Damn, but your body has ripened with marriage," I mumble into her belly.

Cupping her breast, I thumb her nipple and suck a hickey in the dip of flesh near her hip. "I don't think I'm going to be able to hold off licking your pussy."

"No," she rasps.

I hear something in her voice. My gaze shoots up to hers.

"I want you inside me when I tell you my secret."

My cock responds with need, jerking and weeping for her.

"What kind of secret could a precious good girl like you possibly keep from her man?"

She notches the crown of my cock between her thighs, rubbing her wet cunt back and forth, getting it nice and wet for me to thrust up the moment she descends, and then I'm piercing her sweet heat and, fuck, it's as good as the first time. Every time is like the first time.

She gasps as I grab her hips and push her down until I've bottomed out. For the first time, she's not fighting the discomfort of that first moment of full penetration.

"You're finally getting used to my big cock."

"Don't think that's it," she responds, circling her hips for me.

I glance at her bouncing tits, her cunt spread around my cock, her flashing diamond ring and I drop my head back and squeeze my eyes closed. Fuck, I have to fight my body to not pound into her and come within minutes.

Breathing heavily, I open them again and she's smiling at me and getting misty-eyed at the same time.

My eyes sharpen and I work against my body to focus, "What is it, precious?"

"I'm pregnant."

I do a double take. A wave of possessive triumph mixed with an ecstatic flood of love crashes through me.

"Fuck me," I mutter as my animal side takes over. I lift her up and sit her on the edge of the sturdy wooden coffee table, plant her feet on the surface to open her up for me and thrust back inside.

I capture her mouth in a greedy kiss as my hips lurch forward, claiming my rightful partner. My wife. The mother of my child. I glance down at the soft slope of her belly.

My child.

She clings to me as I ravage her, pistoning in and out. I wrap my arms around her, holding her tightly, and lick the sweet-tasting skin of her throat. My fingers slip between her thighs and dance on her clit, teasing her. Her inner muscles start to tighten and ripple around my cock. Her pure blonde hair falls over her face, swirling in my vision, swirling like the whirl of emotions inside me, pleasure mixed with elation—a sense of pure rightness I've never felt before.

She made this all possible.

"My wife. My love. *Mine.*"

Fuck, how I love her.

And the second she comes, I come with her.

Her nails score down my back, drawing blood. I arch my spine in response as I roar to the ceiling and spill into her sweet, supple body.

When I come to from the out-of-body experience I just had, I pull out and catch Star as she slumps over me.

"Oh my God, that was intense," she says against my chest.

Lying on the sofa, I pull her into me and drag the throw over our bodies to cocoon her nakedness from the cool autumn air.

"So you're happy?" she asks, looking up at me with a surprisingly inquisitive look.

"Umm…didn't the intensity of my orgasm tip you off? Or me shouting "Mine" at the top of my lungs?"

She chuckled. "I suppose that might have given me a tiny hint."

I hug her closer. "Baby, you can't imagine how happy I am. I've been wanting to impregnant you the moment I burst through your cherry."

"I guess this means we won't be leaving," she says, her brows knitted together thoughtfully.

"No, we can still leave," I say between clenched teeth. This is gonna make it a helluva lot harder, though. Zoe already visits a few times a week, what with her and Star becoming fast friends. It will break her and my mother's heart if we leave.

"Well, I don't think my mother's ready to move and there's no way we can leave her here. Now with a baby… I'm not so sure I want to leave. Crina and Gabby are here and I don't have the energy to focus on applying to transfer to another school. Plus the Popescus aren't half as bad as I expected. Truth be told, they're more laid back than the Lupu clan."

My heart stops. Sure, I've put a lot of effort into figuring out how we'd eventually move, but I'm nothing if not adaptable. "What are you saying…"

"I'm saying that if you're okay staying, then so am I."

Thank fuck.

I nuzzle into her hair. "Precious, I'm okay staying, but I don't ever want you to stay for me. I can survive anywhere as long as I have you."

She gazes up at me, caresses my throat with the tip of her nose. "No, baby." I moan at the endearment, still not used to the rare times she uses it. "We're having a child and we'll stay here to have it and to raise it."

My eyes blink back tears.

I tease her mouth with a slow, wicked kiss and answer, "Anything for you."

This woman will never cease to be a wonder for me. It took years, but I not only got what I wanted, I got what I needed and I use every day on this earth to make sure I'm what she needs as well.

EPILOGUE TWO

CRINA

I look out at the passing buildings from the moving car, seething with anger.

Married.

On April 20th.

My birthday.

Married to the man I hate.

A bully, that's what he is.

That's what he's always been and, if there had ever been any doubt in my mind that he was anything but a bully, this eradicates it.

Thoughts of cutting off his dick circle around in my head as the car glides down 43rd Street to Saint Nicholas.

And a secret marriage to boot. Even if it's in name only, my parents are embarrassed for forcing me to do this.

Shame on them.

Taking me out of school in the middle of the day to dress me up in this, *this*—I flick a disgusted finger at the delicate lace of my dress—ugly, virginal dress to bind me for eternity to Marku Popescu of all people.

I wrench off the white tulle veil decorating my head and thrust it away. I don't care if his mom is my mother's best friend, and I don't care if they've had this marriage arranged since the day I was born. I do *not* care.

Of course, I expect this kind of madness from my mother, but the real betrayal is from my father.

My chest heaves in shallow breathes. I suck in air as the car rolls around the corner and up the street to the ponderous edifice of the church. Made of brick, the façade is covered with gold-dipped icons on either side and above the door. Topped with a cupola, this is the destination, the holy ground on which my greatest humiliation is about to be consecrated.

The car stops.

The door swings open.

In haughty disgust, I step a toe onto the curb when a hand drops in front of me to help me out. I take it and instantly recoil from the sizzling heat that zaps me.

A head dips down.

Marku.

Curly black hair and eyes so dark they could eclipse the sun. He may be only eighteen, but there's nothing remotely boyish left in this man. Not one trace of the person I'd known as a boy and before that as a baby. Hell, I probably heard him giggling as a baby from my mother's womb.

Gross.

He arches one dark brow in that mocking way of his.

"Fuck you," I spit as I try to shove him out of the way while simultaneously exiting the black sedan. My gaze momentarily catches the sexy tattoo creeping up his neck from underneath the collar of his tux and my rage doubles for having slipped like that.

He tsks, looking down on me with that horrible smirk on his face. "What language out of such a pretty mouth."

"Best not to antagonize her," comes a voice I know only too well.

I narrow my eyes at his best friend, Lucian.

He gives me a grin that makes me want to break his face.

Upon seeing my expression, he takes a step back.

Smart man.

My father finally pushes through them and says, "Back off, boys. I'll take care of this."

Looping my arm in his, I hiss, "How could you," as I have since last night when he broke the news to me.

"There's no other way," he insists, repeating the same thing he said last night and throughout the morning. And looking at him, at the paleness under his skin, I have yet another pang of heart-wrenching pain. I don't know what hurts more, the fact that he thinks he's protecting me or the fact that he's dying.

"And you let Marku's buddies come along to watch my humiliation, but you won't even let me tell my two *best* friends."

He sighs wearily. "They're made men, Crina. You know that."

"Ugh," is my disgusted reply.

Behind me, Marku holds up the veil and says, "You'll need this."

I pierce him with a vicious look. "Why? I don't expect to be a virgin by the time you drag me to the marriage bed."

A vision of a white sheet streaked with blood scrunched in his hand pops into the forefront of my mind, but I thrust that vision away from me.

The cool expression on his face morphs into one of fury.

I stride away from him, but he grabs me by the arm and drags me along with him into the church. He stalks down the center of the nave with me in tow, swings left, and yanks open a side door. Hustling me inside, he backs me up against the nearest wall of the small, tidy office and slams a hand on either side of me.

"The fuck you say to me," he seethes.

"Oh, is that all you're worried about? My virginity? But forcing me into this sham of a marriage, that's okay for you."

"Fuck, baby, you know if there was any other way, I'd have taken it. I'm as much a victim here as you are."

I shove at his chest. "Oh my God, you did not just put the two of us in the same boat. I doubt you'll even stop fucking Luminita or Nadia or whoever your little fuck buddy of the month is."

"I'm not going to fuck anyone but you from this day forward."

That makes me pause for a second. It didn't occur to me that he'd take our future vows seriously. I assumed we'd both go on as we had before. It's not like we'll be living together. I'll be going back to my family and he'll go back to his, at least until graduation.

Wait a minute... Did he have the audacity to call himself a victim?

The fury comes rushing back tenfold.

"Oh, so that's your huge sacrifice? Not fucking other women? And did you call yourself a victim for marrying me? Is that how you see it?"

"For fuck's sake, don't twist every single thing I say, Crina. I know you don't want to marry me right now—"

"Try never," I interrupt.

"Tell yourself what you need to," he mutters.

He caresses my cheek with the back of his hand. "But let me make one damn thing clear. You're mine. You were since the day you were born and you will be till the day you die."

"Fuck no, and if you think I'm going to our marriage bed a virgin—"

He presses a finger hard on my lips, effectively silencing me.

I glare at him, throwing in as much hatred as I possibly can, and I've got a lot stored up for him.

"You'll be a virgin alright, and I'm going to remind you right here, right now, why that is. Get on your fucking knees."

I inhale sharply and struggle to get out of his grasp. He clasps my throat and pins me to the wall.

With a dirty grin, he asks tauntingly, "What's the problem? It's not like you haven't done it before."

I let out a gasp of outrage. "You're a bastard for even bringing that up."

"You're trying my patience, Chuckie."

I cringe at the playful nickname he gave me when we were kids.

"The last time was erotic. This is not." I look him boldly in the eye. "I'm saying *no*. You'll be forcing me if you put me on my knees."

He chuckles indulgently. "Baby girl, we're not American. Consent isn't a thing, but even if it were, we both know you like to be forced."

My entire body lights up in flames. I break out in a sweat and suppress the desperate need to wiggle away from him.

My fingers and toes start tingling with the memory of the only time I had his cock in my mouth. I swallow. Oh

God. That had to be the most excruciatingly delicious experience of my life. I've been haunted by it for years. Hell, it's my go-to masturbation fantasy.

Tugging at the neckline of my wedding dress, I pull it away from my skin and flap it back and forth to get some relief. I rub my thighs together, the gusset of my panties drenched from that one comment of his.

With eagle-sharp eyes, he knows how he's affecting me.

In a guttural tone, he says, "My dirty little angel loves it, doesn't she? Now get on your knees before I push you down."

I shouldn't, I really shouldn't do this, but the bastard has this way of short-circuiting any rational thought and weaving a magical spell around me. I bite my lip and suppress a moan.

He sees it, knows it because he knows me so well, and taking that as a *yes*, reaches for his belt.

Slipping it out of the loops of his trousers, he twirls me around and wraps it around my wrists. I should fight him, fight this, but he knows what he's doing. He knows I'll follow the urge to fight him if he doesn't and he also knows I don't really want to fight him.

He whirls me back around to face him and grasps the skirt of my dress. Inch by slow inch, he pulls it up and groans when he sees the set of white garters and net stockings.

"Fuck me, you're trying to get me to pop that cherry now," he groans as he skims a finger up my leg to the junction of my thighs "But I'm not fucking you for the first time in the back of a church. No, I'll be taking my time with you."

"There won't be a first time, I keep telling you," I snap at him.

"You say that." He briefly closes his eyes as he pushes a

finger into my panties. "And yet, you're wet. Of course, you are."

He slips beneath the silk and plunges inside. I arch my back and cry out at the invasion.

"Tight as fuck," he murmurs against my lips. "Such a good girl and yet so dirty at the same time."

Carefully removing his finger, he slips it into his mouth and sucks. "I'm gonna need to taste that sweet honey."

"No," I cry out, shaking my head roughly because there's no way I'll survive his mouth on my pussy. My hate will barely survive his big cock in my mouth again. Last time, it took me days to get back to the status quo of hatred.

He pushes my panties lower and lets out a groan. His eyes are dilated and enflamed at the same time. Before he can do anything, panic grips me and I pull away just enough to drop to my knees. I can't snatch my skirt up and keep it off the floor with my bound hands, but I don't care.

Let me walk down the aisle with patches of dirt on my pristine dress. Anything is better than going to the alter with the knowledge that his tongue made me come. I know he wants to, he's told me enough times, but I've never let him, knowing I'd never come back from surrendering like that.

"Bad girls who deny me won't get to come."

His dark words almost make my eyes roll back in my head.

I pitch forward and nuzzle my nose along the hard shaft of his cock. Excitement thrums through me like the beat of a drum, each drumroll gets louder and louder in anticipation.

I glance up at him and beg, "Please, Marku."

"Fuck," he mutters as he tears open his trousers and pulls out his long, hard cock.

I should be terrified. The last time we did this, I was aroused for weeks. It was all-consuming. I felt like he'd devoured my soul. The guy's got vampire skills like you wouldn't believe.

But it's too late.

I gaze up at him from my position on the floor and he towers over me, looking so exquisitely dangerous and male. His jacket is off, and the bulges of his muscles are outlined against the fine cotton of his shirt. Unlike any other Romanian made man, he has tats all over his body and they shimmer darkly beneath the pure white of his shirt.

My bodily needs are quickly taking over. I can barely think straight and anyway, he shackled my wrists, taking away my choice. Granting me the relief of not having to choose.

So by the time he says, "Now be a good girl and open for me," I'm impatient to part my lips for the crown of his cock.

He yanks at my neckline, tearing it to expose my breasts. He fondles one, tweaking my nipple harshly, making me twitch in need as he pushes his hips forward, moving past my tongue to my throat. His musky taste floods my mouth, the corresponding scent fills my nostrils. He's surrounding me everywhere with his taste, smell, cock.

"This won't be like last time. You'll swallow the whole of it," he states.

It's big, even I know that just from the little porn I've watched.

I suck lightly around his cock and he grasps my hair, undoing the elaborately made chignon, forcing me to take more. I moan as spit gathers at the corners of my swollen mouth. This is already way more intense than last time.

I breathe in a deep draught of air through my nostrils as he keeps going and going. Fisting my hair, he forces my head back and plunges deep until the very tip of my nose grazes his abdomen.

Holy shit.

"Such a good girl, such a good little girl. Tight throat, tight pussy, and an even tighter ass. One day soon, I'm going to take all three and you're going to love it."

A powerful surge of desire whips through me because I am his good girl. Always have been.

Abruptly, tears sprout from the corners of my eyes, marring my perfectly applied mascara. He does this to me every time. Gets under my skin with dark words that breed even darker fantasies. Fantasies I haven't even put words or images to until he conjures them up like a wicked sorcerer.

"Look at me, Chuckie, let me watch your eyes when I come down your throat," he says, his voice unexpectedly vulnerable.

My eyes snap up to his and then he's thrusting hard into my mouth. I tilt my head farther back, softening my throat even more and then he comes with a bellow. My mouth is flooded and I'm gulping semen down as fast as he spills it.

It tastes like salt and man and Marku.

He pulls out and swipes a thumb over my bottom lip before bending over and claiming my mouth in a brutal kiss. My swollen lips feel even more bruised afterward. Breathless, I'm left feeling stunned and disorientated.

"Damn, that wedding lipstick looks so pretty around my cock," he muses aloud as he stares down at himself.

I see it too. Another jolt of arousal. Another flood of my pussy.

Struggling to get up, I stumble to a standing position

and shut down the moment. "Ugh, you're disgusting. You force me to do this shit and then you have the audacity to gloat about it after. Unleash my hands already."

I turn around for him to take off the belt. Once my hands are free, I tug my panties up and fling the door open. Sprinting down the aisle to the priest is my only option to get away from him. At least momentarily.

The priest's eyes flare in surprise at my appearance. Hairdo ruined, mascara running down my cheeks, lipstick smeared around my lips. I look godawful, from the torn neckline of my wedding dress to the dark smudges on my knees.

My mother rushes toward me, fixing my hair and wiping off the lipstick as Marku saunters down the aisle. She hurriedly slips on the huge engagement ring I threw in Marku's face when he proposed to me and then Marku is by my side.

I stoutly ignore him as the priest begins the ceremony with his Romanian Orthodox incantations.

He switches to English to ask, "Do you take this man to be your lawfully wedded husband?"

I turn toward Marku.

He smiles that smug smile at me, the one I hate more than anything. God, I want to wipe that smirk off his face.

Exploding with rage, I give him a grim close-lipped smile as I twirl my tongue in my mouth, gathering a mixture of saliva and seed.

And then, I spit a glob in his face.

Thank you for reading UNFORGIVABLE! I hope you loved Lucian and Star. I'm working on Crina and Marku's story next, UNREGRETTABLE: A Forced Marriage Mafia Romance. But until then, you can read Tatum's story in The Perfect Heir: An Enemies to Lovers Mafia Romance.

They call her the Virgin Queen because she can never marry...

Clara

I am Clara Hagi, the Virgin Queen. I may not be allowed to marry, but I will be the first woman to rule a mafia clan.

I ache for Tatum, the *consilier* of the Lupu family. I love his piercing black eyes, his tall, muscle-bound frame, his touch, his commands, his beguiling strain of vulnerability —I love it all.

The one time and only time he kissed me—my first kiss —was a mistake.

That's what he called it.

A mistake.

He'll regret those words; I'll make sure of it.

Tatum

Nothing good came from kissing that girl, Clara. A girl whose clan hates mine. A girl who's off-limits. A girl I should loathe.

I live and breathe the Lupu clan, and I do it perfectly. I'm charged with getting the Virgin Queen under control. Once I do, my clan will rule LA, just as it rules NYC.

Every time I see her, I remember. Every time we spar, I want to kiss her. Every time we accidentally touch, I ache for her.

One kiss would never be enough. Maybe bedding her will get her out of my system, virginity bedamned.

But what if I fall for the Virgin Queen?

She deserves better than a tainted man like me.

Want a taste now?

Tatum

"I loathe you," Clara snapped, her hands fisted by her sides.

I was at the wedding of a man who was like a brother to me. I should be joyous. At the very least, I should be drunk.

Instead, I was fuming.

I'd taken a breather in the terrace outside the venue of Luca's wedding reception and came upon Clara. As usual, she'd goaded me with snide comments. This woman was impossible. Haughty and arrogant, she'd been needling me throughout the evening. That didn't include the months in California where she took every chance to make my life a living hell. What had Nicu been thinking, suggesting she spend a few months with the Lupu clan in the city?

I knew she detested me, and the feeling was more than mutual. In fact, I'd guess I had an edge on hating her more. But when she hissed at me like a wet cat, the drive to bring her down a peg surged through me. It was petty of me. For once, I didn't care how it made me or the Lupu family look. I didn't care if I had to get close up and personal to make her feel uncomfortable. Payback was in order.

I slapped a hand on the wall beside her head, penning her in. Thrusting my face into hers, I growled, "You hate me, you say? Sure about that?"

Her eyes flared wide, the bright blue splintered in shards of green and turquoise. She shuddered out a soft breath that coasted over my skin. I stepped closer, until my lips were inches from hers. Before she had a chance to do or say anything to piss me off more, I coasted my lips over hers.

Gripping her delicate jaw, I flicked my tongue against the seam of her lips. She opened her mouth on a gasp. I licked my way inside, and fuck if the taste of her didn't hit me hard. She jolted in surprise. At twenty-one years old, she had never been kissed before.

The realization that I was the first took me aback, but not enough to let me pull any punches. On the contrary, I pressed my advantage.

Tilting her head for better access, I took her wickedly sarcastic mouth harder. A mouth that had spewed comebacks and snippy insults for months, goading me to smother her. But in that moment, I found myself getting lost in her taste. It was delicate and sweet. The antithesis of everything she was. But I couldn't stop myself from delving in harder, maybe a tad too hard.

Not only had she yielded to me, because by now I'd expected her to scream bloody murder, but she'd timidly placed her hands on my chest. It expands with pride. Her fingers spread open, exploring me haltingly. She leaned in, pressing her full tits against me, and tentatively licked into my mouth. I groaned at the innocence of it.

Fuck, I wanted more.

But I wasn't the type of man to do this to a pampered *mafie* princess. That was for the Lupu brothers. They could do whatever the hell they wanted because they were heirs, each one of them. Their father, may his soul rest in peace, was a hard man with demanding expectations. My father was a hard man as well, but without any of the accolades as the Lupu pater. He instilled in me that I could never step out of line.

Perfection was the rule of thumb and mistakes were not to be tolerated.

Of course, I hadn't expected perfection in tasting this sassy little bitch, and that's exactly what I'd gotten. Which was why I should stop. I'd made my point. It was time to pull back.

Only...I found myself in a struggle between the good

son, who prided himself on his reserve, and the bad man, who craved to devour this woman.

I forced myself to pull away, but she moved with me, not allowing an inch of space between us. Clara was like a Lupu, taking what she wanted when she wanted and I wanted to do the same. I was tired of being good and perfect. I wanted to indulge. For once, I was greedy.

My hand smoothed up her side, cupping her plump breast. Talk about luscious. I'd already found myself staring at her tits on more than one occasion, dragging my eyes away an instant before she caught me. Although, I'm almost certain she sensed my gaze on her.

I thumbed her nipple peaking under my ministrations. She moaned into my mouth, the vibration shuddering down my body to my cock. Fuck, my balls grew heavy at the sweet, needy little sounds she made. It dawned on me that she was wet, and abruptly, I needed to feel her silky, wet flesh on my fingertips. I needed the knowledge of how much she wanted me.

Sliding a hand down, I caught the hem of the short, flirty dress she'd worn, little tease that she was, and yanked it up. Then my fingers were over her panties. The heat coming off her scorched me. My pinky finger wiggled between her pussy lips, and fuck, but I felt her juices through the silk.

She was drenched. Soaked.

For me? It was a heady thought.

"Spread your legs," I commanded in a voice I barely recognized.

She shifted on her feet, tilting her pelvis to give me better access. I loved how she responded to my command. I pushed a thick finger in deeper, but the gusset of her panties prevented me, and like a heat-seeking missile, my finger needed more. It demanded that tight, wet flesh to be parted by my digit. Prodding her panties to the side, I pushed inside.

Motherfucker. Slippery *and* tight. The perfect combination. Too bad she had such a nasty little mouth. The thought of putting her on her knees and making use of that mouth of hers, for good instead of evil, crossed my mind. My cock jerked in my pants. Damn, did I want that.

The dirty girl writhed on my hand, her hips twitching as she worked herself on my fingers. It was just how I imagined it, because yeah, I'd fantasized about her in my bed. This was even better. Her tight muscles sucked me in. She was a sensual creature, I'd give her that. I may not like the woman, but feeling her walls clamp around my fingers was close to divine.

I moved my mouth to her ear. "You say you hate me, but your tight pussy is greedy for my touch. Tell me what you want, little girl. Tell me, and I'll give it to you," I promised darkly. With a decade between us, it seemed right to call her "little girl," although I'd never felt the drive to do so before. But here, I undoubtedly had the upper hand. Finally. Because Clara challenged me every chance she got.

Not now, though. Now I had something she wanted, something only I could give her.

My brow furrowed. She could get it from her idiot of a *consilier*, Grigore. The thought of that bastard touching her goaded me to start stroking.

I let out a low, deep growl. "You want something, you come to me. Only me. I'm the only one who will satisfy you, you hear? You will never go to any man but me." The vow fell from my lips unrestrained as I cupped her pussy. "I'll be the one to take this, to fuck this tight channel and burst through your cherry. You'll bleed on *my* cock."

What the fuck?

I didn't talk like this.

I didn't act like this.

Yet, the words spilled from my mouth, like an oath. Like a curse.

I stumbled back, pulling my fingers out of heaven. My cock strained against the zipper of my tuxedo pants, my nuts feeling like they were about to burst, wanting to spray come all over her face and inside her womb. To mark her. To breed her.

Where in the ever-loving fuck was this?

I couldn't have this woman.

I shouldn't even *want* this woman.

She was toxic.

We hated each other.

I scrubbed a hand down my face, scenting her delicate fragrance. I wanted to thrust my fingers into my mouth and *suck, suck, suck* until there wasn't a drop left, until I'd absorbed her juices into my very cells. I dragged them down my face, tugging at my chin to stop myself.

My lungs heaved. What the hell was happening to me?

Face distorted with horror, I rasped, "Fuck, that was a mistake."

She inhaled sharply. The glaze over her eyes vanished as she recoiled in disgust.

"A-A mistake? The first kiss of my life, and such an—" I strained to hear what she was about to say, but she cut herself off, pressing her full lips together. Shame flushed her supple skin a shade of pink right to the tips of her ears. Covering her chest with her arms, she turned on me with fury in her eyes.

"A mistake, you say?" she spat out, pulling her hand back and letting it fly across my face with a resounding *crack* that echoed off the walls of the buildings surrounding the terrace. My head snapped back, skin aflame from the impact of her hand meeting my cheek.

"You arrogant bastard," she hissed.

I rubbed the imprint of her palm on my skin. Just as I'd suspected, it'd been her first kiss. A fissure cracked around my chest, a vicious, vindictive sort of pride spurting through like lava from a volcano. She was right to call me a bastard for pilfering her first kiss. Not only that, but she got more than she'd bargained for. Not only was I the first man to ever kiss this woman, but I was the first to ever fondle her untouched pussy. I was fucking *proud* of that, and I realized with a ruthlessness that startled me that if the opportunity ever came again, I'd repeat it in a heartbeat.

Damn, she was made of pure fire. I'd insulted her with my comment, but a kiss like the one we shared, a break in my control like the one I'd allowed, was dangerous. If anyone happened to come upon us and witnessed what I'd done to her, we'd be at the altar with our wrists bound together and crowns placed on our heads by the end of the week.

She couldn't want that, could she?

I shook my head. No, definitely not. Every single moment she was in my presence, she used it to undermine me, to establish how much she despised me.

Or did she?

Clearly, she didn't hate me quite as much as she pretended because there was no way a woman like Clara, even with our age difference, would allow a man to touch her if she didn't want it. I may have started it as a challenge or simply to shut her up, but she'd kept it rolling.

Shoulders back, chin up, she said, "Oh, it was a mistake, alright. You should be so lucky to ever touch or kiss me again. Don't for an instant think this changes *anything* between us."

Her voice was a mixture of injury and rage, and yet neither of us believed a word of it. Even so, she was a proud woman, and I didn't like the distress on her face. Superiority, smugness, disdain. Those I was used to.

But hurt?

That, I could not stand.

I lifted my hand, about to reach for her, to comfort her, but she faltered, stepping back as if my touch would burn. Before I could say or do anything to try to make things right, she spun on her heels and stormed inside the restaurant, positively enraged.

Unhinged.

She was fucking glorious.

Not only did I have the incredible taste of her still on the tip of my tongue, but I'd turned her against me even more. Discomfort pricked at my heart.

For the first time in my life, I wanted more from a woman.

A woman I'd lost any chance of ever having.

GET THE PERFECT HEIR NOW>>>

MORE BY MONIQUE MOREAU

The Lupu Family Mafia Romance Series

The lives of these powerful men revolves around three core elements: duty, sacrifice, and family. There's little time for women, and no time for love.

Each one of them will be cut off at the knees, humbled by a woman. Oh, how far these mighty men will fall before they learn the age-old lesson that the only way out is through…

The Chosen Heir (Alcx's story)
The Recluse Heir (Luca's story)
The Savage Heir (Nicu's story)
The Perfect Heir (Tatum's story)
The Bastard Heir (Sebastian's story)
The Princess Heir (Emma's story)

Empire Academy Series
A New Adult Mafia Romance Series

UNFORGIVABLE (Starlene's story)
UNREGRETTABLE (Crina's story)
UNFORGETTABLE (Gabriela's story)
UNDENIABLE (Zoe's story)

Steamy Biker Romance Series

Fans of sizzling hot alpha bikers and the sassy, strong women who tame them will love Monique Moreau's steamy MC series.

Kingdom's Reign (Book 1)
Cutter's Claim (Book 2)
Loki's Luck (Book 3)
Stanton's Sins (Book 4)
Puck's Property (Book 5)
Whistle's War (Book 6)
Her Hidden Valentine, A Squad Novella (Book 7)

Join Monique's Mailing list to receive goodies and release information:
https://www.subscribepage.com/moniquemoreau
Follow her on TikTok @moniquemoreauthor
Like her Facebook Page: https://bit.ly/MoniqueMoreaufb
Follow her on Instagram: https://bit.ly/MoniqueMoreauIG
Follow her on Book Bub: http://bit.ly/MoniqueBookBub
Learn all about Monique's books: MoniqueMoreau.com